LAST NIGHT NEVER HAPPENED

NOLON KING

SEAN PLATT

LAST NIGHT NEVER HAPPENED

NOLON KING

SEAN PLATT

STERLING & STONE

Copyright © 2024 by Sterling & Stone

All rights reserved.

No part of this book may be reproduced in any form or by any electronic or mechanical means, including information storage and retrieval systems, without written permission from the author, except for the use of brief quotations in a book review.

The authors greatly appreciate you taking the time to read our work. Please consider leaving a review wherever you bought the book, or telling your friends about it, to help us spread the word.

Thank you for supporting our work.

Chapter One

"Hold still, please."

Nora shifted uncomfortably in her chair. She tried not to frown at poor Mona, who was being very patient as she did Nora's hair and makeup for what promised to be an obnoxious event. It was an ostentatious soirée with a name that broadcast exactly what she could look forward to. The Hollywood Stars and Stripes Gala would not have been remotely close to her jam under the best circumstances, but as the plus-one babysitter for professional prima-donna Daphne Belle, it was just another night in what Nora had long ago started thinking of as a Faustian contract of servitude.

Having only one client would have been arduous enough, but Daphne had less self-control than anyone Nora had ever been responsible for, and that was saying something. Nora couldn't trust her to go anywhere alone — Daphne lived life like it was one big Oscar afterparty, no matter how important the occasion — which is why Nora was still in her workout clothes while sitting in a hotel room awash in gilded opulence, with baroque furnishings that mimicked Versailles, trying not to squirm in her seat as Mona — an impressively patient hair and makeup artist — tended to her face and shoulder-length hair in compliance with Daphne's decree to, "Revamp this look pronto!" because "Time might not be on our side, but beauty sure can be." And finally, said directly to Mona, as if Nora wasn't right there, "She's giving me 'season one reality show contestant' vibes. Let's kick it up to 'season finale' glamor, shall we?"

It had taken two years for Nora to rehabilitate Daphne's reputation, and all that work would pay off tomorrow, when Daphne signed on for the lead role in *Sister Justice*. That triumph would rehabilitate Nora's career too, proving that she deserved a position with Three Mile PR, where she could work with A-list clients again.

"Sit still, hun," Mona reminded her again.

"Sorry. I really am trying." And she was. She just wasn't very good at it.

If Nora could learn to ignore Daphne's most annoying attributes, she could also sit still in her goddamn seat long enough to let this poor woman finish her job.

"Much better," said the stylist as a loud knock on the door turned into an impatient pounding almost immediately.

Nora bounded up from her chair.

"Of course," Mona muttered under her breath.

Nora looked through the peephole to see one of Hollywood's notorious assholes standing in the hallway. She would have left him out there, but Asa Harman was both entitled and insistent — if he already knew that Nora was in the suite, there was no way in hell he would ever stop knocking.

Unless she called security. But in her line of business, invisibility was always Plan A.

Nora opened the door. "What do you want, Asa?"

Instead of giving Nora an answer, the asshole barreled right by her and into the room, barging into Daphne's suite like the bully he was known to be.

He gave Mona a dismissive glance, then turned back around to Nora as she closed the door. "I need your help."

"I'm sorry about him," Nora said to the stylist before grabbing Asa by his arm and roughly dragging him into the bathroom, locking herself in with the smarmy pile of shit who Nora would have hated by reputation alone, despite it being a best practice in her line of work to not judge a person before meeting them.

But Asa was the kind of man she refused to work with under any circumstances. Which meant he had about seven seconds to say whatever he needed to say before she shoved him back out of the bathroom and ejected him from the suite.

"I need your help," Asa repeated.

"Let me guess, you've been caught with an underage girl again."

"They haven't all been underage."

"If she wasn't underage, then you wouldn't be talking to me."

"That's not true." It was obviously true. "You can ask a hundred people how old this girl looks, and all hundred of them — *men and women* — would say 'at least 20.' I kid you not—"

"Get the fuck out of my bathroom."

"I need help," Asa said.

"I couldn't agree more."

"You know what I mean."

"You should be talking to Vivian Piers."

"I tried talking to Vivian, but apparently, she's retired. I ended up talking to someone named Melissa instead."

3

"Right." Nora had heard about that.

Vivian had hit the jackpot. Or so Nora figured from what she could piece together from the scraps of gossip and hushed conversations. A Hollywood bigwig was caught red-handed, channeling money from some undisclosed studio into illegal schemes — the kind that could lead to career-ending exposés.

Vivian wasn't just a leak-plugger; she was a maestro, conducting a financial ballet by shuffling funds through a byzantine series of shell companies until she had scrubbed every cent of that illicit money into respectability. The grateful magnate had paid her off in accounts so offshore they might as well have been submerged.

But there had been a darker layer to the fixer's operations for a while — one that made Nora's skin crawl. Helping Hollywood's male elite dodge bullets in the form of underage scandal had been part of her service menu for years before Nora sniffed out what she was doing. There was no older story in the City of Fallen Angels: an actor with a skyrocketing career getting tangled up in a reckless affair where the risks were monumental. Statutory rape charges, a tarnished reputation, even jail time.

Vivian was the guardian angel such men never deserved, swooping in and brokering a hush-hush agreement between predator and prey. Financial compensation paid under the table, then swept under the rug. Her fee wasn't a one-time transaction. Vivian claimed a slice of that actor's earnings — forever.

It was a filthy business, reeking of desperation, lubricated by money and power.

Vivian might have exited the stage, but her legacy left a stain so deep that not even Hollywood's self-admiring glare could bleach it away.

"Call Melissa back," Nora said. "You were right the first time."

"I called Melissa. She referred me to you."

"That's a lie. And I don't work with clients who lie to me." Nora should have left it at that, but she was like *fuck this asshole* so hard that she could barely help herself.

"I'm glad to hear that Melissa obviously told you to fuck off and that, unlike her former boss, she won't be in the business of helping pedophiles to get their next fix."

"That's not what—"

"Now get the fuck out of my bathroom."

"*Please*," Asa tried again, taking one wrong step toward her.

She reached out and snatched a bottle of Baccarat Rouge 540 from an adjacent table and raised it over her head. "I really don't want to waste this on you. But unless you want to start reeking like a Parisian escort, I strongly suggest you don't make me repeat myself again."

Nora really hoped he wouldn't make her use the bottle of Baccarat. Not because she was worried about wasting it — the perfume would end up as another expense on a tab that the fading star of Daphne Belle could barely afford. It was more that Nora didn't want to have that scent stuck up in her nostrils all night.

"You're going to regret this," Asa grumbled, but he was already on his way out of the bathroom.

Nora took a moment to collect herself, then left the bathroom with a long sigh, entering the living area just as the door closed behind Asa.

"He's the worst," Mona said. "My friend Barrett was the stylist on *Shame Shame*, and they said that Asa had a photo of himself from twenty years ago in his wallet that he wouldn't stop showing to people. Barrett said it was like he seriously expected people to be impressed that he used to look less like a grease-soaked sponge."

More evidence that Asa was broken, still trying to get the hot girl in high school.

Nora reclaimed her seat. "I promise to be good."

"You can be bad all you want. Just stop wiggling around," Mona said, her voice tinged with a reluctant amusement that died before withering into something less decipherable.

"What is it? What did I do?" Nora asked.

"Besides working up a sweat?"

Nora settled into her chair, her muscles going rigid as Mona continued her transformation. Anger at Asa seethed below her skin, but she tamped it down, focusing on the evening instead.

Thoughts of Daphne swirled around like eddies in her mind — once a behemoth of the silver screen, now a fading comet in the Hollywood sky. That could all change tomorrow, assuming Nora did the typically overwhelming job of keeping Daphne in line. With only one night before the pivotal event and an open bar of temptations, Daphne would be at her most volatile, leaving Nora braced for a cocktail of drama.

The door swung open, and Daphne strode in looking like a timeless siren in sapphire silk, defying her decades with an elegance that left Nora in reluctant awe. Blonde curls framed a face that spoke of resilience and strategic reinvention. A spider brooch, encrusted with jewels, adorned her radiant hair.

Daphne's wrist sparkled with a constellation of diamonds so exquisite that Nora found herself questioning just how down and out in Beverly Hills her financial situation could actually be.

"Was that Asa Harmon I heard in here?" Daphne

blurted without preamble or pause for a response. "Let me tell you, working with that guy really curdled my coffee. He was always getting handsy with the talent on the set of *Wolfpack*. Not me, I mean the *young* talent. Whatever you've ever heard about Asa, I'm sure it's true — I went straight to the director, no detours, and said, 'This isn't amateur hour, Antonio! We either get rid of this jerk, or I'm booking a one-woman show called *Sayonara Daphne*!'"

"You're a hero to everyone," Nora said.

"Asa only got a slap on the wrist because Antonio wasn't about to recast him, but Asa got full revenge on me by talking the director out of my next role after I was already cast because he's three times the asshole."

Nora already knew the story and didn't need to hear it again. But she did need to redirect Daphne before she ended up saying something regrettable in front of Mona.

"Of course," the stylist muttered again as Nora stood, then led Daphne into the recently vacated bathroom.

Nora closed the door behind them. "Asa may not be a client, but—"

"He better not be. He got me dropped from *Into the Void* for being too old. I was 35 years old, for God's sake. So, why was he in my suite?"

"That's what I was about to say. What Asa and I discussed is confidential. Even if he's not a client. Are you ready for the gala?"

"I was born ready!" Daphne giggled.

"I need you to tell me the rules."

"I'm not a baby, Nora. I know the rules."

"Of course you do. That's why I'm asking you to recite them for me."

"You do realize I'm an actor, right? Memorizing lines is what I do for a living. It would be irresponsible of me to not remember my lines."

"I won't remind you about any of your irresponsible behaviors in the past or that you haven't worked for a while."

"You just did both of those things."

"Tell me the rules, Daphne."

The actress sighed. "No drugs, no alcohol, no flirting, no fucking, and no talking to reporters."

"Great. And here's a new one: No talking to Asa. I don't want his inevitable scandal to rub off on you."

Daphne snorted. "I'm much too old for anything of Asa's to rub on me. And your rules are going to turn a really fun party into a total bore."

"I'm just making sure that nothing goes wrong tonight. We can't afford for anything to happen before you sign the contract for *Sister Justice* tomorrow."

"I don't know why you think I'm—" Daphne stopped talking at the sound of Nora's buzzing phone. "Who is it?"

Like Nora was going to tell her.

She looked at the screen and saw a text from Asa: *Last chance to change your mind.*

She blocked his number, then turned to Daphne. "I need to finish letting Mona change what I look like."

"*Enhance*, darling."

"Says you." Nora turned around and left the bathroom.

Then she sat like a statue for a quarter hour, barely moving a muscle.

"You earned an A+ there at the end," Mona said.

After squeezing into her dress, Nora felt even more uncomfortable than she had while getting her hair and makeup done.

"Your tits look outstanding in that dress," Daphne told her right after Mona left them alone.

"Glad to hear it," Nora replied while texting their driver, *On our way.*

On the elevator ride down to the bottom floor, a young girl stared in admiration at Daphne for the entire trip until the doors dinged open to the lobby, and Daphne could no longer help herself.

"Yes! I'm her."

The girl's mom offered Daphne a friendly, yet slightly apologetic smile. "I think she was just admiring your brooch."

As they walked away, the little girl (who clearly had no idea that Daphne Bell was a famous movie star) whispered to her mom much louder than she realized.

"That spider jewelry was *soooo* pretty, Mommy!"

Chapter Two

THE LIMOUSINE GLIDED to a halt one block from the theater, its headlights casting a transient glow on the bustling crowd ahead.

The Stars and Stripes Gala unfurled in all its chaotic grandeur, an ostentatious sea of sequins and silk that far surpassed any spectacle Nora had mentally prepared for, even after a childhood growing up with a movie actress mom. When she was eight, watching her mother leave for all-night parties gave Nora a stomachache. She'd never been able to sleep, knowing that Katherine Bauer would come home stumbling drunk or incoherent, expecting Nora to put her to bed.

Babysitting Daphne was a piece of cake compared to taking care of her own mother. Nora would still have to put Daphne to bed, but at least she could make sure Daphne was a sober pain in the ass when it happened.

Thanks to her mother's addiction, Nora had a distinct talent for compartmentalizing her fears until they transformed into an unyielding gravitational pull, strong enough to steer her through any crisis.

At a glance, her youth might suggest a resume light on experience, but that belied the hidden arsenal of invisible victories she had stealthily amassed while working as Vivian's once-indispensable apprentice. It had been Nora's hand correcting Hollywood mishaps at a staggering ratio, outperforming her boss threefold at least.

Until she stumbled upon Vivian's most secret clientele, and the revelation made her immediately tender her resignation. Nora was replaced with Melissa the very next day.

Under a canopy of twinkling stars and strategically arranged spotlights, the white carpet unfurled outside the theater. A-list actors, visionary directors, and glamorous influencers converged in a tsunami of sequins and flashing cameras.

Reporters with lacquered smiles brandished their microphones like royal scepters while flanking the spectacle, angling for the perfect soundbite or candid shot to capture just one more second of the world's fleeting attention.

Daphne looked out the window in awe, a fair share of which was reserved for herself. "It's been years since I've been invited to this thing."

"Obviously," Nora replied. "That's why you hired me."

The limousine stopped, and the driver got out to open their door.

Daphne stepped out onto the white carpet first, preening and posing with a swish of her voluminous gown, treating the runway like her personal stage as mobs of paparazzi served as an adoring audience.

A sea of cameras and eyes washed over her as Daphne sashayed down the carpet with a playful wink and a sultry pout to deliver her usual breed of good-humored glamor. But once the questions came in a chorus amid those flashing cameras, Nora needed to step in and help her navigate the press.

"Who are you wearing?"

"Are you dating anyone?"

"What's next for Daphne Belle?"

The questions were benign at first, but then Nora turned toward the wrong reporter — Tim Bowen would wrestle the worst possible responses out of Daphne if she allowed that to happen. The tabloid hound had a grin that never reached his calculating eyes. He was slinking through the crowd toward Daphne, smartphone in hand.

Nora reached out to pull her in the other direction, but they had already reached the end of the carpet, meaning there was barely any attention left to lavish upon Daphne, so she soaked up what she could get from a stray photographer.

Naturally, Daphne started walking toward Tim, leaving Nora behind.

Nora caught up with her right as Tim finished what she hoped was his first question. "So, how has it been since you went on the April Hayes show and spilled all those spoilers for *The Silhouette Files?*" Tim's smug smile was on full display.

Daphne had shit the bed when talking to April about her new film a couple of years ago. She was playing a character who realized that her own past was the key to solving every mystery in the movie, but the last five minutes of the film were ruined in the first five minutes of Daphne's appearance on April's talk show.

"No comment," Nora answered for her.

He turned to Daphne. "Any comment about how you chastised women who participated in the Me Too movement for not having enough backbone?"

Nora wasn't fast enough that time.

Daphne started laughing. "After a couple of bumps—"

"She means 'no comment,'" Nora said, glaring at Tim.

"Hey there, Nora!" Tim laughed like an asshole. "Don't get your panties in a bunch, the camera's still sleeping."

"Can we please retire 'panties in a bunch'? It's a tired, sexist cliché that trivializes women's legitimate concerns by reducing them to underwear malfunctions."

Daphne shrugged. "I like it."

Nora kept glaring at Tim as she took Daphne by her arm, successfully this time, leaning in to whisper as she led them away from the reporter.

"*I told you not to talk to Tim.*"

"Nope." Daphne shook her head. "I memorized all of my lines, and that one was *definitely* not in your little script. You can't hold me responsible for keeping track of what I'm supposed to do and not do if you're just going to keep adding a bunch of new rules all the time."

"Consider Tim Bowen officially added to the list."

Nora looked toward the entrance and noticed another cluster of paparazzi who tended to live on the sleazier side of their dirty little industry. "Let's just wait a minute before going in."

"You don't want anyone to talk to me," Daphne said.

"I actually don't want *you* talking to *anyone*."

Nora was miffed at Tim. The reporter knew how hard she had worked to rehabilitate Daphne's image and didn't need him sabotaging her efforts. They each had a job to do, and if he ever wanted her help in the long future, she would have as a Hollywood fixer who was only now *finally* getting a reputation then Tim needed to not be a dick.

She took out her phone and sent him a text; one word, two syllables: *asshole*.

The three dots promising his reply appeared, then disappeared, reappearing for a blink before vanishing a final time as a kissy face emoji buzzed onto her phone.

"I wasn't trying to break any rules." Daphne often liked to defend herself shortly after getting corrected by Nora once she had effectively worked out an argument in her head. Just like Nora's mother used to. "I just thought that I would explain to Tim that my former agent, Marty, kept warning me to stay far away from Me Too or it would hurt my career. That's the only reason I said what I said on that—"

"Stop talking. That's the lesson here, Daphne. You pay me to answer questions for you. As of tomorrow, this phase of our relationship will finally be in your rearview mirror. After you've signed for *Sister Justice*. Until then, I should remind you that you haven't landed a single role since your apology tour."

"I know the story because I'm the one who wrote it!" Daphne finished Nora's regular rant: "I'm on the verge of bankruptcy; I'm about to be a washed-up Hollywood star; I'll be living under a bridge wearing the only fancy gown I still own if I insist on talking. Is that what you were going to say next, Nora?"

"Something like that."

Daphne was sulking, but Nora needed her client to smile. All part of the job.

She glanced around the lobby before nodding at Heather Sparks, standing alone and surprisingly unmolested by the crowd. Her flowing golden locks framed striking blue eyes and a cherubic smile. Heather's magnetic blend of innocence and magnetism had landed her multiple magazine covers during her first year on the scene and then every one of the dozen years since.

They started walking toward her at exactly the wrong

moment, just as Heather was waving for the nearest server to deliver another glass of bubbly.

The server turned to Nora and Daphne as they stepped up to Heather.

"Nothing for us." Nora shook her head as Heather grabbed a glass and handed it to Daphne. Nora plucked the glass from her hand. "She's been sober for eleven months."

"That's her code word for 'bored,'" Daphne scoffed.

"Her streak won't be ending tonight."

Before Heather could respond to Nora, Scarlett Anderson appeared in front of them, radiating red carpet mystique with a nuclear insincerity.

"I am *so* happy for you," Scarlett gushed, waving a hand at Daphne before putting it on her arm.

Daphne shrugged Scarlett's hand away as the starlet continued.

"There is not a single actress in the world that I would rather see play Sister Justice. And I'm sure there are millions of other women just like me."

"There's no one quite like you." Daphne's laugh was almost as loud as its *eat shit* subtext.

"I don't know if you heard, but I actually auditioned for the role before I found out that they wanted someone old and had my manager pull me out." Scarlett laughed too, but Daphne had won that round of their little chuckle-off. "I'm just *loving* this move into motherhood parts, but Daphne can have all the grandmas, thank you very much!"

"Can I have your grandma?" Daphne asked like it was a serious question. "Because I bet your Prada panties that I could—"

"What else can we talk about besides grandmas?" Nora interjected.

It was time to interrupt their volley regardless, but

Nora also saw Lavigne, the sleaziest among the paparazzi so far, slinking by.

Nora worked not to curl her lip in disgust. Lavigne's greasy mane fell haphazardly over his forehead as he lurked in the periphery around their table, his camera lens protruding like a predator's eye and his compass always pointed toward *scandal.*

Instead of the reporter's usual collage of threadbare garments (choosing to be a slob despite some ungodly sums he had earned for exclusives), he was wearing a suit.

But Lavigne blended into the shadows better than most.

"How did you get in?" Nora stood from their table to ask him.

"As a server, of course." He gestured to his suit and displayed an empty tray. "I'm surprised to see that you let Daphne off her leash."

"Go stalk someone else!" Daphne snapped.

"It's only a matter of time before you fuck up again," Lavigne replied with a smile.

Then, the human buzzard sauntered away from their table.

Chapter Three

Nora felt as if she were tiptoeing through a psychological minefield, each step threatening to trigger one of the volatile egos around her.

Scarlett and Daphne's spat continued to dance on the razor's edge of civility, each barb wrapped in a photogenically poisonous smile. The actresses lived across from one another, so Nora had seen plenty of their bitter back-and-forth before. Yes, their feud was real *and* intensely performative.

The volley of venom left Nora with frayed nerves.

Lavigne, that opportunistic insect, could resurface any moment like a cockroach skittering out of the sewer, eager to capture the least flattering second of their lives.

The reporter was out of sight and out of mind, but Melissa was walking right toward their table. Once a colleague, then a rival, and now — what? She had been an apprentice to Vivian, an enabler of the worst Hollywood had to offer. However, according to Asa's insider intel, Melissa had chosen to redraw her ethical boundaries. Hurray and a half for her, if that was true.

Nora didn't know, and in this business, lies could even be hidden in the truth. Was Melissa an ally cloaked in frenemy's clothing, or still apprentice to a monster, merely biding her time before revealing her fangs?

Melissa nodded as she sat in the empty seat next to her. "Hey, Nora."

Unlike the gown that Daphne had cajoled Nora into wearing, Melissa was clad in a tailored suit that hugged her trim figure and made it clear that she was working the event instead of being celebrated as one of its stars.

Nora was jealous of Melissa's ability to dress however she wanted, but when it came to professional skills, both women navigated the industry's underbelly with discreet efficiency after having studied under the best. Both were armed with encrypted smartphones that never left their sides, and both had an incredible knack for reading people. But Nora still gave herself an admittedly biased edge.

"So, did you really inherit all of Vivian's clients?"

Melissa nodded. "All the ones I wanted."

"And how are you finding your transition to boss?"

"Exhausting, overwhelming, and exactly what I was hoping for," Melissa replied as a server walked by their table with bottles of water.

She stopped in front of Nora and handed her a bottle, then a second one for Daphne, who was apparently gone from the table.

Melissa looked bemused as Nora cast glances about the room until she finally spotted Daphne engrossed in a conversation with her partner in crime, Caroline Crosby.

The actresses were of a similar vintage, but they wore their years differently.

Caroline's auburn hair was still vibrant but now streaked with strands of rebellious silver. And her eyes had been seasoned by a life of soirees, still gleaming with mischief after all these years. Her strapless gown was boob-to-ankle gold sequins that shimmered with the slightest movement, designed to outshine everyone around her in all but the lowest of lights. And just in case someone failed to notice her dress, she'd added a chunky necklace encrusted with champagne diamonds and a matching bracelet that she waved around every chance she got.

Nora supposed that anyone who spent their life as Daphne's sidekick would have to go to extremes to capture any attention at all, given that they'd be constantly competing with Daphne's insane antics.

Caroline and Daphne often got out of hand when they were together, and Nora felt certain that their wave of mutual mirth right now could not possibly be crashing into anything good. Daphne was also eyeing her friend's champagne with obvious envy, and as close as they were standing next to each other, the odds of her snatching Caroline's glass to steal a greedy sip or three in the next few seconds felt next to definite.

"I'll be right back," Nora said to Melissa, then walked over to Daphne and gently took the champagne flute out of her hand just a blink after she had lifted it from Caroline.

"I don't need a babysitter!" Daphne snapped at Nora.

"That's exactly what you need," she disagreed, eyeing Lavigne and imagining the headlines he was surely penning in his head for yet another one of his clickbait articles, dropping details about tonight while teasing the more delicious tidbits posted in the morning. "And no talking to the wait staff either."

"What kind of treat do I get if I behave?"

"Your career," Nora answered her.

"Thank you, Warden Bauer."

Another reporter appeared between Nora and

Daphne, clad in a tailored suit that fit in with the crowd well enough without rivaling the stars.

"Good to see you, Daphne." He used his grin like a microphone. "Dennis Totter from HollyBuzz — we haven't seen you out in public for a while. What makes tonight so special?"

"Daphne decided to take some desperately needed downtime away from the spotlight so she could focus on her personal growth," Nora answered on her behalf.

"And why was that?" Totter pressed.

Daphne opened her mouth, but again, Nora got there first.

"She needed to spend time understanding how much her words hurt women."

"Is that right, Daphne?"

Daphne stood by Nora's side like a good girl, nodding like a bobblehead as a soft voice came over the speakers (elegant enough that it sounded conspicuously devoid of a British accent), requesting that guests at the gala please locate their designated seats for dinner, so that the ensuing auction could finally commence.

"Great." Daphne chuckled. "Looks like they're holding our stomachs hostage until we empty our wallets."

To Daphne's great delight, she and Nora were seated next to Caroline and Melissa. But before a conversation could ignite at the table, the emcee emerged onto the stage. Glenn Stahl was the host of Influence This, but instead of his usual jeans and band T-shirt, he was clad in a sequin-studded tux that only the charity-raising side of Hollywood could forgive.

With a chiseled face, his devil-may-care smile, and a bearing somewhere in between rockstar and philanthropist, his charisma filled the space as he boomed, "Ladies and Gentlemen, tonight, your generosity will transform lives! We're not just raising funds. We're raising hopes while sending ailing children to a magical week full of smiles at circus camp! There is no limit to how much good we can do here tonight, so let's open those hearts wide and those wallets even wider!"

Stahl beamed at the crowd as the first auction item was rolled onto the stage.

"Feast your eyes on this exquisite oversized mirror. A magnificent work of art and craftsmanship dating back to the 19th century. Framed in ornate hand-carved gilt wood, its surface boasts a flawless beveled glass that not only reflects your image but also transports you into an era of unparalleled opulence. This isn't just any mirror; it's a grand statement piece and an heirloom investment that promises to elevate any room it graces, capturing the essence of both historical grandeur and timeless beauty. Can I get an opening bid for $12,500? That's $12,500..."

"I want to be transported into an era of unparalleled opulence! I want a grand statement piece! I want to capture the essence of both historical grandeur and timeless beauty!" Daphne shouted all three of her exclamations in a row.

"No bidding," Nora told her.

Daphne sulked throughout the mirror's bidding, which ended at just over thirty grand, then through the remaining items. Nora's stomach growled through most of it, so she was thrilled when the final piece of inventory was auctioned off (a luxury cruise in the Mediterranean aboard the *Dionysia*) and servers were setting food on the tables with flair.

Nora had already forgotten the name of the Michelin chef in charge of the gala, but his culinary artistry met patriotic elegance in a lavish spread of artisanal canapés from miniature crab cakes with Old Bay aioli to petite tamales alongside an impressive raw bar featuring oysters from both coasts. Then, wagyu steaks for the main course, paired with truffle-infused mac and cheese with bourbon and maple-glazed vegetables. Vegans and vegetarians were treated to a foraged mushroom risotto that smelled earthy and delicious.

The conversation stayed breezy through dinner. Caroline kept Daphne distracted and laughing all through the meal, almost like she and Nora were on the same side for once. Nora was almost enjoying herself by the time their server was setting a gorgeous plate of red, white, and blue macarons on the table.

Everything was going great until Roberta — a late-coming interloper to the table who had worked on a movie called *Killer Queen* with Caroline over a decade ago — blurted a question at Nora before her ass was even in the seat.

"Did I hear a rumor about you interviewing at Three Mile PR?"

Nora was capable of bending the truth without actually breaking it for her clients, but she was less willing to conduct such acrobatics for herself.

"Yes. That's true."

"Wait a minute …" Daphne's expression got lost somewhere between befuddlement and hurt. "Are you dumping me?"

"No," Nora said. "Of course not. I'm taking my clients with me."

"Don't you just have one client?" Melissa managed to make her question sound serious, possibly even tinged with concern for her friend.

"It wouldn't be the worst thing in the world." Caroline shrugged. "Daphne's only like ten percent as much fun as she was before Sergeant Nora took over her life." She put a hand on her friend's shoulder and gave her a couple of pats. "No offense. It's not your fault."

"Of course, it's not my fault. I'm the one who —" Daphne stopped talking as an already rowdy band took the stage to a wave of hearty applause.

"I didn't know the Stray Bullets were playing," Melissa said.

"I thought you knew everything," Nora replied.

"I'm fine with surprises that have no way of affecting my job."

The music was loud, grating on Nora instead of helping to wake her up like she'd been hoping it would. There was no alcohol in her blood right now, but she had consumed too much sugar for sure, and the crash was clearly creeping up on her.

"Thanks." Nora barely acknowledged their server with a nod as the woman handed her another two bottles of water, one for her and another for Daphne. The server looked bone-tired but still managed to hold a best-effort smile throughout the two-second exchange.

They must have run out of the good stuff because this Oasis brand came in embarrassingly cheap plastic bottles. Whoever was in charge of this fancy gala must surely be cowering in shame somewhere, making a list of the people who needed to be fired over that little faux pas.

Nora handed Daphne her bottle.

"Are you kidding me?" Daphne whined. "The night's almost over. And I *still* can't even have a tiny sip of champagne?"

"That's a firm no, Daphne."

"Fine." Daphne started drinking her water, pouting harder now that Caroline wasn't around to distract her.

Daphne turned away from Nora and stared at the

dance floor, her head bopping up and down in time with the Bullets on stage.

"How much longer do you want to stay?" Nora asked as the silence between them started to feel weird.

Daphne didn't answer.

Not that first time nor the second time a few moments later when Nora asked her again.

She looked closer to see that Daphne no longer appeared bothered, with her eyes far away and her body sort of sagging.

"I don't feel so good," Daphne said, suddenly clutching her skull. "And why is it like a thousand degrees in here?"

Then she was up from the table and wandering toward the exit, calling out to Nora from behind her. "I need some fresh air!"

Nora was pissed. Was Daphne messing with her and pretending to be sick, or had she taken some sort of pharmaceutical cocktail when Nora wasn't looking?

She caught up to Daphne in the alley behind the theater, standing beneath a wash of murky lighting from the glow of strategically placed sconces on the brick.

Nora arrived just in time to grab Daphne as she nearly collapsed onto the ground, now giggling hard from her depths.

Yeah, she'd definitely taken something.

Nora got out her phone and texted their driver.

I need you to come and get us. We're in the alley behind the theater. I'll walk out to the street and meet you there.

She hauled Daphne to her feet, working through various ways she could spin this story without inviting too many questions, finally settling on "food poisoning."

Nora made her way toward the street, but two steps in, a strange feeling overcame her. A buzzing filled her ears, and the world started to spin.

She clutched at her head and stumbled forward, with no control over where she was going or how she was feeling as her knees crashed onto the alley floor and dizziness swept through her entire body.

Wild laughter bubbled out from inside of her, and Nora couldn't contain what had escaped in a flood of emotion through her veins.

"Crap." Nora cursed under her breath.

Whatever Daphne had taken, she had also passed it to Nora. Every cell in her body felt raw and exhausted as she managed to pull Daphne up and into her arms.

Nora started walking.

She might have lost her shoe, though it was hard to know for sure with those bright lights drenching the alley in sunshine and swallowing the both of them.

Nora kept pulling Daphne along with her, clomping toward the car and…

Chapter Four

The Los Angeles sun blazed down onto Nora's skull as she slowly blinked awake, disoriented despite being able to vaguely grasp her downtown location. She was sprawled across a park bench. The drone of traffic and scurrying feet buzzed around her.

She collapsed back down, cradling her aching head in both hands as if to massage the pain away. She squeezed her eyes shut, breathing steadily to regain some semblance of balance and clarity.

She couldn't remember anything after leaving the gala last night.

A prickling sense of being watched prompted her eyes to fly open.

She lurched up from the bench, spotting a homeless man observing her.

He was weathered, his beard a tangled maze of gray and brown, lines etched into his leathered skin to map a difficult life. His wild yet perceptive eyes narrowed on Nora, making her feel oddly cared for yet deeply unsettled.

"Big night?" Then, when she didn't answer, he added, "I thought you were dead when I first saw you."

"Nope. Just feels that way. You have any idea how I got here?"

"Nada." The man shook his head. "I only saw you after I thought you were dead."

"Did you take my purse?"

"I would have," he admitted with a shrug. "But only if you were dead, in which case you wouldn't need your money no more. I've never been a thief or nothing like that, and that ain't why I came up to you."

"Then why did you come up to me?"

"If you were dead, then I would have to tell someone fast or get far away so that no one would think that I had anything to do with it."

"Which one were you going with?"

He shrugged again. "Hadn't decided. But if you were still alive, I figured you probably needed some help."

"Thank you?"

"No problem. Sorry your purse is missing."

"Honestly, I care more about my memory." Nora rubbed her head again, angry as a slurry of blurred remembrance settled around her. Daphne had obviously drugged her, then dumped her downtown so she could go off somewhere and party.

She looked down to see ketchup stains all over her dress.

At least, she thought it was ketchup …

"Looks like blood," said the man.

"It's not blood." Nora was circling a vague memory of her and Daphne eating hamburgers at some point last night. "It's definitely ketchup. Do you know where my phone is?"

He brightened, but then his words didn't match at all. "No idea."

"Never mind." Nora reached into her bra and pulled out her phone. The impressive shower of glitter that rained onto both her lap and the bench was a big surprise.

She swiped her thumb across the glass, ready to give Daphne a piece of her mind. But the phone, out of charge, was a brick in her hand.

"What's your name?" Nora asked the man.

"Thanks for asking. It's been a while." He grinned. "Name's Frank."

"It's good to meet you, Frank. Would you happen to have a phone I can borrow?"

He shook his head. "Sorry. My last phone was one of them, Razors."

"Then how about if I borrow one of your jackets?" Nora nodded to a rickety shopping cart brimming with an eclectic tapestry of multicolored attire from both genders of all sizes. She saw a scant few bright neon fabrics among the patchwork, but it was mostly fading colors and fraying threads.

Frank dug through his cart until his fingers found a large coat. He held it high like a prize. "It's the least smelly one!"

"Thank you. I really appreciate it." The woolen fabric was coarse and matted beneath Nora's fingers. She lifted it to her nose, trying to steal a whiff without being obvious. It smelled worse than she'd feared: a vile blend of body odor and car exhaust steeped with urban grime ground deep into the threads.

She slipped her arms into the oversized sleeves, the coat enveloping her as she tugged it closed, trying not to imagine its journey through his vagabond existence.

"Sorry, I don't have any shoes." Frank gestured to her naked right foot.

"No problem. I never mind walking. Which way to Beverly Hills?"

Frank pointed. Nora nodded her thanks and started walking west, on the verge of tears but successfully swallowing them down.

She was Nora Goddamn Bauer, and Nora Bauer didn't cry or panic.

Nora Bauer took always took action.

That's what she kept telling herself as she approached a nearby homeless camp nestled amid the steel bones of downtown skyscrapers. Ramshackle and sprawled out on a broken stretch of sidewalk, the camp hosted every size and shape of tent, forming a makeshift neighborhood.

The air smelled of urban decay and human resilience. As the pungent aroma wafted into her nostrils, it alerted Nora to how badly she needed to pee.

She looked around, looking for someone with a phone or a place where she could empty her bladder. Either would do.

She spied a woman talking on her phone in front of an open-flapped tent and approached her, then stood a few feet off to the side, trying not to bounce on her feet and now needing to urinate even more than she had just a few moments before, on account of having to actively wait for the woman to finish her call.

"Do you mind if I borrow that?" Nora asked a moment after the woman hung up.

"How much you got?"

"Nothing." She gestured down at her stained gown. "All I have is this dress."

"I like that dress," the woman replied.

"But it's all covered in ketchup."

"I like ketchup." She squinted at the stains and added, "Looks like blood."

"It's ketchup."

"Let's trade. I have lots of clothes in there. Pick whatever you want." She gestured for Nora to duck inside the tent where they could ostensibly trade clothes.

Stepping inside the dimly cramped space, she surveyed the disorganized piles of clothing strewn about, stained and tattered and reeking.

Rifling through a mound of faded dresses, a hundred percent of which had holes, she settled on a baggy sweatshirt and ill-fitting track pants. Nora slipped out of her soiled gown, and once naked, she could see that the ketchup had not only soaked through the fabric, it had also crusted into something grosser and more brittle on her skin. Vaguely sinister even, the way it flaked away, crumbling between her fingertips and leaving residue that seemed a little too vibrant for ketchup.

Could it really be blood?

The rough, baggy fabrics chafed her smooth skin but still felt like a fresh start compared to the ketchup-stained dress. She emerged from the gloomy tent with a sense of relief, determined to make her way back to the real world and shed her disheveled appearance.

After she called Eric.

The woman looked pleased as she handed Nora her phone.

In a world where most people couldn't remember numbers beyond the important ones they had grown up with, Nora took pride in knowing most of her Rolodex by heart — not that anyone ever used the word *Rolodex* anymore.

Nora never knew when a number might be needed

without access to her phone, even though she never went anywhere without it. Preparing for every contingency was her ply and trade as a fixer, which is what was making this current situation of living in the dark about last night so goddamn untenable.

"This is Detective Guerrero," Eric answered.

"It's Nora. Bauer."

"You never need to give me your last name, Nora. Where are you calling me from?"

"How possible would it be for you to pick me up right now?"

"If I say yes, are you going to tell me you're in Vegas or worse?" Eric asked.

"I'm at 3rd and Grand."

"Why are you there?"

"I'll tell you when you get here."

"I'll meet you in front of the Broad Museum."

"See you there." Nora hung up and returned the phone to its owner.

"Who was that? Your butler coming to pick you up in the limo?"

"I told Jeeves he could have the Bentley today, so it'll just be me and Detective Guerrero."

The woman had no idea what to do with that.

"Thanks for the phone." Nora gave her a nod and started toward the museum, stopping on the way at a gas station to use their bathroom.

Eric must have used his license to speed, because he arrived just a few minutes after her. He leaned over and opened the passenger side door for Nora while she admired his chiseled features and strong jawline. He looked better to her than most of the actors who loved to prance all about.

Nora got into his Dodge Charger and closed the door.

Eric pulled into the street.

"Was there any kind of ruckus at the Stars and Stripes last night?" she asked.

"Not that I heard of, why?"

Nora didn't want to tell him that Daphne spiked the water. It was just too damn embarrassing. What kind of fixer let that happen to their client, let alone to themselves? "No reason."

"There's always a reason. Why am I picking you up downtown?"

"Fine, there's a reason. But mostly, it's just because I had too much to drink, and it was all Daphne's fault. I'll tell you what happened later. Right now, you only need to know that I'm going to murder Daphne."

"Wait." Eric sounded serious even though he wasn't. "Are you confessing to a crime before committing it? Because I'm not sure that's such a good idea."

"I won't actually pull the trigger. I just want to put the fear of God in her."

Eric laughed. "I don't think Daphne fears God under any circumstances."

And despite her mental fog, Eric made her laugh all the way to the Sunset Sovereign Hotel.

"Thanks for saving me," she said.

"I just gave you a ride. I'm sure you saved yourself from whatever Daphne dragged you into just fine without me."

Nora smiled in parting, then walked away from the car.

She entered the hotel lobby and went straight to the front desk. April was still working. The twenty-something apparently never stopped smiling.

"I'm so sorry, I lost my hotel key."

"Of course, Miss Bauer," April said. "Let me get you another one.

"Have you seen Daphne by chance?" Nora asked.

"Not since yesterday."

"Thanks." The bad feeling in Nora's stomach was turning into something worse.

Chapter Five

Nora entered the hotel suite and went directly into her room, surprised to find the remnants of hamburgers and fries sitting on the bed, which was gross for multiple reasons. It was hard to believe that she'd have left such a mess even while under the influence of whatever had knocked last night right out of her, but it was hard to argue with the evidence atop her comforter.

They must have eaten the burgers here, but she had no memory of coming back to the hotel, let alone their suite.

She plugged in her phone so it could charge, then opened the door to the adjoining bedroom, hoping to find Daphne. Instead, it looked like the place had been tossed.

Clothes were heaped in towering piles across the bed, with a landslide of fabric in every color threatening to topple over. The nightstand held a chaotic array of half-eaten plates of food — crumbs littering the surface, with a slice of cheesecake missing no more than three bites, drips of raspberry sauce staining the wood like blood on a wound.

The dresser was buried under an explosion of glittering

bangles and dangly earrings scattered among the clutter like gleaming confetti. Bottles of nail polish and makeup brushes caked in powder and eye shadow mingled with crumpled candy wrappers, making the entire room look like a tornado had ripped through it, leaving Daphne's debris in its wake.

Nora was unconcerned about an actual break-in because this was Daphne's MO.

She returned to the bedroom and checked her phone, which was charged enough to make a call at eleven percent.

But dialing Daphne sent her straight to voicemail.

"This is Daphne. If you're a friend, leave a message, and I'll call you back. If it's business, call my agent. If you're a fan, of course you are. Why wouldn't you be?"

"Hey, Daphne. This is Nora Bauer, your fixer, the person who you pay to keep you out of trouble instead of ditching her downtown so you can get your party on. You better be calling me and trying to make this right *before* you get this message!"

Nora hung up and went back into the bathroom so she could wash off last night.

She got undressed and stepped into the shower, turned the knob to unleash a torrent of hot water, almost scalding, enough to cleanse her of all the lingering tension as it cascaded over her skin and rinsed away the caked dirt and stench.

Steam filled the air as she scrubbed, her movements mechanical yet cathartic as fragrant notes of eucalyptus and lavender mingled with the mist to form as purifying a ritual as she could ever hope to find in a hotel bathroom.

She shut off the steaming shower and reached for an impossibly plush towel, then buried herself in its embrace and luxuriated in a texture that felt a world away from the scratchy fabrics she had dragged across her skin in that woman's tent less than an hour ago. Though she was still unsettled, the soothing heat had relaxed her tense muscles and cleared enough of the fog from her mind to leave Nora feeling slightly renewed. Still, true grounding continued to evade her.

She packed her suitcase, then took the elevator down to the garage, where she loaded the luggage into the trunk of her Infinity and slid into the leather driver's seat.

She plugged in her phone to continue to charge and set the GPS to guide her.

The engine came to life with a satisfying purr at the press of a button.

She threw the car into reverse, then exited the gloomy garage into glaring daylight, gripping the wheel as scattered memories from last night slowly surfaced, fragments that began interlocking like a puzzle inside her mind.

Nora's first stop was the theater that hosted the gala.

But the building loomed dark and silent, devoid of the pulsating energy from last night. She cruised through the nearly vacant lot, spotting a handful of stranded vehicles dotted across the asphalt, probably left by partygoers needing rides after too much of a good thing, or separate arrivals turning into single departures as amorous couples rushed to get horizontal.

Nora pulled up alongside a janitor using languid sweeps to cram his dustbin with debris. She glimpsed two discarded condoms, gracelessly tumbling into the bin.

She pulled up a few feet in front of him and killed the engine, working to mine his name from her memory banks. She couldn't find it.

"Hi there! I'm Nora. Can I ask your name?"

"Jason." The janitor looked shocked that Nora (or anyone) would care who he was.

"Great to meet you, Jason. I think I left my purse here last night. Would it be possible for you to let me in to look? I'll be fast. I just need a minute or two."

"Of course." Jason looked perfectly happy to help with her simple request.

He opened the door and let her inside, but after 10 minutes of furious searching, which was already a lot longer than she had promised Jason, she had gone through every area inside the theater where she could remember going last night but found nothing.

Jason was in no hurry to get rid of her. "Come on. I'll take you to Lost and Found. I don't remember seeing any purses like the one you described, but I wasn't the only one piling the haul in there last night."

He opened the door to a dimly lit room filled with an eclectic display of misplaced opulence: a glittering sequined purse sitting beside a silk bow tie; a single satin glove laying crumpled and alone; an assortment of gadgets from smartphones to wireless earbuds, and even two expensive-looking cameras.

Nora actually squealed as she spotted her missing handbag, then scooped it off the shelf. She looked inside, saw that her cash was still there, and pulled out a $20 bill for Jason.

"Thank you so much for your help."

He took his bill with a smile. "My pleasure."

Then Nora walked back outside and rounded the corner into an alley behind the theater, where she found her missing shoe.

She walked through the alley to the next street, vaguely remembering getting into the limousine as it pulled up to her and Daphne.

But then Nora could hear the echo of the bone-chilling words that had left Daphne's mouth last night through a gale of laughter as they stumbled toward the limo.

"I have a great idea," the actress had said.

But Daphne's ideas were never great. They were potentially career-ending.

In the last month alone, Daphne had suggested writing and performing a one-woman show where she would embody every character from Shakespeare's *Othello*, either completely oblivious to or disregarding the nuances of race and representation. She had also floated the idea of producing a reality TV show featuring her: *Daphne's Diva Boot Camp* would feature young actors undergoing humiliating challenges for a chance to be her personal intern. She was clueless to the fact her idea would only result in a full display of her ego without any actual mentoring.

Daphne had been inches away from disaster before Nora stopped her from launching the toxically ill-conceived # DaphneDoesn'tAge campaign, in which she planned to post side-by-side pictures of herself now and from decades ago with some noticeable yet unacknowledged digital retouching.

Nora went back to the car and tossed her shoe into the back seat.

She started the engine to get the AC going and tried to call Daphne again. Voicemail again. Goddamnit.

Nora put the car in drive and almost instantly found herself ensnared in a creeping line of vehicles. She inched forward until she finally spotted the cause: a Rolls Royce parked conspicuously by the roadside with an asshole's vanity plate: *LVNGLGND*. An odd spectacle for sure, but still not worth snagging attention from every passing driver.

Nora tightened her grip on the steering wheel, impatient and unimpressed.

She honked her horn and got flipped off by the driver in front of her.

But at least he sped up a bit and quit with his rubbernecking.

She tried Daphne yet again, this time knowing her call would go to voicemail and wanting to leave a message.

"You know who this is," Nora growled. "You better not be out there causing any more disasters for me to mop up. We're supposed to be done with this shit today. Call me back so I can stop imagining ways to murder you for putting me through this one last nightmare. If I don't hear from you in the next hour, then the reason you won't be signing that *Sister Justice* contract is because you'll be dead."

Of course, Daphne knew that Nora would never actually kill her, especially not after leaving the threat on a voicemail. But she had run out of other ways to make her client listen, and considering last night, Nora had already decided that the contract signing would be their final hurrah together.

She hung up and focused on the road, feeling immediately unsettled by that same inner sense that had made her aware of Frank on the bench.

She looked up into her rearview mirror to see a dark sedan that might have been following her. Or not. The vehicle was far enough back that Nora could very well have been paranoid but close enough that her instincts might also be right.

Several evasive maneuvers later, the sedan was still behind her. Even after she circled the block. But then, after the second right turn, it drove in the other direction.

Nora still couldn't remember what had obviously been a very long night. It made sense that she would be paranoid, imagining things that weren't really there.

And her pounding headache was only making things worse.

She pulled into a drive-thru Starbucks two blocks down. She rubbed her temples while idling in line and ordered her coffee iced so that she could consume the caffeine faster.

Nora pulled back out onto the road to find that same black sedan behind her again.

Unless it was another car because, of course, it could have been and probably was.

There were black sedans everywhere, including to her left and right, just a few cars ahead. Three blocks later, she still wasn't sure if the sedan was actually following her.

Probably the goddamn paparazzi.

Nora was more deliberate with her maneuvers this time. She circled the block, making two lefts and then four rights before returning to her route. She finally managed to lose the tail she was increasingly certain was indeed in pursuit.

The only thing evasion cost her was the rest of her iced coffee that spilled as she turned.

She cursed Daphne under her breath, then gunned it even faster for Beverly Hills.

Chapter Six

DAPHNE WOKE up on her living room floor with a splitting headache, her dress torn and stained with what had to be ketchup. She scraped at the crimson blotch, bringing it to her nose and inhaling a metallic aroma before licking her finger and tasting the undeniable tang of iron on her tongue.

What the actual fuck?

She sat up straight and began to pat herself down, checking herself over from head to perfectly manicured toe. She had a few scrapes on her arms, but despite the instant fear flooding her veins with the thought that she might have been half of a murder victim, the spot-check determined that the blood on her clothes couldn't possibly belong to her.

But that's all she knew.

Daphne couldn't remember a single goddamn thing that had happened after dinner. Even after several long moments spent squeezing the bridge of her nose, it was still like most of last night never happened.

And that was weird. Not just that Daphne couldn't

remember, but that she was dealing with this seriously disorienting strain of hangover at all. She sure as hell didn't remember getting drunk. Nora would never have allowed that.

If left to her own devices, Daphne would have loved a glass of bubbly. And it was hard saying no to Caroline all night, so she had taken one of Caroline's little happy pills, but that could not have possibly knocked her out or caused the axe to the back of her skull she was feeling right now.

The pill had done exactly what Caroline promised, giving her a nice little buzz. But Daphne had swallowed that little present shortly after she'd arrived at the theater and had begun to feel the effects waning before the Stray Bullets stepped out onto the stage. It should have worn off by the end of the event.

She felt surprisingly irritated by the entire situation right now, especially at Nora. She paid that little know-it-all a lot of money. The very least she could have done was to put her only client to bed.

But thinking that gave Daphne a sickening sense in the pit of her stomach, because Nora was annoyingly *over*-responsible. Of course she would have put Daphne to bed. So, where was Nora right now?

Probably freaking the fuck out somewhere.

Daphne winced, cursing her headache as she shoved a hand down the front of her dress to scratch at a sudden itch and pulled it back out in a rainbow shower of glitter.

Daphne giggled at the sight.

Wherever she had been last night, it really must have been one hell of a party.

That would explain the hangover. But how had she convinced Nora to let her go?

She couldn't wait to start remembering it. But first, she needed to get a hold of Nora and start smoothing things over with her before she got all uppity and tried to fire Daphne as a client.

She blustered about Nora always bossing her around, but there was no doubt that the woman was great at her job. A lot like her mom, but in some ways, also her opposite. Nora had definitely saved Daphne from what would have been a few seriously public blunders, like #DaphneDoesn'tAge.

Even Caroline admitted that Nora had helped her dodge a bullet with that one.

Daphne's saving grace lay in what that girl Melissa had pointed out at dinner last night. She was almost for sure Nora's only client, which meant the odds of the fixer ditching Daphne right now were basically nil.

Unless she really was going to sign with an agency, and they started her with some clients that Nora considered less high maintenance.

Admittedly, that wouldn't be hard to do.

Daphne went to the kitchen to grab a bottle of water from the fridge and found her phone on the top shelf, sitting next to a set of car keys and a pint of strawberries.

She looked at the screen and saw that her battery was at two percent power. Enough to check her voicemail.

She laughed as Nora's message ended, both amused and frightened by her tirade. Daphne always found it best to laugh at that particular cocktail of emotions, often when playing her characters onscreen but always in real life.

She went to the shower and stood under the water, washing off what was *definitely* blood, though again, that made her question where so much liquid life could have possibly come from.

There was *a lot*. Not a Carrie at the prom quantity, but a single-victim slaughter, at least.

She thought hard, but her night ended rather jarringly

with a memory of Nora dragging her down an alleyway to the limo.

No. Daphne massaged the shampoo into her scalp.

She had a memory after that of Nora lying in an alley, giggling.

Wait. There was also something after that … Caroline following them down the alley to the limo.

She rinsed her hair, thinking even harder, scouring her mind until she found an image of them all driving to Burt's place last night.

That made sense. Caroline had an invite to one of Burt's wild parties, which Daphne always loved but had been missing out on for the two years that Nora had forced her to sober up. All she got to do was scroll through photos of his bacchanals on Instagram instead of making those memories herself.

She and Burt had been on and off lovers for years, decades, if Daphne stopped avoiding the math. But he was also one of the few true friends she had in Hollywood. In a town of fleeting loyalties, her compass always pointed toward Burt's magnetic north.

She got out of the shower and dressed, eager to give Caroline a call. Surely, her bestie would know what had happened last night.

Her phone was still mostly dead, but even a little juice was enough to get the thing ringing. But she got Caroline's voicemail on the first ring, and Daphne barely knew what to do with that. Because *shit, fuck, damn*, Caroline ALWAYS answered her phone. That bitch would pick up while on the tightrope in a circus act.

Daphne figured she should give her phone just a little more juice before calling Nora, and naturally, there was no better way to kill a few minutes of charge time than by tending to her growling stomach.

She started digging through her kitchen with a strange sense of melancholy at the life she had built for herself slowly slipping away, with the evidence more abundant in the kitchen than anywhere else in her house, mostly because she had to let the cook go three weeks ago.

Fumbling through her opulent but mostly deserted pantries, Daphne opened cupboard doors to an eclectic inventory of canned delicacies like escargot and truffle-infused foie gras sitting adjacent to neglected jars of quinoa and chia seeds. Expensive bottles of truffle oil and aged balsamic vinegar jostled for space amid economy containers of coffee and cereal. A smattering of international teas and exotic spices lined one shelf, but Daphne never actually drank any of that leafy plant broth.

A small fortune's worth of culinary treasures, and yet nothing appealed to her cravings more than a stale bag of Doritos she grabbed from the corner of her lowest shelf.

She opened the bag and shoved her hand into the bottom before popping a handful of chips into her mouth, crunching as she looked out the window at Nora climbing out of a sleek black Infiniti, obviously furious as she stomped toward Daphne's front door.

Daphne tried to beat her there, but the door flew open to reveal a fuming Nora as Daphne entered the living room.

"What the hell happened last night?" Nora snapped.

Chapter Seven

Daphne stood a few feet from the still open doorway, staring at Nora, stuttering a couple of times but not managing to make a single coherent sentence despite her trio of aborted attempts.

"You've done a lot of questionable shit in our two years working together, but spiking my drink? That's not just too far, Daphne, it's *illegal*."

"Why would you think I spiked your drink?" Daphne sounded not just baffled by Nora's accusation but almost aghast at her audacity.

"Maybe because *you spiked my drink*!"

"Why would I want to do that?"

"Because you wanted to go off and get your party on."

"That's bullshit!" Daphne snapped, still sounding offended. "And fuck you for thinking that I would do something that shitty to you!"

"What's the last thing you remember?"

"I remember us in a limo together with Caroline." She shrugged. "After that, I woke up at home covered in blood with glitter all over my boobs."

"It was ketchup."

"You wish it was ketchup." Daphne laughed. "That was definitely blood."

Trust Daphne to not get that waking up covered in blood and with no memory of how she'd gotten there was a *bad* thing.

Nora didn't want to think about what Daphne's life had been like before the actress had been forced to hire her.

"How do you know it was blood if you don't remember what happened last night?" Nora asked. "And why are you laughing?"

"How many movies do you think I've made, honey? Ketchup is for fries, squibs are for dramatic exits, and blood is nature's way of either reminding us that we're alive or in a fucked-dry-without-lube sort of situation. This tastes like blood, and I think it's funny that you don't know the difference."

"We should call Eric," Nora said.

"Your detective boyfriend? Why would we call him? Are you horny?" She laughed.

"Because of all the blood?" Nora explained, surprised that she needed to.

"It's just a little blood."

"Are you kidding me? I don't know about you, but there was a lot on me last night. My dress was covered with it. Are you sure you don't remember anything?"

"How many times do I have to tell you? I woke up with this hangover a few minutes ago, then you showed up. That's literally all I know."

Daphne sounded believable enough that Nora's extremely sensitive bullshit meter still wasn't blinking.

However, Daphne was also an excellent actress when

cast in the right role, and no one was better at playing Daphne Belle than Daphne herself.

But if Daphne was telling the truth, that was bad news too. Because it meant that someone else had decided to drug both of them.

Why?

"I need more coffee to deal with this," Nora grumbled. "Preferably hot this time."

"Is there another kind of coffee?" Daphne made a face.

"Do you know how to work that thing?" Nora nodded at a coffee machine sitting in a corner on the counter that looked like it could occupy a shelf at the Apple store.

"Of course, I know how to work it," Daphne said on her way to the machine.

"Would you mind making us a pot then?"

Daphne stared at the coffee machine, her eyes glazing over at the myriad of buttons and dials that looked more like a spaceship control panel than an everyday appliance. She jabbed at a couple of gleaming knobs, which caused the machine to hiss and sputter without producing any actual coffee. Just as Nora had suspected.

Nora gently nudged her aside. "I can figure this out."

"Of course, you can figure it out. You're a fixer, and that's what you do. Fix things."

"Well, sure," Nora kind of agreed, "but the coffee maker isn't broken. Fixing things isn't the same as spending the required time to figure out how something works."

Nora proved her point by getting the coffee started before turning to Daphne. "So, what could we have ingested that would knock out our memories like this, and how could we have ingested it?"

Daphne came alive like she'd been waiting a week to answer that exact question. "Oh, honey, there are too many options to count. It's like going to the Jelly Belly store. Ambien is great for those nights when your brain keeps doing the cha-cha and won't quiet down. Xanax is for when the world gets too loud, and you need it to hush up for a few hours. Valium is like a fuzzy blanket for—"

"I'm not asking for recommendations. I'm trying to figure out how whatever it was got into our system."

But it was like Nora hadn't even opened her mouth.

"Ativan, darling, that one is like swallowing a lullaby. Klonopin might be what we're looking for here. I have no personal experience with that, but one of my friends — and I won't tell you who because it isn't Caroline — said that Klonopin is like tossing your memories into a blender and hitting *puree*. Phenobarbital sounds like a ritzy drink, but it's actually a ticket to forgetting."

"Okay." Nora tried to reset the conversation. "Disregarding the wide array of potential pharmaceuticals we could have ingested, let's focus on *how* we could have ingested them."

"How am I supposed to know that?" Daphne asked. "I'm an expert on taking drugs, not drugging people. By the way, I found some car keys in the fridge right after I woke up. Do those belong to you?"

"Nope." Nora shook her head. "My keys were in my purse, which was back at the theater."

"Weird." Daphne shrugged.

Nora went over and opened the refrigerator door to grab a bottle of water and remembered the two different servers on two separate occasions with two contrasting brands of water last night, one bottle perfectly upscale and aligned with the evening and the other decidedly out of place.

"What if our water was spiked?" Nora asked.

"Why would someone want to do that?"

"I'm not sure," Nora said, at least half to herself. "I'm thinking on it…"

"Maybe it was Scarlett Anderson," Daphne answered her own question with a laugh. "Vengeance for my getting the *Sister Justice* role instead of her. Fuck her, by the way. Scarlett is the same age as my youngest sister but twice as much of a cunt."

"That word is never okay."

"It's sometimes okay," Daphne defended herself.

"Scarlett isn't out of the question. But I think Asa is our most likely suspect."

"Asa might chase after girls who just got their learner's permits but drugging them? Not to defend the guy, but I don't see him doing that."

"Asa said that he was going to get even with me," Nora said. "And this sure feels like getting even with me."

"He wasn't even at the Gala."

"But he showed up to the suite beforehand, and he knew where we were going. It wouldn't have been hard for him to buy one of the servers off."

Nora poured herself a mug of coffee, then went to get her phone, which now had just enough juice for her to make a call without worrying that her battery would drain down to nothing at any second.

Asa answered on the second ring, sounding arrogantly excited by the sound of her voice. "So, I guess you reconsidered my offer?"

"Not in a million years. I'm just calling to let you know that I'm about to have you arrested for assault."

"Assault?"

"That's right, *assault*. Last night. This is a courtesy call."

"It doesn't sound courteous at all. But I suppose I can handle the manners for both of us. So, please tell me,

Nora: I flew to Mexico right after leaving your hotel, so how is it possible that I was sipping margaritas with several sexy señoritas at the same time that you claim I assaulted you?"

"You're a pig."

"Maybe so, but that doesn't change my timeline."

"What about your threat?" Nora said.

"I never threatened you."

"You gave me 'one last chance to change my mind.'"

"That?" Asa laughed. "I said it in a movie once. I thought it might work on you like it did on James Franco."

Nora hung up and started searching through social media by hashtags from the gala. But judging by the pictures, no one else seemed drugged, or to even be misbehaving. Oddly enough, she didn't see any photos of her or Daphne beyond the white carpet images that had been taken outside before the auction even started.

So as of this morning, the gala had not ended in irreparable damage to either one of their reputations. There was still hope to salvage whatever this was.

But Nora felt confused. If it wasn't Asa, then who the hell drugged them?

She could understand his motive a lot easier than Scarlett's, considering how much the actress would have to lose and how little there was to gain for spite.

Nora turned around to ask Daphne if there was anything else she should know about her relationship with the other actress, but Daphne was nowhere in sight.

Nora ducked out of the kitchen and peeked into the living room to see that the front door was wide open. *Shit.*

Nora ran outside past the garish stone cherub guarding the entrance, its chubby rock body painted in clashing neon hues, with rosy ceramic cheeks and pudgy limbs, garishly at odds with the mansion behind it.

Daphne was already at the end of her driveway, about to march across the wide boulevard toward Scarlett's.

"Stop!" Nora cried out.

Daphne ignored her, crossing the street to Scarlett's mansion. Just like Nora's mother had always ignored her when she got a crazy idea in her head, trusting that Nora would be there to clean up whatever mess she'd made.

Nora was a grown-up now, and her mother was dead. But somehow, she was back to dealing with the same infuriating bullshit.

She gave chase — she was faster than Daphne but probably not nearly fast enough to reach the front door first, considering Daphne was already at the edge of Scarlett's gorgeous green lawn and halfway to the fat white pillars lining her front porch.

"Stop!" Nora called out again, trying to run faster.

But Daphne was already inside the house as Nora reached the property.

She chased Daphne past the threshold and into the grand foyer, with opulent chandeliers dangling from frescoed ceilings and a gilded staircase spiraling upward from the polished marble floor.

Scarlett's house was gorgeous, but it felt like a showcase. Daphne's mansion at least felt like a home.

"What do you think you're doing?" someone yelled.

Nora turned toward the maid, but instead of answering her question, the woman started screaming at the top of her lungs.

Nora started to run past the maid but then stopped to face her instead — not just because screaming might bring the cops, which she definitely didn't want to deal with right now, but because she felt compassion for this woman who might fear for her life without knowing that Nora could never mean an innocent, hardworking woman like her any harm.

"This isn't a home invasion, and you're not in any danger," Nora assured her. "I'm chasing my crazy client, Daphne Belle before she screams at your crazy boss upstairs."

The maid nodded, her eyes full of understanding. "Good luck."

Nora raced upstairs, reaching what she knew to be Scarlett's bedroom, thanks to the sound of Daphne screaming at her before Nora arrived.

Scarlett was in bed with a man. Nora couldn't see who it was because he was cowering under the covers, but she saw an empty tuxedo draped over an overstuffed chair in the corner.

"I have no idea where you went last night after you left the table!" Scarlett yelled at Daphne, and by the sound of it, Nora figured it was the first time she had managed to get a word in. "You got drunk and left, then you never came back."

"It was food poisoning. Daphne didn't have anything to drink last night." Nora took Daphne by the arm and started to drag her back out of the bedroom.

Her phone pinged as she crossed the threshold. Nora pulled it out of her pocket and looked at the screen. It read, *One million or this gets sent to Sheryl Stewart.*

Her phone buzzed with another text, this time a video.

Nora probably should have waited to press play until she and Daphne were back outside instead of watching the video while still standing in the doorway, but she couldn't help it.

Not that Nora needed to see the whole thing.

The screenshot showed Daphne dancing topless on a

tiki bar with her boobs smeared in glitter, and that was more than enough.

Chapter Eight

"Are you planning on building a summer camp in my hallway?" Scarlett yelled from her bed. "ROSALINA! Why did you let these people into my house?"

Nora grabbed Daphne again and dragged her toward the staircase.

"Slow down!" Daphne wailed. "I can walk — there's no need to drag me away like I'm fresh kill on the Serengeti!"

"Have a good day!" Rosalina waved at them as they reached the bottom of the stairs. Nora kept marching her charge toward the door.

"And *bien dia* to you *tambien*!" Daphne waved, turning back around to face Nora once they were both outside. "When do we get to see the video?"

"I can't believe you." Nora shook her head. "It's *always* something. We had *one* day, Daphne. *One* day, and then we were home free. Why the hell did you do this?"

"Why don't you give me a look-see at the video? I'd like

to know what I did." Daphne was laughing, still not getting the gravity of this situation.

Judging by the last two years of their time together, Nora was the fool for expecting anything different. She pressed *play*.

The video had obviously been taken last night because Daphne was still wearing her gown from the gala, or at least most of its bottom.

Under a warm orange glow from the tiki bar's lanterns, Daphne danced about with her usual flair, loud laughter exuberantly harmonizing with the rhythm of island drums. Statues jostled behind her as if wanting to boogie down by her side.

The crowd was already hooting and hollering, but the screaming came hard and fast as Daphne lowered the top of her dress, lapping up the attention as she sashayed across the artfully weathered bamboo with an uninhibited allure, an orange glow washing across her bare body, drops of moisture rolling down her skin like liquid gold.

"I don't remember doing any of that." Daphne shook her head with a frown, looking truly perplexed. "But my tits do look fantastic, don't they?" She gestured at her ample bosom that defied gravity much more so than most of her peers. "# DaphneDoesn'tAge, am I right?"

Daphne was smiling. Unbelievable.

"Focus up, Daphne. Someone drugged us so they could set you up to blackmail you with this video." *And I let them do it because, apparently, I suck at my job.* "I wish I knew where we were in this video."

"Oh." Daphne shrugged. "That's Burt's place, for sure. We obviously went to his afterparty when we left the gala."

"We agreed that we were not attending any of Burt's afterparties until your contract for *Sister Justice* was signed," Nora said through gritted teeth.

"We only had one night to go!"

"Exactly!" Nora exclaimed to make the opposite point. Then she started walking toward Daphne's house.

Daphne definitely didn't have a million dollars, and if Sheryl saw that video, she definitely wouldn't have the lead role in *Sister Justice* — and Nora would definitely have no career when that happened.

She had to figure out who the blackmailer was and get some leverage on them before they realized Daphne wasn't going to pay. Which meant finding whoever had drugged them, and if it wasn't the blackmailer, forcing that person to point them in the right direction.

"I don't know why you're so upset," Daphne said as she caught up. "Sheryl isn't going to let a little thing like that stupid video get in the way of my signing—"

"Please tell me you're kidding right now. Please give me some indication that you understand the stakes here. That there won't *be* a movie, or at least not one with you starring in it, if that video gets released to the public."

"You're making a big deal about this." Daphne waved a hand at Nora. "The world has seen my tits before. These babies have swung on and off camera in front of both ladies and gentlemen, long before YouTube."

"Right. And long before you were being cast with as nun who has a heart of gold."

"You can have a heart of gold and still shake your money makers. Julia Roberts was a hooker with a heart of gold in *Pretty Woman*, and she did a *lot* more than shake them. I bet Richard Gere wanted her to—"

"I think a hooker is the opposite of a nun, and I believe that 'sex worker' is the proper term these days."

"Is that a Me Too thing or just a regular woke thing?" Daphne asked. "And if you think I'm being sarcastic, I'm not. That's an actual question."

"It's more like a 'look around and read a room' kind of thing."

"So what are we supposed to do now?" Daphne asked.

Good question. She'd bought them a little time. But she needed to get her damn head straight before anything else. The pity party was over. It was time to do what she did best, and that meant fixing this.

"I'm going to make this problem go away," Nora said.

"I sure hope so. But I was also hoping that maybe we could get a bit more specific. I feel like I'm about to cash in my punch card. This is exciting."

"I'm sure you will love to tell me what that means."

"You know, like when you get frozen yogurt, and you go a dozen times, and they give you credit with every purchase, then the 13th time you get a free frozen yogurt?"

"Of course," Nora replied.

"You've given me little fixes before, but this is the *big* one, right at the end, just like in a really great story." Daphne seemed genuinely excited, so clearly, she was delusional and still not getting it. "So what's the plan?"

"I'm working on it."

"You do know that I don't have a million dollars."

"You have more than a million dollars, Daphne. Just not in cash, and at the rate you're going through it, not for long. But even if you had twenty million in your purse, we're not paying. I'm better at my job than succumbing to blackmail. We're going to find out who took the video."

She took out her phone before Daphne could ask the next question, texting the mystery number back with, *Who is this?*

No response.

Thirty seconds into waiting, Daphne said, "It looks like they haven't gotten back to you yet."

"Thank you, Daphne."

Let's talk, she texted.

But still nothing.

Let's meet and negotiate, Nora tried again.

Three dots appeared, but they were gone in a blink.

So she tried another tactic: *We need a few hours to get the money.*

One hour, they replied.

We need at least two.

The blackmailer gave her a thumbs-up — a fucking thumbs-up — on the last message.

When she found them, she was going to feed them their own phone. After she deleted the video.

Nora searched the phone number on Google in every one of the seven separate ways she regularly used since, every so often, one of those methods would surface a result that the others did not. If nothing came up in all seven, the number didn't exist.

Nothing came up.

"You sure you don't recognize this number?" Nora repeated the question as she showed her screen to Daphne again.

"I've never seen it." She shook her head. "I don't even recognize the area code."

Nora texted Eric next, inserting the number and typing, *Could you look this number up for me?*

??? he texted back.

In a bind and need answers fast. No broken laws. Pinky swear.

"So, is Mr. Detective sticking it in you yet?" Daphne asked.

"I think you should call Burt and see if he knows who was at his party last night."

"Good idea," Daphne nodded. "But not *great*. Hardly punch card redemption status. But it is a good start."

Nora ignored her. Both of them froze as the phone rang in Daphne's ear.

"It's going to voicemail," she announced in a stage whisper before leaving her message. "Hey there, Burty-Boo, this is Daphne Cake and O-M-G, I know I'm calling like ten seconds past the crack of dawn, but that's because Nora made me, and you know how she is, so we'll just catch up with you later."

Daphne hung up the call, looking suddenly upset.

"You didn't ask the question," Nora said.

"It's not like he can answer without calling us back." Daphne waved a dismissive hand. "We'll ask when we get there. Burt is probably sleeping. His libido might still be in its twenties, but the rest of him needs the beauty sleep."

"Let's get going," Nora said.

A few minutes later, they both had coffee, water, and sunglasses, with Nora behind the wheel of her Infiniti as they drove to Burt's place. After a quarter-hour in the car, Nora felt certain that Daphne was acting, pretending to be in a better place than she was, smiling her way through a dark cloud.

"Here. You should take one of these." Daphne handed her a bottle of pills. "They're like an abracadabra for your headache, I promise."

Nora took the bottle, lowered her window, and tossed them out onto the street.

"What the hell did you do that for? Those cost me a fortune."

Daphne sagged in her seat, seeming a lot more downtrodden than seemed appropriate for the moment, and again, Nora thought that there was something more wrong here than was readily apparent.

And without enough clues to go on right now, *everything* mattered.

"What is it?" Nora asked. "What aren't you telling me?"

"What do you mean?"

"Something is on your mind."

Daphne sighed. "We have another problem."

Of course, they did.

Nora glanced into her rearview mirror and saw a black sedan behind them. "Is it the car following us?"

Daphne looked into her side mirror just as the sedan made a right turn. "You're just being paranoid. It's a side effect of the drugs."

"Then what's wrong?"

"My spider brooch is missing," Daphne admitted. "It's not mine, and—"

"That brooch is worth a cool two million dollars," Nora finished.

Chapter Nine

Nora and Daphne had been arguing for a while before they pulled up in front of Burt's mansion in the hills, but it had been at least seven full minutes since Daphne had managed to say anything new.

"I don't remember where I last saw it, and I swear I didn't mean to lose it!"

For the umpteenth time (Nora had seriously lost count, despite trying to maintain a tally for a while because she figured it might come in handy when arguing with Daphne later), Nora took a breath.

"I have never once in this discussion suggested that you *tried* to lose the brooch. I am asking clarifying questions that might help us home in on its possible location. Two million dollars is a lot of money, and thus, an embarrassing amount of scandal."

"You think I don't know how much two million dollars is?" Daphne screamed. "That's half of what they paid me for *Duchess of Dysfunction*. And what's the worst-case scenario here, Nora? The brooch is insured, and someone makes a bunch of money on the jewelry without even having to sell it?"

"Assuming they *wanted* to sell, which they probably didn't. And regardless, you having lost the brooch will only hurt your reputation."

"Good point," Daphne finally agreed.

"I'm sad to say this, considering it's still so relatively early in the day, but your missing jewelry is only our second most pressing problem."

Nora got out of her car and took in Burt's estate, sick with terraces and panoramic views. At nighttime the glittering lights must look gorgeous, but right now, a thick fog hung over the city.

"It's weirdly quiet," Nora said.

"What does that mean?"

"I don't know yet." Nora felt oddly unsettled by the sight of so much detritus strewn all about, even though she had seen much worse at many Hollywood bacchanals while babysitting clients.

Last night's debauchery was displayed in a series of exhibits: underwear on the ground twisted into indecorous shapes (an orgy outside?), empty champagne bottles strewn about the driveway, and several vehicles parked like the discarded toys of overgrown children that they were.

A military Jeep sat off to one side, in crudeness amid the luxury sedans and sports cars, casting a darkly brooding silhouette across the winding driveway.

Nora wasn't sure why she expected anything different from Daphne, but she didn't even bother to knock on Burt's door, storming into his mansion the same way she had marched right into Scarlett's.

Did no one in this town ever lock their doors?

The interior was even more trashed than the driveway, with posh furniture overturned and partygoers lying like fallen soldiers on a liquor-soaked battlefield, their shallow breaths punctuated by the occasional groaning snore or muffled moan. At least a third of the bodies were naked.

Daphne picked up a mostly full champagne bottle and tipped it back, but the bottle didn't quite reach her lips before Nora plucked it out of her hand and put the champagne out of reach on the counter, assuming Daphne didn't lurch for it.

"Spoil sport," Daphne said instead.

"I have no idea where we're going to find Burt in this pile of bodies."

"Oh, I know where he is!" Daphne exclaimed, like that wasn't the exact information that they had been waiting for.

"Then *please.*" Nora tried not to sound too exasperated. "Lead the way."

Daphne guided them through an interior maze of hallways until they emerged outside to see an incongruously placed military tank hulking beside a bubbling hot tub, its metallic surface gleaming with menace under the Californian sun.

Burt lay sprawled atop the behemoth, clad in a silken bathrobe and oversized sunglasses, his chest rising and falling as he cradled a rocket launcher like a pillow in his arms.

"Be careful," Nora called out to Daphne as she nudged her fellow thespian awake.

Wrong move. Sudden pressure on the trigger without warning sent a rocket screaming from Burt's launcher through the air, its fiery tail tracing a deadly arc before smashing into the distant hills and erupting into a brilliant ball of flame and smoke as the hillside trembled, then roared as loose dirt, rock, and vegetation cascading down to the ground in a tsunami of earth.

A cloud of dust billowed into the sky as Burt hollered like Yosemite Sam.

"You couldn't have planned that better!" He made it sound like a compliment. "But I'm surprised to see you ladies so early. Did you sleep before coming back?"

"Oh, I slept all right." Daphne shook her head. "But I have no idea what happened last night."

Burt hopped off of the tank and propped his rocket launcher up against its side while walking toward the back door of his mansion alongside them.

"We saw a video that was taken here at your house last night. Daphne is doing a dance on the table without her—"

"I dare say that might have been the crown jewel of last night." Burt cut her off as and started to holler like Yosemite Sam again, chuckling as he shook his head in disbelief. "Daphne was up on that bar dancing like it was 1999, and that was before she lost her top. But you sure as hell gave her a run for her money."

"Excuse me?" Nora didn't understand.

"You were the showstopper." Burt gave her a grin. "Or you would have been if you hadn't kept your clothes on."

"Christ on a cross." Nora shook her head.

Even after scrubbing through her memory banks, including a speed of light revisiting of an adolescence she had longed to forget, Nora settled on the reality that this moment now was the most mortified she had ever been in her life.

"Who brought us here?" Nora asked, trying to ignore her humiliation as she added a second question before waiting to get an answer for the first one. "And who videotaped us?"

"The limo dropped you two off with Caroline, and you

were already plenty happy when you got here. I don't know what you all were on, but you were on a lot of it."

"Including Caroline?" Nora asked.

"*Definitely* including Caroline. And anyone could have filmed that little meringue. The party was packed." He grinned with pride. "My parties are always packed. I think the real question is, who sold the video to a bad actor? No pun intended. I don't think this has anything to do with an actual actor. We tend to play bolder than we really are. Am I right, Daphne?"

"I'm plenty bold." She jerked a thumb at Nora. "This one keeps me from being bolder all the time, though."

"I don't think you guys are using that word in the same way," Nora said as her phone buzzed with a text, one of the two she had been waiting to get. She would have preferred to hear from the blackmailer, but a message from Eric was still a win. Sort of.

No luck with the number. Obviously a burner phone.

"I don't suppose you ladies have brought back my car?" Burt asked.

"Your car?" Nora blinked back at him.

"Specifically, the absurdly expensive Rolls Royce Shadow with the vanity license plate that reads LVNLGND."

"Living Legend — I always loved your license plate!" Daphne touched him on the arm. "It tells a true story in just seven characters."

"You asked to borrow it," Burt said to Daphne before turning to Nora, "and you took the keys."

"I know where those are!" Daphne declared. "We saw the keys at my place. We'll get your wheels back right away. You always have the best taste and the most wonderful toys."

Daphne glanced over at the tank, almost like an impulse she couldn't even help.

"You want to shoot the tank, don't you?" Burt asked her with a hopeful smile.

"I don't think I'm allowed." She shook her head, the disappointment clear in her voice.

"I get it," Burt replied, somehow managing to acknowledge them both with a shrug.

"Thank you, Burt," Nora said, taking Daphne by her arm again and then walking away. "You've been a massive help."

Chapter Ten

"I can't believe you!" Nora said as Daphne led her back through Burt's house to the front door. She was grateful for the guide. Without Daphne, there was zero chance she'd have made it to the foyer without getting lost a couple of times.

The pile of bodies sprawled in the entryway had dwindled just a bit, but Nora saw no evidence as to where the stray partygoers may have wandered off to.

"I can't believe you lost that brooch plus a fucking *Rolls*," Nora snarled.

"*You* had the keys. Burt just said."

"That doesn't mean I was the one driving."

"Oh, it absolutely does! You know I never drive, so if we took that sweet ride anywhere, then *you're* the one who drove, which also means *you're* the one who lost the car. So there."

"So there? Are you twelve?"

"No one knows how old I really am, baby!"

"I've seen your birth certificate on three separate occasions. I know exactly how old you are. And the Rolls isn't lost."

"Oh yeah?" Daphne looked across the Infinity from her side as she opened the door.

"Yes. I know where it is, so that's where we're going next. Even if the Rolls is only priority three in this ever-escalating shit show, it's a problem we can solve by driving there."

Nora got into the car.

"We have to go to my place first," Daphne said as she sat. "The Rolls explains those keys in my fridge. We should also call an Uber to meet us at my place."

"Why?"

"You know I don't drive."

"Really? You don't say."

"So, how would we get the Rolls and your car both back?"

Nora grumbled to herself, but she didn't disagree because Daphne was right, and she was feeling silly for not having caught that herself. She had been Daphne's chauffeur for much of the time she had worked for her. Not that Nora had ever signed up or even agreed to the duty. A once or twice favor after Daphne was forced to let her driver go had eroded into an everyday expectation.

On the other hand, it meant she was literally in the driver's seat, so she had more control — Daphne couldn't go anywhere without Nora agreeing to take her there.

"Honey, with what I'm paying you, the least you could do is chauffeur me around a bit," Daphne had said, the first time as a joke but shortly thereafter as a matter of fact.

"It's too soon to call for an Uber," Nora told her as they pulled out of Burt's driveway. "It'll take us half an hour to get back."

"I'm just looking at our options. This gives us more time to choose."

"You are exhausting."

"I'm being helpful. What kind of car do you want?" Daphne asked.

"The kind that gets us to the Rolls Royce that you never should have borrowed."

"That *we* never should have borrowed. SUV or van?"

"I don't care."

"How about an Escalade?"

"Please, no," Nora said.

"You don't like Escalades?"

"We don't need a luxury ride to retrieve the Rolls."

"Are you hearing yourself?" Daphne scoffed. "If we're going to retrieve a Rolls Royce, then anything shabby is just inappropriate."

Nora managed to ignore her for the rest of the way there. She sighed as she pulled into Daphne's driveway, where a Toyota Camry was waiting.

"I told you it was too early to schedule a car."

"This way, we won't have to wait," Daphne explained, as though the driver behind the wheel of his Toyota, giving them an impatient glare, had nothing better to do than wait for them. "The trick is that you just have to tip enough that they don't care how long you've been making them sit there. So it works on a sliding scale."

Daphne got out of Nora's car and called out to the Uber driver. "Two minutes!"

Then she ducked into the house and disappeared for an excruciatingly long time (just under ten minutes) before joining Nora in the back of the Uber.

"She promises to overtip," Nora said as Daphne jogged toward the Camry.

Daphne got in and slammed her door. "Sorry to keep

you waiting, but nature called, and let me tell you, it was more like a shout!"

The driver exhaled with a gust and pulled onto the street.

Less than a mile out of Daphne's neighborhood, Nora felt something prickling at the base of her neck. She turned around and — of course — spied a dark sedan driving behind the Camry.

"Can you pull over?" Nora asked.

The driver sighed, clearly having surrendered in this battle with the famous actress and her fixer running him around, then pulled over without a word.

The sedan flew by fast enough that Nora barely nabbed a glimpse of the hoodie-wearing driver.

"Thank you. We can go again now."

He pulled back into traffic and drove the rest of the way to the underpass near the museum where Nora had seen the Rolls Royce amid a long line of lookie-loos earlier that morning.

"I hope it's still there," Nora said under her breath, mostly to herself.

"You and me both, sister!" Daphne exclaimed with the approximate volume of a church choir.

They got out of the Uber and Daphne tipped their driver 100% of the fare.

Nora thought it should have been more.

But she exhaled with relief upon seeing the Rolls parked about fifty feet away. She approached it with Daphne trailing behind her. They reached the vehicle in unison, but Daphne was the one to point out the sight that had gave Nora chills.

"That's blood," Daphne said about the long smear across the trunk. A stark crimson streak marred the pristine alabaster sheen of the Rolls. "Do you think that's the same blood that was on our dresses?"

Nora didn't answer, popping open the trunk. Inside was the corpse of an unfamiliar man.

A single blink, then she slammed the trunk again.

"Was there a dead guy in there?" Daphne asked the obvious.

"Yes," Nora nodded.

"That couldn't really have been a dead guy." Daphne shook her head as if willing the reality to wander off and leave them alone. "Maybe it was something else. You did slam that trunk awfully fast."

"That was a body."

Daphne gestured down at the trunk. "Open it."

Nora complied, looking around as she lifted the lid, then leaning into the yawning space and inspecting the body while Daphne did the same thing right next to her.

"At least we know where the blood came from," Nora said.

"We don't know for sure that the blood belonged to this guy."

Nora turned to her. "Do you remember there being more bodies? I should call Eric."

She took her phone.

"No, you don't!" Daphne snatched the phone away from Nora. "This is for all the times you took my glass of whatever away from me, except that what I'm doing right now actually makes the world a better place."

"How is that?" Nora asked.

"You can't call your private dick because if the police know what happened here, then we'll both be charged with murder. And yes, I understand that he's not actually a private investigator. I meant more like you use him privately."

"He'll listen to me," Nora argued.

"We were covered in blood, a fact that will definitely come up during questioning when they ask us where our clothes from last night are. And we were the ones who had Burt's car. Do you think that I haven't been in this movie before?"

Nora was starting to panic. Her heart pounded, each wild drumbeat echoing the rising tide of dread that was sinking its talons into her throat. It was one thing to screw up with a client and crash their career. Committing murder and hiding the victim in the trunk of a movie star's borrowed car was a mistake on a whole new level, one she had no idea how to fix.

Daphne grabbed her by the shoulders and shook her, yanking her out of her panic. "You're the fixer! You can fix this."

She had to fix this. Because if she didn't, they might both be going to jail. No alibi, no memory of what had happened…

"We just need to sort out what happened to us." Nora nodded as she gathered herself. "Then we can go to the police."

"We can't do that. Considering you're my fixer, I really wish you were getting this faster. The cops will never buy that we can't remember anything. It's the stupidest alibi ever, and if this were a script, my agent would throw that shit in the trash."

"You're right. But it's kind of dangerous to be driving around with a dead body."

"We can take the Rolls back to my place. Leave it out back while you figure out what's happening, and then we'll decide what to do next."

Nora nodded again, glad that she and Daphne appeared to be on the same page for once. Although, how surreal was it that Daphne was the one thinking straight while Nora was freaking out?

Maybe the drugs weren't completely out of her system.

They got in the Rolls, and Nora started the engine.

She pulled out onto the street and into traffic.

No surprise, that same dark sedan was following them.

For less than a minute before, an Escalade emerged from a side street like a sudden storm and slammed into the sedan.

Metal shrieked, and glass shattered, sending the sedan spinning out of control.

Masked figures in black spilled out of the Escalade, with guns brandished by their apparent leader, aiming his pistol at Nora as he walked calmly toward them.

Daphne screamed as she slammed her foot atop Nora's on the accelerator, the dual pressure sending the Rolls Royce rocketing forward.

The engine growled as it devoured asphalt like Pac-Man swallowing pellets, hurtling toward the nearest on-ramp.

Daphne retracted her foot, allowing Nora to take command again as she zoomed onto the highway.

The Escalade followed.

Chapter Eleven

NORA AND DAPHNE raced down the interstate with the Escalade hot on their tail. They were suddenly in serious trouble, and Nora had no idea why any of this was happening.

The kinds of crises she was used to dealing with involved sending sex workers out through the back door and keeping naloxone handy so she didn't have to call an ambulance — and possibly attract paparazzi attention — when a client accidentally overdosed. The kind of out-of-control bullshit that her mother used to get into.

Nora would've given anything to rewind this day back to the point where the only problem she had to solve was a video of Daphne shaking her glitter-encrusted tits.

She glanced over at Daphne, who had her phone.

"What are you doing? Don't just sit there, call the cops!"

"I already told you we can't call the cops, Nora! We have a goddamned body in the trunk! Unless you've got a magical trunk fairy, I don't think dialing 911 is our best move right now."

"Do you want to get out of this alive?"

"Definitely. But I'm not going to prison. I'm sure you can outrun them." Daphne patted the dashboard. "This puppy knows how to bark."

Nora glanced in her rearview mirror again. "Do you think I should take the next exit, but at the last possible second?"

"Not the next one, but the one after that." Daphne nodded, sitting up straighter in her seat now.

Nora's hands tightened on the wheel, her knuckles whitening as she gripped it in anticipation.

"Left!" Daphne shouted. "Hard left now!"

Nora jerked the wheel without hesitation.

The tires barely whispered against the asphalt as the Rolls rounded the curve.

"Right!"

"Now straight!"

"Left again!"

Daphne kept barking orders while Nora's eyes darted between the road ahead and the rearview mirror.

But the Escalade remained in hot pursuit.

"Where are we going?" Nora asked.

"I have no idea." Daphne shrugged. "But I always wanted to direct!"

"Your directorial debut is about to get us killed." Nora took a breath to steel herself, then began to plot her own course.

Her eyes darted around, searching for an escape route as she veered sharply right, plunging the vehicle into a dim, narrow alleyway, brick walls on either side of them seeming to close in as they soared toward the street at the end.

And for a second, it seemed like Nora had lost the Escalade.

But her victory was short-lived.

She gunned the engine and sped toward an open parking lot, failing to see the elevated curb ahead. She tried to avoid it with a desperate swerve. Too late.

The Rolls lurched violently as its undercarriage met the concrete with a gut-wrenching CRUNCH.

The purring engine made a tortured groan. And the car refused to budge.

"You know, sweetie, if you just throw some glitter on it with a gentle pep talk, I bet she'll start right up again."

Nora ignored her.

"Maybe you should try—"

"YOU DON'T EVEN DRIVE!" Nora took a breath. "Sorry. I just need a moment to think."

"You would be feeling a lot better right now if you hadn't thrown all of our pills out the window."

"Your pills, Daphne."

"What? Now I'm in trouble for offering to share? You must not have been a very good kindergartner."

"Can you PLEASE let me think?"

"Geez. Sorry." But Daphne could only stand the silence for so long, in this case, just over a minute. "So, what are we going to do now?"

Nora took another breath, then she swallowed and said, "We're going to leave the car here, with the keys in the ignition."

"Why would we do that?"

"Because we're going to report it stolen. Hopefully, Burt has insurance."

"Of course, he has insurance, but I still don't think that—"

"Do you have any better ideas?" When Daphne didn't dare to even try: "We'll wipe the car clean of our fingerprints and get the hell out of here."

"But what are we going to do with the body in the trunk?"

"Did you want to put it in your purse?" Nora asked. "We're leaving the body right where it is."

"What if our DNA is on it?"

"We opened the trunk and looked, but we never touched the body."

"Maybe not today. But what about last night?"

Good point, but also, goddammit.

"Why don't we take the body with us?" By the sound of her voice, Daphne didn't consider that a ridiculous question. She even doubled down after Nora ignored it. "I'm serious. We should take the body with us."

"I can't even tell if you're being serious right now."

"Oh, I'm serious, honey."

"I'm going to check and see if the coast is clear. Then I'll come back and get you. Sit tight and don't move. Can you do that?"

"I guess."

"No guessing, Daphne. I'm asking you a yes or no question. Will you be able to cool your jets until I get back in like two minutes from now?"

"Yes, mother."

"You're twice my age," Nora said.

"And yet you're the one saying 'cool your jets.' You're like a hundred times my age when it comes to fun-squashing." Daphne laughed to herself. "You're like a librarian in charge of the 'shush' department."

"I'll be back." Nora walked away, not wanting to dignify Daphne's accusation that she was a killjoy yet again, despite feeling the need to remind her that this was exactly what she paid her to do.

Everything would be different in just a few hours from

now. The *Sister Justice* contract would get signed, and Nora would be on her way to working at Three Mile PR.

Her feet pounded the pavement, heart galloping as she hurried up the street in search of the Escalade, half-relieved and half-frightened to see it in her periphery. At least she had eyes on it instead of the other way around.

She watched the SUV circle around like a sinister vulture.

It parked on the street, and panic swelled within her. She squinted into the distance and watched a trio of men spill out of the vehicle. Their masks were off this time, but they were all too far away for Nora to see them.

Shit.

She needed to get back to Daphne.

Nora ran back to the Rolls, but Daphne was gone.

Double shit.

Did the men in the Escalade somehow manage to grab her? Had Nora failed again?

She couldn't text because Daphne still had her phone.

She should have called Eric. Now they were—

Daphne came bouncing around the corner with a shopping bag in each of her hands.

"YOU WENT SHOPPING?"

"Of course, I went shopping. I know how to multitask."

"How is that multitasking?" Nora asked.

"I had to get supplies for our plan," Daphne explained as she pulled a man's trench coat out of the bag, along with a pair of sunglasses and a small bottle of cologne. "Like I said, I think we should take the body with us."

"And like I said—"

"I'm not going down for a murder I didn't commit, Nora. This right here is a punch card situation, whether you want to help me fix it or not."

"So you want to dress the body in your drugstore Halloween costume because you think that's going to get us out of this?"

"Haven't you ever seen *Weekend at Bernie's*?"

"The *Weekend at Bernie's* strategy didn't even work in *Weekend at Bernie's*."

"It worked just fine," Daphne said. "That's why there was a sequel."

"If we touch the body, it will be considered interfering with a police investigation at the very least."

"You're just proving my point."

"How am I proving your point?" Nora asked.

"Would you rather get dinged for interfering with a police investigation or become the prime suspect in a murder the press will never stop talking about if I'm involved?" Daphne opened the trunk. "I already cleaned his face off with the wipes that Burt always keeps in his glove compartment. And I called us an Uber. So help me get this body out right now."

Nora felt like she had no choice but to comply.

Whoever the man was, he appeared to have been shot in his chest.

Together they pulled the trench coat over the corpse, then doused it in cologne and stuck the sunglasses on his vacant face.

The Uber pulled up, and the driver cast a curious look their way, eyeing the woman even more suspiciously as they manhandled the figure into his car. Daphne draped herself dramatically over the corpse while issuing a series of dramatic giggles.

"Oh, you know Roger!" she drawled in a classic Daphne Belle performance tailor-made for their driver. "Always overindulging at parties!"

She gave the drunk man a playful nudge, making

"Roger's" sunglasses slide down his nose. The driver grunted as Daphne finished her show, proudly displaying her chest as she said, "He just needs to sleep it off. By the time we get back to my place, he'll be back to motor-boating these babies big time!"

Chapter Twelve

THE DRIVER MUST HAVE STOLEN a hundred glances at Daphne's boobs in his rearview mirror, but she didn't mind — it was better than if he'd spent that time looking at "Roger" and possibly noticing that he was dead. Besides, she was only another couple of minutes away from escaping from some of the worst parts of this giant mess she found herself in, and through no fault of her own, this time.

That was a nice change.

This was something that had happened *to her*, and Daphne was the one getting herself out of it, despite having a full-time fixer on her payroll. This time, *she* was the one bailing Nora out.

She could barely believe that Nora had wanted to leave the body in the trunk of Burt's Rolls Royce. Had she never seen *CSI*? Or *Law & Order*? Forensics always found *something* that got the killer caught.

And yet Nora was furious with her for the entire ride, fuming by the time their driver took one last glance at Daphne as he pulled up in front of her house.

She distracted him by leaning forward, giving him a final glimpse along with an extra big tip that she could afford a lot less today than yesterday, while Nora did the heavy lifting, dragging the body out of the car. Daphne loudly laughed and declared that Old Roger had definitely fallen into the deep end of the cocktail pool this time.

Once the driver had taken off, she and Nora worked to move the body into the house.

"Did he gain weight?" Daphne asked halfway there. "He feels heavier."

"Maybe he was snacking in the car when we weren't looking."

Why was Nora still fuming? They'd pulled it off, hadn't they?

"That does sound like Bernie," Daphne joked, wishing Nora would relax.

But instead, Nora snapped, "We're not calling him Bernie."

"You can call him whatever you want." Daphne shrugged. "I'm calling him Bernie."

It took her almost two minutes to open her front door because she wanted to use the app, but then the app wanted Daphne to give it an update, which she didn't even intentionally agree to.

They dragged the body over to the couch and plopped it onto its side.

"It looks like he's sleeping," Daphne said.

"That's about as dead as a body can look. That nap is forever. We're lucky if our Uber driver isn't calling the cops right now."

"Are you kidding? He's probably two blocks away adding some mayo to his knuckle sandwich."

"I can't even with you." Nora shook her head.

"I'm not being full of myself. You should see my DMs. They're rated R."

Nora sighed.

Daphne started toward her kitchen. "We can leave him on the couch until we figure out who the hell he is and what the hell is going on. And by 'we,' I mean 'you.' I'm making breakfast."

Daphne opened the refrigerator door as Nora entered the kitchen behind her.

"Are we expecting guests?" Nora gestured to the full carton of eggs, thick restaurant bacon, and some rather delicious-looking mushrooms already on the counter as Daphne dug through the fridge for more. "You can't possibly be hungry right now."

"Breakfast is for you. You're gonna need some serious sustenance to figure this shit out."

"What if I'm not hungry?"

"You'll be hungry once you start smelling it. While I cook, tell me what you're going to do to fix this."

Chapter Thirteen

Nora closed the bathroom door and sat on the toilet lid.

She still wanted to call Eric, but Daphne was right. No one would believe their story. *She* could barely believe their story.

At first, she'd been afraid that she'd hit their dead friend while driving last night.

Except that didn't make sense once she accounted for the total lack of front-end damage on the Rolls. The only blemish Nora had seen on the vehicle before driving it right into a crisis point was that blood smear on the trunk.

"Bernie" had been shot. But she didn't have a gun.

Did Daphne have a gun? If so, Nora sure as hell should have known about it.

"You can figure this out," she told herself in the mirror, steeling her eyes and doubling down on the message. "You're Nora Fucking Bauer, and you can fix anything. You decide what you're going to do, and then you do it. When confronted by an obstacle, you find a way over, under, or around it. There is no problem you can't solve once you discover the first thread to pull. You're inches away from figuring this out."

But there had been at least one problem she couldn't solve in her life: convincing her mother to clean up her act and be the adult in the family. And every second she spent with Daphne felt like being twelve again — watching her out-of-control mother careening breathlessly toward disaster while partying her life away, with Nora chasing after her, knowing that when she caught up, she'd find nothing but wreckage.

Her mother had died before Nora had been old enough to solve that problem.

But at least she could fix things for Daphne.

She took one last look at herself, along with a final breath, then abandoned the bathroom and went back into the kitchen, where the scent of frying butter slapped her nostrils as it mingled with the tantalizing aroma of caramelized onions.

Her stomach started rumbling, a primal yearning as she sat at the bar. "Do you have a gun?"

"Of course, I have a gun!" Daphne left the stove and started toward the pantry. "You would have a gun too if strange men sent you pictures of your own damned feet from a week ago."

She pulled out a box of Honey Nut Cheerios and shoved her hand down inside it. A second later, Daphne was holding a gun.

"Jesus," Nora said.

"I've never even used it once." Daphne handed it to her. "Here."

Nora put it under her nose, but it didn't appear to have been recently shot, and didn't smell like oil or anything else. Just the faint whiff of metal. Barely noticeable.

Nora handed the gun back to Daphne. "Put it somewhere safe."

Daphne shoved it down her shirt. "I already know what you're going to say, but it's only until I finish making your omelet."

What had she been thinking, handing the gun back to Daphne?

As Daphne went back to cooking, Nora walked over and withdrew the weapon from her client's cleavage.

Then she started to pace, thinking out loud. "Last night, you were just an actress about to make a comeback, but today you're a blackmail victim and possibly a murder suspect — and it all started at the gala. We need to make a list of suspects. Who could have drugged us?"

"Who couldn't have?"

"Scarlett—"

Daphne nodded in approval. "I'm glad you put her first on the list."

"These aren't in any kind of order."

"Subconsciously, they probably are."

"Fine." Nora didn't see the point in arguing. "Maybe it's subconscious because she was the first person you accused this morning."

"It was Scarlett's fault for being a bitch last night. She didn't want the job because they wanted someone old? She's just jealous of me, so fuck her, I would throw Scarlett Anderson into a pit in the ground with Harvey Weinstein—"

"Please don't ever say anything like that again."

"—and not even think twice—"

"You should think at least a *thousand* times before saying that shit."

"—because Scarlett Anderson is one of those people

who is mean just because she can be, and people like that suck a bag of old man dicks with all the gray little—"

"I've got it, Daphne. And again, *Jesus.*"

Daphne left the stove, came over to Nora, gently took the gun from her, then went over to the pantry, and returned it to the box of Honey Nut Cheerios, before heading back to finish the omelet.

"I'll put it somewhere later," Daphne promised, in a voice that let Nora know that there was a one hundred percent chance that the gun would still be in that box the next time she looked. "So, Scarlett. Who is number two on our list?"

"The second person on our randomly ordered list is Caroline."

"What?" Daphne turned back to Nora. "Why Caroline? She shouldn't even be last on the list."

"Caroline was there, and she had an opportunity."

"But no motive."

"You never know someone's motive. Caroline is on the list whether you like it or not."

"I've known Caroline for almost thirty years. She would never do this to me."

That wasn't worth arguing with either. But no way was Nora taking Caroline off the list. "Asa is next."

"If I agree that Asa could have done it, will you take Caroline off the list?"

"Tim, Lavigne, and you."

"ME? What the fuck, Nora?"

That note of innocent outrage was perfect. Too bad Nora saw through Daphne's bullshit. "Everyone is on the list."

"You're not on the list," Daphne said dramatically. "How do I know you didn't set me up so you could move on to new clients? And we have no idea who killed the man on my couch."

"I didn't drug myself. And I was already going to move on — I didn't have to do anything to make that happen."

Daphne scowled. "What's next?"

"The only way I know how to fix this is to start at the very beginning and figure out what happened last night. Caroline was with us, so there's no better place to start than with her."

"I already tried calling her earlier this morning, but I didn't get an answer. Definitely weird because that bitch always answers her phone."

"What about her assistant?"

"Sophia? *That* bitch would be there to smell every one of Caroline's farts if she could. She's like a tenth-degree sycophant if that's how degrees work."

"Is everyone a bitch now?"

"No." Daphne shook her head. "Just my friends and people who suck."

"So I should call Sophia?"

"I'll call her." Daphne was dialing just seconds later.

She put the phone on *speaker*.

"Hey, Daphne. I was just about to call you," Sophia answered.

"Because you wanted to know why I don't age?" Daphne laughed and winked at Nora.

Nora ignored her even harder than she was ignoring the grumble in her stomach.

"I was wondering if you knew where Caroline is?" Sophia said.

"That's why I was calling you. She's not answering her phone."

"I've been ringing her for over an hour now, and I'm starting to lose my shit. She has a meeting with Evans

Glenn today, and that guy is already kind of a cock to her. He'll be a full-effect shitface if she gives him a chance."

"Hey there, Sophia. This is Nora."

"Hey, Nora."

"I'm going to text you my number. Can you give me a call when Caroline comes back? We'll do the same if we see or hear from her first."

"Of course."

"Thanks." Nora hung up the call and then texted her number.

"Now what?" Daphne asked.

"Now we call the catering company for the gala."

"What do they know?"

"The waitress who served our table last night," Nora said. "Specifically the one who handed me the two bottles of water. Oasis brand."

"So technically, *you're* the one who poisoned me. If we're talking about who gave me the drink."

"How is that relevant?"

"You're always saying that everything is relevant." Daphne shrugged. "I didn't realize that you meant only for the stuff that *you* think is relevant."

Nora sighed and checked the gala email to find the catering company's name, then called them.

"Saffron and Silk, this is Jessa. How may I help you?"

"Hey there, Jessa," Nora said, "I was hoping you could help me."

"I hope I can help you, too."

"I was at the Stars and Stripes Gala last night, and I was hoping that I could talk to the woman who served me."

"Can I ask why?"

Nora hesitated. The woman had no reason to give her the information and every reason to protect her employees.

"I found her necklace on the floor near our table, but she'd already gone. The chain must've snapped when she brought us water."

"What did she look like?"

"Tall, dirty blonde hair in a ponytail, athletic." Nora realized how many of the servers that described as the words left her lips. Most of the wait staff who worked at Saffron and Silk were actors and actresses waiting for their big break.

"You don't have a name by chance, do you?"

"Sorry, I don't."

"We're prepping for an event right now. Most of last night's staff will be serving at a luncheon one hour from now. If you want to drop the necklace off there, I could give you the address?"

"I would *love* the address, Jessa. Thank you."

"Just ask for Stan when you get there."

Nora tapped the address into her phone as Jessa delivered it to her, then ended the call only to realize that Daphne had disappeared again.

Nora went outside to the car and saw that the actress was sitting in the passenger seat of Nora's car.

Nora opened the driver's side door. "You're not coming."

"Bullshit." Daphne shook her head.

"I have work to do."

"So do I, Nora. I'm in this as much as you, whether you like it or not. I also pay you. And if those two facts aren't enough for you, then I'm punching my card. Don't care about the punch card? Then FINE." She was suddenly twice as loud. "I'm not staying here by myself with a dead body!"

Daphne might have been acting, but if so, Nora appreciated the performance.

"Fine." She closed her door and started the car. Her stomach growled, reminding her of the breakfast Daphne had been preparing. She'd been right — as soon as Nora had smelled the onions browning in butter, she'd been starving.

But she could eat once they'd made some progress.

Nora drove to the address that Sophia had given her, eyes on the rearview mirror every few seconds the entire way, keeping them peeled for any sight of the black sedan, the Escalade, or any other predatory vehicle.

When Nora felt sure they were clear, she called the police to report the Rolls Royce stolen. But apparently, that was a task she should have given to Daphne.

"Let me handle this," the actress said while grabbing the phone from Nora, clearly delighted that she could speak car when her fixer could not.

"I apologize for her ignorance, good sir. But I can answer all of your questions posthaste. The vehicle in question is a Rolls Royce Shadow. The right rear taillight is slightly dimmer than the left. There's also a *tiny* scratch, I mean barely a pube, it's so small, but even a pussy hair scratch is noteworthy on a Rolls if you know what I mean, and you'll find that one just behind the front passenger-side wheel."

She winked at Nora, then hung up and handed over the phone.

"How the hell did you remember all that?" Nora asked.

Daphne grinned. "You only *think* I don't pay attention."

Chapter Fourteen

Nora steered into the service entrance behind the Château Luminaire, an architectural masterpiece with white columns and vast marble steps leading up to a set of grandiose double doors. She'd expected a venue approximately half as opulent as the one hosting last night's gala, but instead, this place made the former building appear downright dressed down, regardless of all those spangles and stars.

Large bay windows offered fleeting glances of the elegant chandeliers inside, and the stone cherubs peeking out from behind cascading ivy looked a little like the one guarding Daphne's front door.

Nora killed the engine and turned to Daphne. "Wait here."

"We already talked about this a bunch of times: *I'm coming with you.*"

"This time, you'll have to be with me in spirit. You'll draw too much attention, so I'm pulling my card as the authority here and insisting that you listen to me this time."

"Fine." Daphne crossed her arms and slid down low in her seat.

"I'll be back fast." Nora got out of the car without waiting for her reply. She circled around the building to a simple door, at least compared to the regal entry in front, though the back door was still studded with ornate ironwork that must have cost a fortune.

A perfectly coiffed man was already approaching Nora the second she entered. He was surprisingly young considering his confident bearing, his coal black hair neatly combed back, a crisp tailored suit hanging from his impeccable postured frame.

"Excuse me," Nora said as he approached her. "I'm looking for a gentleman by the name of Stan."

"I'm Stan. How may I be of service?"

"I attended the Stars and Stripes Gala last night, and I was looking for the server who took care of our table."

"I see." He narrowed his eyes. "Was our service less silken than we promised?"

"The service was impeccable!" Nora gushed, needing this man to feel happy that she was here asking questions. "I came down here to personally commend Saffron and Silk for doing such an incredible job last night, so if those compliments extend to you, please take them with my full heart. But I also wanted to see if I could speak to our server, so I could thank her for taking what would have been an incredible evening regardless and turning it into one of the most memorable nights of my life."

Stan opened his mouth, but Nora needed to get the rest of her spiel out.

"*Truly*. She was *amazing* and not at all what I would expect from a catering company. No offense. She just really seemed to care that we were having a great time at our table, and the best photos of our whole night were all taken by her. You really do curate your waitstaff remarkably."

Stan gained at least an inch in both his shoulders and his smile. "Do you happen to have her name?"

"Wish I did." Nora shook her head. "I've been racking my brain all morning. She was tall, with dirty blonde hair in a ponytail. I know that describes a quarter of the female servers last night."

"Or more. Is there anything else you can tell me about her?"

"I could see how bone-tired she was, not that she was showing it. I'm used to seeing that same kind of fatigue on set. Whoever this waitress was, she managed to hold her smile even though it probably weighed a hundred pounds."

"That is also very kind of you to say." Stan touched his chest as if the compliment belonged exclusively to him. "I do believe you might be speaking about Jennifer. If so, she's right through those doors."

He turned around and pointed toward what Nora assumed must be a dining room. "If not, you're welcome to come back, and we'll brainstorm a bit more. Sound good?"

Nora smiled even wider at him. "Sounds great."

She headed toward the open doors, not so much as pausing upon crossing the threshold because doing so would have put her shock on full display, but she was still bowled over with surprise once inside the expo area.

There were plenty of tables, but Nora didn't see a single one intended for eating. Instead, she saw a rainbow of sexual innovations as far as her eyes could see, with each table showcasing a variety of avant-garde intimate products, according to their banners and bright neon signs. It all looked especially garish, blinking beneath those ornate chandeliers that cast colorful shadows across a wide variety of similarly themed displays.

A highly polished waitstaff wove its way through the throng, trays glinting under the ambient light, carrying sparkling concoctions garnished with exotic-looking fruits, arrays of gourmet canapés, and appropriately themed delicacies like honey butter drizzled over figs.

Nora scanned the crowd until she spied the familiar face of her waitress from last night: *Jennifer*.

She made a beeline toward the server.

Jennifer turned around.

Their eyes locked, and a visible jolt of recognition crossed the server's features, draining her face of color. She fumbled the grip on her tray, sending canapés scattering amid a clatter of metal and porcelain.

Jennifer bolted, and Nora gave chase.

The waitress tore through the crowd amid an explosion of gasps and shouts from startled attendees. She narrowly dodged a stall showcasing velvet harnesses and sent the entire display tumbling, barely managing to recover her balance.

Nora raced by a scantily clad and extremely exuberant brunette. The woman paused her performance mid-gesture to stare after the caterer fleeing the high-strung millennial.

They raced past a curtained demo area until Jennifer arrived at a nondescript door.

She threw it open to reveal a dim alley.

Nora reached the door just before it finished closing, then she was racing down the alley after the waitress again, the sound of her footsteps bouncing off the brick walls on both sides of her.

The waitress rounded a corner midway through the next alley.

Big mistake. Jennifer was going top speed into what Nora already knew to be a dead end.

Jennifer slowed as her shoulders hunched in resignation.

Nora approached her, panting. "Why did you run? What happened last night?"

Her voice was shaky yet sincere. "All I remember is a woman handing me a bottle of water to give you and Daphne. It wasn't our usual brand, so I figured it was probably some promotional thing. We see that kind of partnership all the time."

"But you weren't sure about it. And there's something you know right now that you're not telling me." Nora spoke like she could see right into Jennifer's mind. "Guilt sent you running off like that."

Jennifer swallowed.

"Tell me about the woman who gave you the bottles of water," Nora ordered her.

"What do you want to know?"

"What did she look like?"

Jennifer seemed to think about it. "She was white, maybe a couple of inches taller than me, but I wouldn't say that she was remarkable or even memorable in any distinct way."

"Everyone has something that makes them memorable. Think harder. What was the color of her hair? What was she wearing?"

Jennifer pinched the bridge of her nose, obviously bothered by her own lack of recall. "She was blonde, but the kind of person who turns invisible once you're no longer in front of them. Like, she wanted to blend in on purpose, I guess. She had a black dress, but that could describe half the people there."

"I had the same problem describing the servers from last night, but I still managed to find you. And that doesn't explain your guilty look or why you ran."

"I noticed you both seemed … I don't know … off, I guess."

"Off when?"

"Not long after I gave you the water. It was subtle at first. You just both seemed kind of sluggish, first Daphne, then you. But both of you ignored me for like a full minute while I was talking to you before getting the giggles. Your eyes got glazed over, and you wandered away. You and Daphne first. Caroline followed you a few minutes later. That's when I went looking for the woman who gave me the water because I knew something had to be up, but I couldn't find her anywhere. I was afraid to ask around because I didn't want to get into trouble. I kept telling myself that you guys were fine, but I barely slept at all last night. I was sort of wondering if I would see you again."

"And when you did, your response was to run?"

"Instinct can be a bitch," Jennifer didn't quite explain. "Am I in trouble?"

"If everything is as you said, then you're fine. But if you remember anything, and I mean *anything*, no matter how small it might seem, please give me a call." She gave Jennifer her number, who thumbed it into her phone.

"Of course. I promise."

Nora circled the block back to where she had parked the Infiniti, only to find the passenger seat empty.

Panic flooded her system as she pictured the Escalade or that black sedan screeching to a halt in front of Daphne and hauling her out of the vehicle.

Except there wasn't any broken glass or sense of disturbance around the Infiniti, only a long and permeating silence.

She dialed Daphne, and the call connected, but a wall of background noise and confusing chatter was all that Nora could hear.

"Hello!" she shouted into the phone. "Daphne, where are you?"

The cacophony on the other end made it clear that Daphne could not hear.

And Nora knew exactly where to find her mischievous companion.

Reentering the expo, Nora saw Daphne amid a sea of enthusiastic fans, blowing sultry kisses at the adoring crowd, many of them waving boldly designed dildos wildly through the air while waiting for the actress to sign them.

The laughter was even louder from all the way across the room.

Nora strode over and took her by the arm. "Alright, diva, show's over."

She held her expression of indifference while dragging Daphne behind her, who was still blowing kisses at the crowd all the way to the door.

"Do you understand the kind of attention you're drawing?" Nora yelled at her once they were both outside. "Will you please stop—"

"Nora, darling, can you please be just a little more sex-positive? You would have sounded like a grandma in the 90s. Not *my* grandma. That old lady was a total slut!"

"This has nothing to do with my being sex-positive or not! It has to do with—"

Nora stopped when the phone in her pocket rang, triggering a Pavlovian response.

She took it out and looked at the screen, saw a text

with the name *Lavigne* flashing across it. She swiped for the message.

Her heart sank when she read it: *I've seen the tape.*

Her hand tightened around the phone as she breathed into the inescapable reality that her worst fears had just been realized.

"*Fuck*," she whispered.

Chapter Fifteen

Meet me at the downtown convention center. 30 minutes. We need to have a chat, Nora texted Lavigne.

"What if he doesn't show up?" Daphne asked.

"I give the odds of that happening at no better than ten percent, and if the unlikely should happen, we can figure it out then."

"Fair enough." Daphne shrugged. "I like this slightly chiller version of you. Because it sucks less, you feel more worth the money."

"I'm glad to hear that."

"Who are you calling now?"

"Melissa," Nora said as Melissa answered.

"That's my name."

"I was hoping you could do me a favor."

"Getting right to the point. I like that."

"We both have shit to do," Nora said.

"Indeed. What's the favor?"

"I need you to watch Daphne for me."

"I don't need a babysitter!" Daphne shouted.

"She needs a babysitter?" Melissa asked.

"Like you wouldn't believe."

"THAT'S NOT TRUE!"

"Oh, I can believe it. Vivian told me stories." Melissa laughed. "But that's not the only reason I'm willing to extend this professional courtesy."

"Are you telling me that I'll regret asking before you even agree?"

"I just signed a client I can't name, and they are about to do something I can't repeat. So the odds are better than excellent that I'll be calling in this favor fast. But you should definitely bring Daphne down to my office."

"I assume that's Vivian's old office."

"Like I would give this space up." Melissa laughed again and hung up the phone.

Daphne was still pouting. "I don't need a babysitter."

Nora felt a wave of déjà vu tinged with frustration. On the rare occasions when Nora had won an argument with her mother, pouting inevitably followed. And like Nora's mother, when Daphne finished with her sulk, she would go right out and do something ridiculous again, getting herself into even more trouble.

Nora didn't feel even a little bit bad about insisting that Daphne did, in fact, need a babysitter.

"I'm not letting you anywhere near Lavigne, and I need to have a little talk with that asshole. I don't want to take you to Melissa's office any more than you want to go there."

"Why would you care?"

"I'm sure Vivian's name will still be all over the door and on the signage."

"I thought she taught you to be an uber fixer," Daphne said. "Did you have beef besides all her kiddie-diddler defending?"

"Is that not enough?" Nora kept going. "If I had stayed

with Vivian, she would have eventually turned this Anakin Skywalker into a Darth Vader."

"Are you calling yourself a Jedi?"

"I'm calling myself a Padawan. I'll be a Jedi one day."

They drove to the office, and as predicted, the name *Vivian Piers* was plastered everywhere.

"You should really consider putting your name on the door," Nora said to Melissa as she entered with Daphne.

"It's at the top of the list, right behind dealing with the person I can't name and doing favors for my colleagues when they call me begging me to help them."

"I wasn't begging." Nora turned to Daphne. "Stay put." Then back to Melissa. "You can handcuff her if you need to."

"No, she can't," protested Daphne.

"Do I get to know what's going on?" Melissa asked.

"PR Emergency," Nora replied.

"Bullshit." Melissa nodded. "But I'll keep an eye on her."

"You'll probably want to use both hands. She's a tricky one. I'll be back soon." Nora walked toward the door.

"Fuck you!" Daphne called after her.

Nora felt a stab of satisfaction. If only she'd been able to hand her own mother off to someone like Melissa, who'd have actually been able to rein her in long enough to give Nora a break.

She got back in her Infiniti and drove to meet Lavigne in front of the studio where he shot his bottom-feeding show *Los Angeles Live*. Her heels clicked on the polished concrete as she crossed the space, passing the bustle of production assistants, cameramen, and stage personnel, most not sparing her a second glance as she sidestepped a cart laden with heavy equipment pushed by an enthusiastic intern.

Then she saw Lavigne sauntering toward her, his usual aura of smug self-assuredness hanging like a low cloud around him. Beads of sweat dotted his forehead, making his skin shine under the studio lights. Nora tore right into him.

"You can go ahead and release that video, asshole. Then I'll get you registered with the Everyone Knows You're a Fucker Guild right after I let the world know you drugged a major Hollywood star to get your footage."

"*Whoa.*" Lavigne raised both hands and shook his head. "I don't know anything about any drugging."

"Bullshit. You just didn't think you would get caught this fast."

"When exactly do you think I drugged you?"

"Last night after dinner."

"I didn't make it to the end of dinner, and there are plenty of witnesses that can testify to that."

"Where did you go afterward?" Nora asked.

"It doesn't matter where I went afterward. Only that there is no possible way I could have drugged you because I wasn't even on the premises."

"Where were you?" she tried again.

"I got kicked out of the gala after I was recognized by a director."

"I'm assuming you mean a director you've publicly shit on?"

"There are few other kinds." Lavigne laughed like an asshole.

"Let's pretend you're wrong about it not mattering where you went after getting your ass kicked out of the gala. Spill your alibi."

"I went to a bar and got drunk, and yes, there are plenty of witnesses."

"So what about the video?" Nora asked.

"Someone texted it to me last night. I saw it when I woke up this morning." Lavigne took out his phone, then swiped the screen to show her a text: *Tell no one and do not release until after 4 pm.*

Well, at least now Nora knew how long she had to fix this mess.

He shrugged. "I figured that you and Daphne had whooped it up a little too much after the party. Do you really believe that she's a victim in this?" Lavigne leaned in and whispered, "We both know Daphne. That's exactly her kind of fun."

Four in the afternoon was after Daphne would sign for *Sister Justice*, so that meant they were planning to release the video anyway. And it looked like the number that had texted Lavigne was the same one that had sent the clip to Nora.

"You could have had the server drug us before you were thrown out." The skepticism was evident in her voice. According to Jennifer, she had received no payment.

Lavigne tried his theory again, but Nora cut him off at the pass.

"Daphne wasn't faking," she insisted.

But Lavigne pressed the issue. "She can be one hell of an actress, and from all that I've heard and seen, that is *more* true when it comes to the people in her life than it is on screen."

"I was drugged too, asshole. So I know for damn sure that Daphne wasn't 'faking it.'"

"Sorry." Lavigne raised his hands again, but this time, his concern appeared honest. "Did anything, you know, bad happen to either one of you?"

"No." Nora shook her head. "Nothing like that."

"You sure?" Lavigne asked, still seeming sincere. "Is there anything I can do?"

"You can help me figure out who took that video."

"I have no idea," Lavigne replied.

"Why did you text me when the sender specifically said to tell no one?"

He flushed with embarrassment. "Professional courtesy, I guess."

"What do you mean by that?"

"It's bad," Lavigne said without explanation.

"What's bad?"

"The footage." He swallowed. "Something much worse has already been leaked to the press."

Lavigne opened the Entertainment TV app on his phone and passed Nora the trending video of Nora dancing last night at a strip club called The Disco Stick. On the lower third of the screen, a ticker read, *Top Hollywood agent Nora Bauer caught cutting loose at a strip club.*

"Apparently, you and Daphne cut quite the scene last night."

"How many people have seen this?" Nora asked.

Lavigne turned around and pointed to the Jumbotron, where Nora was horrified to see the same footage in King Kong-sized high-definition looming above them. Her earlier sense of mortification was only a fraction of the basement-dwelling her soul was bottoming out with now.

His concern earlier had seemed sincere. Did he have a better nature that she could appeal to?

"Can you please not release the footage of Daphne?" Nora asked Lavigne.

"What's it worth to you?"

"I won't negotiate." Nora shook her head. "I *can't* negotiate. But if you promise to sit on the story, then maybe I'll consider giving you a double scoop of something deliciously exclusive in the future."

"Just 'maybe'? Sounds like kind of a shitty deal for me."

"It's the best I've got. But you can have my word as a fixer that the day you get that big story, you'll be goddamn glad about the deal we're about to make right now."

Lavigne laughed and extended his hand. "Count me in."

They shook hands, then Nora got in her car and drove back to Melissa's office, wondering who could have (and would have) released that footage of her.

She looked at her phone once more before starting the engine and noted a missed call from Eric but no text or voicemail.

She called Sheryl, who sounded frantic. "What do you need, Nora?"

"To move our appointment."

"My day is packed."

"Do you have *any* wiggle room? *Please?*" Nora wanted to add, *You know how Daphne is*, but that would hardly make the case for her being an invaluable signatory on today's contract.

"I have a tiny window at 12:20."

"I'll take it."

Chapter Sixteen

IT HAD BEEN a while since Daphne had visited Vivian's office.

She tried to count the years while sitting in the chair at Melissa's desk, waiting for her to finish yet another phone call, but she stopped caring after she couldn't decide between four and five.

Vivian had been in charge of Daphne's press once upon a time, and Daphne had considered the two of them friends. But the second she got caught in that Me Too mess, Vivian dropped her like a falling star. Business was business, and Daphne would have been fine with that, she supposed, except that Vivian was still willing to help pedophiles get away with obliterating all those childhoods. So fuck her, and fuck this office twice.

But Daphne had always liked Nora a lot, definitely more than it was good for her to know, and Nora was also right that working for the Emperor didn't automatically make you Darth Vader. So maybe Melissa would be fine.

Nora had feigned ignorance when Daphne got dropped by Vivian, like she didn't have a clue that no one else in the world would take her, while Daphne pretended not to notice Nora's fierce ambition to penetrate the industry. Mutual exploitation remained an unspoken agreement, but that didn't diminish Daphne's affection or gratitude for a bond she depended on. Not that Nora ever needed to know that.

Melissa turned around to the mini fridge, pulled out a bottle of water, cracked the top, and took a swig. Then, she got a second bottle and offered it to Daphne. Oasis.

Daphne felt her stomach turn at the sight of the label, remembering how sick she'd felt after drinking the drugged water. She shook her head.

The fixer opened her mouth, looking like she was about to ask Daphne a question, but then she snapped it back closed as her phone started to ring.

"Yes," Melissa answered. Then, after several long moments of listening and nodding to herself, she finally said, "I can assure you that everything has been handled… Yes, of course."

She ended her phone call and took another sip of her water before turning to Daphne. "So, what was up with you and Nora last night?"

"I'm not sure what you mean."

"Why did you leave the party early? You guys were just suddenly gone from the table."

"I got food poisoning." Daphne could be a fixer, too.

"Nope." Melissa shook her head. "That's a PR answer."

"How was the gala after we left?"

"It was fine. You know how those events are."

"I do!" Daphne laughed knowingly. "I can't get enough of them. Looked like you came not quite dressed to party down, though."

"I came to work," Melissa explained.

"You're not supposed to work at a gala." She laughed again. "Did you notice anything funny going on? Anyone watching us?"

"Maybe I did, but you know how it goes. It's hard to know what you saw without context. So why don't you tell me what's really going on, and I can scour my extremely observational brain to see if anything matches what you're looking for?"

"Oh…" Daphne made her face look disappointed, almost exactly like when she'd found out that the hunk next door was about to move away for good in *Got MILF?*. "So you don't have anything?"

Melissa's phone rang before she could reply.

"This is Melissa… Oh shit. Thanks. Bye."

She hung up the phone and turned her office TV to an interview with Scarlett Anderson on *Tinsel Talk*, one of the more insipid Hollywood gossip shows highlighting the biggest news from last night.

"How did you feel about losing out on the role of *Sister Justice* to Daphne Belle?" a reporter asked Scarlett on the white carpet.

"Oh, I wouldn't consider it a loss at all," Scarlett said. "I'm so happy for Daphne. She's had a long career of playing hard-won roles. I imagine playing *Sister Justice* will help Daphne reconnect with that quieter self that she's been talking so much about the last couple of years."

"Bitch," Daphne said to the screen.

"Scarlett is my client," Melissa reminded her.

"That doesn't mean that she isn't a bitch," Daphne said.

But then the news switched over to the next story, and Daphne could tell by Melissa's face that this was the main attraction: Nora dancing at a too-familiar looking strip club.

Melissa started laughing loudly, stopped to listen to the newscaster, and then laughed even louder. "Actual O-M-G. I totally didn't know Nora had it in her."

Daphne felt increasingly furious as she tried to untangle the sight — it wasn't the tiki bar at Burt's place. Definitely The Disco Stick, though she had no memory of going there last night.

More importantly, she couldn't stand someone humiliating Nora like that. It was one thing for her to shake her glitter tits at Burt's mansion — laughing off people's reactions to her own scandalous behavior was fun. And more importantly, it was part of her brand, or whatever the young people were calling it now.

But Nora had never signed up to be in the spotlight like that, and she never would have gotten up on that stage if someone hadn't drugged her. Nora would never in a million years have chosen to do that. (Although Daphne had to admit, the girl had some pretty good moves when she let herself get into it.)

But filming it to humiliate Nora was cruel. Daphne vowed she was going to make whoever had done it pay.

"Do you know—" Daphne's question died as Nora barged into the office.

She took one look at the screen, then marched over to Melissa's desk and snatched the remote to turn it off. "Thank you for babysitting."

"Please tell me that you're going to explain that to me." Melissa nodded at the black screen.

"Are you calling in your favor?"

Melissa shook her head. "Definitely not."

"Then we're out of here." Nora grabbed Daphne and hauled her out of the office.

"Talk to you later!" Melissa called out behind them.

"What happened with Lavigne?" Daphne asked on their way to the car.

"It was a bust. Lavigne received the video, but he has no idea who sent it to him."

"How do you know that you can believe him?"

"A lot of ways, only one of which is that Lavigne showed me the text, and it came from the same number that sent the video to me."

"What did he want?" Daphne asked.

"Nothing."

"That's because Lavigne is sweet on me."

"Did you get anything off of Melissa?" Nora's phone rang before Daphne could answer her question. Panic exploded inside her as she looked at the caller. "It's Eric. What if he found the body?"

"More like he found a TV channel." Daphne laughed.

Nora blushed, something Daphne had never seen Nora do before. Then she declined his call and sent it to voicemail. Another new one, ignoring her private dick.

"Where are we going now?" Daphne asked as Nora started the engine.

"The Disco Stick."

"Naturally." Daphne clapped.

But two miles down the road, they spotted that dark sedan behind them in unison.

"See the dent in the side?" Nora asked. "That's definitely the same vehicle that collided with the Escalade."

"Who do you think it could be?"

Nora's eyes darted to the rearview mirror as her fingers clutched the steering wheel.

Then it was pedal to the metal as the Infiniti surged forward, darting into a narrow alleyway as Nora swerved to avoid stacked boxes, barely squeezing by a dumpster before she spun the wheel hard to execute a swift U-turn.

Then, a sudden right, plowing through an ankle-deep puddle, into a parking structure, and up the spiraling ramp to the roof, where she hid behind a concrete barrier, holding her breath like that might actually matter.

After five minutes of waiting, there was no sign of the sedan.

Daphne shifted impatiently in her seat. "I think you lost them, Bullitt. Can we go to The Disco Stick now?"

Nora waited another few minutes, then drove to the strip club.

She pulled into a small lot across the street, glancing over at the retro signage as she parked. The neon lights were off, and the lot was mostly empty, making the exterior look drab in comparison to its lively nighttime atmosphere.

"This place is one of my favorite haunts from the old days," Daphne said, eager to see Caspian. Caspian always had some of the good drugs on hand, and he was always willing to share.

"You've been here before last night?"

Daphne shrugged. "Caspie is an old friend."

"When were you going to tell me that you recognized it from the video?"

"When you asked, darling."

Nora gave her an angry look before getting out of the car and slamming the door. She glanced around as if looking for that dark sedan or the Escalade, then headed for the front door of The Disco Stick.

Daphne hurried to catch up, although she did glance behind her once or twice, just in case their pursuers had decided to tail them on foot.

She was definitely getting the hang of this fixer stuff.

Chapter Seventeen

Daphne felt slapped across the face by the silence as they entered.

It was practically deafening compared to the riotous energy that was usually pulsating through the club. Devoid of its usual pounding music and raucous crowds, the expansive interior felt hollow, a cavernous tomb dedicated to debauchery without any faithful to keep the party gods appeased.

Poles stood vacant, missing their usual cadre of gyrating, glitter-adorned dancers. And without the animated ambiance, the space felt chillingly inert.

"This place sure feels different in the daytime," Daphne said.

"I imagine the clashing prints and patterns look a lot better under the glow of that rainbow disco ball."

"I realize that you're being sarcastic, but it totally does."

Nora stopped walking as her phone rang. She fished the device from her pocket and wrinkled her nose when she looked at the screen.

"That look on your face makes me think it's your private dick calling." Daphne winked. "Am I right?"

Nora ignored her like usual, answering the call with a reluctant-looking swipe.

"Hey, Eric," she said, turning her back to Daphne and walking away to take her call in a shadowy corner, then returning two minutes later looking even more constipated than she had before.

Daphne grinned at her. "Let me guess: you didn't ask him to fuck you?"

Nora started walking toward the back office again.

Daphne followed. "I'm just kidding! Geez. Tell me what he said! Did he see your video?"

"Of course, he saw my video."

"I bet he loved it. I bet he's watching it right now and—"

"DAPHNE." Nora kept walking.

"What else did he say?" Daphne asked as they stopped in front of a door labeled **PRIVATE** in neat block letters, practically the only thing straight in the entire club. "No more jokes, I promise."

"Eric offered to discreetly ask around and see if he can find out who filmed and/or released the video."

"And then you offered to blow him?" Daphne laughed. "Sorry about that one! I couldn't help it."

Nora knocked on the door but only hit the wood once with her knuckles before it swung open to reveal the club's owner, Daphne's old friend Caspian.

"YOU FUCKING BITCH!" Caspie had a silvery gray pompadour and lived in a tailored suit. He pulled Daphne into a hug, clearly delighted to see her. "Did you forget something last night?" He turned to Nora with a wicked grin. "And *you.*"

Nora flushed with embarrassment and gestured past the open door. "Do you mind if we talk in your office?"

"Will you promise a follow-up performance if—"

"No," Nora cut him off.

"Fair enough." Caspian led them inside.

"How long have you two known each other?" Nora asked as she took a seat next to Daphne in front of his desk. Caspian made himself comfortable on the other side.

"Daphne used to dance here," he said.

"*Shh.* It's a secret." Daphne put a finger to her lips and laughed. "Don't tell."

"You were a stripper?" Nora exclaimed.

"One of the best," Caspian said.

Daphne shrugged. "Barely anyone knows."

"Cherry Kiss was the queen of the pole and the heart of my dance floor."

Daphne swatted a hand at him. "You stop!"

"I was glad to see that you still have the spark!" Caspian turned from her to Nora. "And you certainly have a future stripping if your PR career falls through."

"That's one floor show you'll never see," Nora said.

"*Again,*" replied Caspian and Daphne in unison before a gale of laughter.

"We have no memory of coming here last night," Nora redirected them. "When did we get here?"

"No memory?" Caspian repeated.

His posture shifted as he seemed to suddenly understand the gravity of this situation.

"Can you tell us what time we got here?" Nora asked.

"If we look at the security footage, but I didn't even know that you two were here until Luba came in and told me about the patron on my stage dancing while Daphne Belle took selfies with the dancers."

"You know more than you're saying." Nora narrowed her eyes at him.

He shook his head. "I assure you that I absolutely do not."

"Why would Caspian lie?" Daphne asked.

"Can we speak to one of the dancers from last night?"

"Sure." He shrugged. "But the first shift starts tonight, so it doesn't matter which one of them you want to call, I can assure you she's sleeping."

"Do you know what time we left?" Nora asked.

"The three of you left together around midnight."

"The three of us?" Nora said. "Was Caroline here?"

Caspian nodded again.

"Did any of the dancers happen to mention where we were going, sweetheart?" Daphne asked. "You know how loose Luba's lips are, I'm sure she said *something*."

Nora rolled her eyes. But then Caspian seemed to brighten with recollection, and she blinked in surprise.

"I do remember Luba saying something about you guys going to Action Channel."

"I don't know what that is," Daphne said.

"Me neither," Caspian said. "But Luba said you were going to buy drugs."

"Caroline is the missing link to our lost memories." Nora nodded. "And our best bet at finding some answers."

"I hope she's okay," Daphne said.

But Nora seemed more busy than concerned as she took out her phone.

"Who are you calling?" Daphne asked.

"Hey there, Sophia. You haven't heard from Caroline yet, have you?"

"Put her on speaker!" Daphne demanded.

Nora complied.

"—No," Sophia continued, sounding half out of her

mind. "And I'm starting to get really worried. She missed her morning meeting and still isn't answering calls."

"Have you tried tracking her phone?" Daphne shouted, even though she was just as close to the receiver as Nora.

"Of course. But she switched it off."

"We were all together up until midnight, according to the dancers here at The Disco Stick," Nora said.

"That doesn't make me feel better," Sophia replied.

"Maybe—"

Nora was abruptly interrupted by the frenetic entrance of a lithe blonde dancer.

"What are you doing here so early?" Caspian asked her. "And isn't it your day off?"

"It is. But I forgot my shoes, and if I leave them here tonight, that bitch Luba will steal them for sure."

"You know the rule, Ali, no shit talk." Caspian gave her an admonishing look.

Ali ignored him and turned to Nora and Daphne. "There's a media circus outside. I'm sure they're here for you."

"For moi?" Daphne laughed.

"No." Ali nodded at Nora. "I mean for her."

Nora looked like she wanted to die.

But Caspian came to their rescue. "You can't go out there, not with those vultures waiting. My car is parked out back. You should take it. No one will see you leave."

He escorted them outside, and Nora decided to look Caspian's gift horse in the mouth without even consulting Daphne.

"We can't take that," she said.

"Just because it has a little personality?" Daphne waved a hand at the station wagon, covered in mirrors and glitter. An oversized silver disco ball and stick were perched on the hood, with the words *Follow Me to the Disco Stick!* scrawled on the side in flamboyant neon lettering. The interior had leopard print seats and a steering wheel covered in rhinestones.

But Nora was still just standing there, staring at Caspie's car in horror. *Rude.*

"We're wasting time," Daphne prompted Nora before climbing into the car, then calling out to Caspian. "Thank you, honey!"

Nora gave him a nod, trying not to cringe as she got into the driver's side.

"I'm disappointed in you." Daphne closed her door. "This doesn't seem like very fixy behavior. Where's the PR spin? Maybe this is the perfect car for us to escape in."

"You're right. This hideous disco-ball-on-wheels is the perfect camouflage for us to escape the circling paparazzi."

"It's like a Trojan Horse."

"That's not quite right," Nora said.

"Has anyone ever told you that you're a know-it-all?"

"You. An average of four times a week."

"It's like I'm paying to be friends with a TED Talk."

Nora turned the engine, and an ancient digital clock came to vibrant life on the dashboard. It was exactly 10:00. "We have two hours and twenty minutes until our meeting with Sheryl."

"Got it." Daphne nodded. "We're signing the contract four hours before 4:20."

"I'm serious."

"Clearly." Normally, Daphne would've managed to get at least an eye roll out of Nora with a line like that. The fact that she was dead-panning after learning that they'd gone to buy drugs last night underscored how serious Nora thought this was.

Which made it hard for Daphne not to worry a teensy

bit. But letting Nora see that her worry was rubbing off wouldn't help.

Nora took out her phone.

"Are you actually setting a timer?" Daphne laughed at her.

"To ensure that we don't lose track of this crucial appointment that determines your professional fate? Yes, I think a timer might be a good idea."

The engine suddenly died. Now, Daphne had to remind herself not to look their Trojan horse in the mouth.

Nora went to turn it again when Ali knocked on the window.

"Caspian said you were talking about Action Channel," she said after Nora rolled it down. "It's a spot in Santa Monica where the La Cabronas sell drugs under an underpass. Here…"

Ali handed them a piece of paper with cross streets scrawled in lipstick.

"Thank you, Ali."

Nora turned to Daphne and said, "How is it that you were so high you were dancing topless last night, but you still felt the need to buy *more* drugs?"

Chapter Eighteen

DAPHNE AND NORA had been going at it for a while now.

Officially, Daphne paid Nora's salary, and the bitch needed to listen to whatever her boss said. But unofficially, Daphne knew that without Nora, she would probably be dancing on a sinking ship with two left feet and that it might be best to shut her yap and do whatever the fixer told her to.

But Nora, as usual, was acting like a cat at a dog parade.

"I'm not saying that we shouldn't go to Action Channel, Daphne. I'm saying that we can't go charging into a dangerous area without knowing what we're doing or having a plan."

"And I'm not saying that we don't need a plan. I'm just wondering if maybe we can come up with one on the way."

"If you have a plan, I'm listening. But blindly rushing into a place we don't know is not the kind of strategy I'm looking for," Nora said.

"We were there last night."

"In a compromised state."

"Exactly." Daphne nodded, glad that Nora was finally getting it.

"Exactly what?" Nora said. "I don't understand."

"If we were all fucked up going to Action Channel after leaving the Disco Stick, then we need to pick up the trail immediately or risk losing it."

"I am seriously not following your logic."

"Don't feel bad." Daphne waved a hand to let Nora know that her being dim right now was no big deal. "It's not your fault. Are you ready for Action Channel?"

"You're treating this investigation like some blithe little adventure. Are you aware of the gravity—"

"Honey, I don't even know what the word blithe means!" Daphne laughed. "It's just one of those words I kind of sort of get by context. Right now I'm guessing it means 'fun'?"

"I'm glad this is fun for you!" Nora sighed, needing a deep breath before she finished venting at Daphne. "We still have an unexplained dead body on your couch. So can you please just snap the hell out of it!"

"Fine." Daphne pouted. "You tell me the plan then."

"We're going to Action Channel. I just want us to be careful." Nora was already on her way out the door.

"I never said that we shouldn't be careful, Mom. Geez."

Daphne kept quiet as Nora drove them out to Action Channel, the shadowy Santa Monica underpass looming ahead, its dark arches casting deep shadows onto the graffiti-soaked walls.

A faint murmur of passing cars made for a haunting hum overhead. The place looked sketchy but not overly perilous.

"It looks quiet." Nora killed the engine.

"If this were a movie, I would say, *Too quiet.*"

"I appreciate you saying it anyway."

"Why do you look so bothered?" Daphne asked. "It doesn't look like there's anyone around here."

"Could our vehicle be any more obnoxiously conspicuous?"

"Is that your Chandler impression?"

"What?" Nora said.

"Chandler. From *Friends*? Could I *be* any more Chandler right now?"

"I never really watched *Friends*." Nora shrugged. "It was a little before my time."

"*Friends* is timeless!"

Another shrug. "I'm more of an *Office* girl."

"Sacrilege!" Daphne gasped.

Nora got out of their disco ball on wheels and scanned the desolate area while Daphne trailed behind her, both of them looking for any evidence as to why they had come here last night.

"Shit. Look." Nora pointed to a gnarl of shadows under the overpass and started walking toward it. Once there, she picked up a silver pump from the ground. "Is this Caroline's?"

Daphne walked over to give the shoe a closer look, but she didn't need to. Of course it was Caroline's, with intricate sequined patterns that even Daphne thought seemed like a bit too much.

"That's Caroline's."

"Well. Fuck." Nora stood. "I don't know whether I should feel glad that we found her shoe or scared that we didn't find Caroline."

"She's probably fine! Wherever she is," Daphne replied, mostly to reassure herself.

"What's that?" Nora turned toward what sounded like shuffling sneakers on the asphalt.

Daphne followed Nora's gaze to see a lanky teenager emerging from the deeper recesses of the underpass. Sunlight and shadows danced across a network of acne on his angular face. His dark brown hair was matted, and his clothes were a sloppy ensemble of oversized flannel, faded jeans, and beat-to-shit Converse.

"Y'all looking for something special?" His voice had the raspy edge of someone who smoked too young and far too often, his gaze lingering too long on Nora's purse.

"We're not here to buy. We're looking for someone. Were you here last night?"

He sized them up, his lips curling up into a sly grin. "My memory's not so good. Remind me again, what's in it for me?"

Nora pulled out a twenty. "Did you see us? Do you know who we talked to?"

"Twenty bucks?" The kid laughed in Nora's face. "That won't even get you my name. Definitely not my memories."

Nora looked like she wanted to tear the little hoodlum's head right off his shoulders as she reached into her purse and grabbed $200 in cash. "Double down or fold asshole."

"Fair game." He held out his hand.

Nora yanked the money away from him. "Who was working here last night?"

The kid gave her another smirk, then made a call, turning his back to them and obscuring his words as he mumbled into his phone.

Then he ended the call and turned back to them. "Cool your shit. He's on his way."

"Who's on his way?" Nora asked.

"He'll be here soon." The kid took out a carton of Marlboros. "Wanna smoke?"

"We'll wait in the car," Nora told him, then went to the station wagon.

"Don't mind her. She's tighter than my jeans on Thanksgiving!" Daphne called out to the kid as she followed Nora.

"Seriously?" Nora said once they were both back inside the station wagon. "You really felt the need to offer the kid an apology on my account."

"I just didn't want him to think it was his fault that you're being moody."

"I'm not being moody."

"You should tell your face," Daphne said. "What are you worried about most right now — besides everything in the world?"

"I'm worried that whoever that teenaged criminal called is going to show up in the Escalade that's been haunting my nightmares."

"It hasn't been haunting your nightmares because you haven't been asleep. And don't be so judgy. You don't know that the kid is a criminal just because he dresses like Macklemore."

"He literally just offered us drugs."

Daphne shrugged. "Caroline offers me drugs all the time. That doesn't make her a criminal."

"She isn't *selling* them to you." Then, a beat later. "And she's still breaking the law. Drugs are illegal."

"Not all of them," Daphne argued. "And not even the best ones."

"Maybe—"

"Maybe what?"

Nora nodded at the car pulling up next to the kid. Not an Escalade, but a vintage 1970 Cadillac Coupe de Ville.

With sinuous curves and a regal presence, the chrome-trimmed luxury liner looked as much like a boat as it did a car.

"If that car had a voice, I bet it would sound like Barry White," Daphne said.

A tall, imposing man stepped out as the kid jabbed his finger at the disco mobile. He was tall and dark, with a chiseled jawline framed by a mane of longish black hair. The hint of a beard added to his brooding, Mediterranean mystique.

"Maybe coming here was a mistake," Nora said, already getting out of the car.

Daphne followed. And for a second, even she felt scared.

But that was silly because Tall, Dark, and Handsome were obviously happy to see them. "It is so nice to be in the company of you ladies again so soon!"

He came up to Daphne first, pulling her into a familiar embrace and kissing each of her cheeks with what felt like genuine affection.

Then he turned to Nora and offered her the same, a friendly hug followed by his European kiss.

The man smiled at them. "I trust you enjoyed your fish scale?"

"I'm sorry. You'll have to forgive me. Last night is still a bit foggy," Nora said.

He chuckled. "I can imagine it is."

The kid laughed behind him, but the sound rang out with the hollow notes of duty — he had no idea what was funny.

Daphne nodded at Nora. "She means that we can't remember dick about shit. We both slept through the movie, so there's no reason to ask us what happened."

"You don't remember what happened last night?" He

stood taller, his shoulders stiffening and jaw going harder. "You don't remember your time with Chiflado?"

"Are you Chiflado?" Daphne asked. "Sorry if that's a dumb question, but—"

"Are you questioning the purity of my fish scale?"

Daphne and Nora traded a look.

"My shit don't cause no memory loss, so if you're saying Chiflado—"

"No, Chiflado. That's not what we're saying." Nora shook her head, gambling that the guy's name really was Chiflado and that he just liked to speak about himself in the third person. "The drugs were perfect. Best I've ever had."

"Damn straight." Chiflado grinned. "My clients never forget their experiences."

"Can you tell us where Caroline is?" Nora asked.

"She was here with you all last night, but I can't tell you much. I split when things got rowdy at Action Channel."

"So you have no idea where Caroline might have gone?" Daphne asked.

"I assumed you all left together in the Rolls after the bedlam. So, no." Chiflado shook his head. "Her disappearance perplexes me."

"It perplexes me too," Daphne agreed.

"Tell me more about the bedlam," Nora said to Chiflado.

"Why you need a recap?" Chiflado snapped. "You wearing a wire? You trying to entrap me?"

"Definitely not!" Daphne cut in. "We would never do that to you, Chiflado. You can take my word for it."

"How am I supposed to take your word for anything? It ain't like—"

"Here!" Daphne flashed her tits. "No wires."

Chiflado grinned and turned to Nora. "How about you?"

The kid leaned forward.

"How about fuck you both?" Nora said to Chiflado and the kid.

Chiflado laughed. "Well then, I am afraid we are at an impasse. I cannot disclose anything more until I am certain that neither of you are recording me."

"Fine. But tell that little fucker to turn around first." Nora gestured at the kid, then flashed Chiflado like Daphne had after he gave her the signal. "Now spill it, asshole."

"You should be nicer," Daphne admonished her. "We're all getting what we want here."

Nora turned back to Chiflado, looking at him expectantly until he finally started talking.

"After you bought the fish scale last night, the Amigos Latinos showed up out of nowhere—"

"Amigos Latinos?" Nora repeated. "I've never heard of them before."

Chiflado shrugged. "They seemed to know who you were."

Daphne grinned. "Honey, everyone knows who I am."

"What did they look like?" Nora asked.

"Big dudes." Chiflado shrugged, but before he could elaborate, and just as Nora was wondering if they could be the same men that had jumped out of the Escalade, that very SUV came barreling into the overpass.

The kid bolted off in the other direction.

Chiflado whipped out a pistol, then spun around and started firing shots at the Escalade while yelling at the women to get the hell out of there.

Nora nodded at the station wagon and yelled, "RUN!"

Chapter Nineteen

A RIOT of gunfire ripped through the stillness.

The shockwave echoed through the underpass.

Nora and Daphne hurled themselves behind a graffitied concrete pillar, chests heaving in tandem with the heartbeat drumming in Nora's ears.

The dusty air thickened with tension, punctuated by the reek of burning rubber and smoky residue.

In a fleeting pocket of silence between the raging gunfire, Nora locked eyes with Daphne and nodded: *time to run.*

A lone bullet smashed into the glittering disco ball atop the wagon and detonated with a spray of glitter and glass shards, casting minute rainbows amidst the chaos as it showered down on them.

Daphne shrieked, instinctively shielding her face with her forearm, but momentum carried her forward.

She reached the wagon, her fingers grasping the cold handle, only to find it locked.

"GODDAMMIT!" Daphne bellowed.

The Escalade growled as it skidded to a halt, tires

screeching as the doors flung open to masked men cloaked in darkness, balaclavas hiding all but the cold determination in their eyes.

Before Daphne could move, they were on her, yanking her backward.

Nora watched helplessly from behind the station wagon as Daphne's attackers subdued her, muffling her piercing screams with a large, gloved hand.

The metallic taste of fear filled Nora's mouth as the Escalade sped away.

* * *

Inside the SUV, it was oppressively dark, intensifying Daphne's sense of claustrophobia.

"Where's Julio?" demanded one of the men, his breath foul against her face.

"I don't know any Julio!" Daphne's quivering voice held a note of defiance.

"Lies!" another spat, "We saw you with him last night."

"Was I wearing a spider brooch in my hair when we were together by chance?" Daphne pointed to the empty spot in her do where the brooch used to be. "Did any of you boys happen to see it?"

To her surprise, one of the armed men gave Daphne a nod. "I saw the spider thing in your hair last night right before everything went to hell."

"That's great news!" Daphne exclaimed as if these men weren't holding her prisoner. "Did you—"

The Escalade lurched forward and sent her flying back into the wall.

One of the men turned around to look out the rear window.

Daphne looked too, expecting to see the cops. Instead it was Nora in hot pursuit, and the disco wagon somehow managed to look even more outlandish behind them.

"Definitely not the cops," said the masked man at the window.

"Of course, it isn't the cops!" Daphne laughed, hoping they wouldn't jump to the conclusion that Nora was undercover. "That's just my PR manager, Nora."

The Escalade made another evasive maneuver, peeling hard into the next lane and pressing Daphne back against her seat.

"I think you have me mistaken for someone else!" she tried, even though they knew exactly who she was, down to the brooch they had seen in her hair last night.

"Can someone shut her up?" The nice guy nodded at Daphne, except now he wasn't being so nice.

"Last chance," said the man nearest to the formerly nice guy. "Talk now, or we'll take you to someone who will make you cooperate."

"Well, I hope whoever it is got better grades in charm school than you monkeys—"

That's all she got before one of the men was roughly binding Daphne's wrists behind her back while another shoved a hood over her head, plunging her into darkness.

Panic bubbled up in her chest, but she tried to drown it in memories of the countless auditions and roles she had survived. This right now was just another scene.

She wondered if her mascara was running under the hood.

And then she started choking on her fear, realizing with the sudden force of lightning striking the back of her skull that the danger here compared to what she had ever faced on set was a little too perversely real.

Under the muffled hood, Daphne could hear the men conversing in rapid Spanish, but it was much too fast for her to catch more than a few words. There weren't any easy ones like guacamole or quinceañera, but she did hear the words "negocio," "peligro," and "recompensa" along with Caroline's name, and determined that the men were taking a moment to bargain.

"Do you boys happen to know where Caroline is?"

The men kept jabbering en Español and ignoring her.

"Excuse me?" Daphne tried again, smelling her own surprisingly terrible breath while trapped beneath the hood, hoping that Caroline could corroborate her innocence and let these kidnappers know that she had never even met this Julio guy, even if she had met a lot of other Julios that she both could and couldn't remember (there were a *lot* of Julios in Los Angeles). "I asked if—"

The hood was abruptly yanked off of her head.

"You want to know where your friend is?" That first balaclava guy was back to being nice again. "What do you have to tell us in return?"

"Thanks for taking that off. That felt like the kind of spa treatment that Gwyneth Paltrow might like."

"What can you tell us?" the man repeated.

"I'm happy to spill the beans, let the cat out of the bag, and even reveal the secret ingredient in my potato salad recipe, but that's all assuming I know the things you're hoping I know, and right now I can't remember a thing about last night. At least not the part you care about. The part I do remember was sort of boring. But that's because of Nora. Don't let that clown car in hot pursuit give you the wrong idea; she's normally an instruction manual."

"You better say something fast!" He grabbed Daphne by the arm.

"I'm saying a lot of things!" she protested. "And I'm saying all of them fast! I am trying to help you. Seems to me like we're on the same side, even if you guys kidnapped me and you're all wearing masks. I'm looking for Caroline.

If you know where she is, then you can just tell me, and maybe that will jog my memory about—"

"Maybe this will jog your memory." The man holding her arm raised his gun with the other hand but didn't actually strike her.

"What's your name? I feel like we should be on a first-name basis the way you're manhandling me. Can I call you Diego?" Daphne turned her head to the side. "Look, Diego. You obviously need whatever it is that's in this old noggin of mine, and I would just love to hand it over. So maybe I'm right here, and you helping me to find Caroline is our best bet—"

Her stomach lurched with a sudden need to vomit.

Daphne doubled over to take a breath. She couldn't see outside with the rear window now closed, but the Escalade was hurtling down the freeway at breakneck speed. Surely they must have lost Nora in that shitbox by now. It wasn't like she was behind the wheel of Burt's Rolls.

The Escalade swerved hard, and Daphne slammed into the door.

"OWW!" she wailed.

Her ears were assaulted by blaring horns and tires shrieking against the asphalt, with Spanish curses from the men blending into the chaos.

Nora was apparently relentless in her pursuit. Daphne didn't dare look behind them for fear that Diego would think she was resisting and hit her in the face with the butt of his gun. She couldn't do press conferences with a black eye.

Unless she played it off as a training injury, the result of learning her fight choreography for—

A horrifying staccato of gunfire exploded from both vehicles.

The men ducked down, returning steady fire from inside the van.

This was getting dangerous. And loud.

The thunderous exchange of bullets transformed the Escalade's interior into a throbbing cocoon. Daphne prayed for Nora's safety as she was thrown back and forth each time the Escalade swerved again until the SUV finally settled into a smooth purr. They must have given Nora the slip.

Then silence for fifteen minutes or so— Daphne not daring to open her mouth and the men obviously having nothing else to say. For now, anyway.

She nudged away her relief as the car stopped.

The door was yanked open, and before Daphne could gain her bearings, the suffocating hood was shoved back over her head.

The air was heavy with the musky reek of oil and stale water, which seemed to thicken with every step the men forced her forward.

Then the hood was removed, and Daphne had to keep blinking until her eyes finally adjusted to the dim, eerie glow.

The room was vast, with high ceilings supported by rusty beams and walls dripping with moisture. Ancient machinery stood silent guard in dilapidated pieces around the room.

Before her stood a large man with skin that seemed almost gray in the dim light, a gnarled scar creating a ravine down his right cheek, and eyes that were devoid of all empathy as he scanned Daphne like a chef assessing his protein.

"Little bird." His voice came in a gravelly whisper that seemed to claw at her. "You will tell me where Julio is. Otherwise…" His gaze leisurely swept the sinister array of implements and instruments spread out on the table. "I will have to break your wings."

Daphne's heart pounded against her ribcage, breaths coming in ragged gasps with the realization that she might never deliver another punchline again.

Light glinted menacingly off the blades of both straight and serrated knives, the cruel curve of hooks, and the cold-looking pliers, all sitting on the table to communicate the unimaginable agony awaiting Daphne if she refused to cooperate.

Chapter Twenty

THE ABSURDITY of Nora's pursuit behind the wheel of Caspian's disco wagon, its disco ball having been blown to shards, only seemed to heighten with every passing second that she managed to stay behind the imposing Escalade.

The humming engine sounded like a groaning plea, but the wildly swerving SUV had yet to lose her. And it was flat-out impossible for Nora to stay inconspicuous while behind the wheel of the clown car.

The Escalade disappeared from sight, and Nora let the driver believe that he'd lost her. A gamble for sure, with maybe a one-in-three chance the SUV would turn into the seedy warehouse district, and she would never see it or Daphne again.

But it was still her best shot, and she made the right call, just spotting the Escalade as it turned into a long row of what appeared to be abandoned warehouses.

She kept a cautious distance, following far behind and keeping watch until she saw the men get out of the van, dragging Daphne out onto the ground and putting a hood over her head before they disappeared inside the nearest dilapidated building.

Nora killed the engine and hunkered down in her seat, deciding that she would do the smart thing and give Eric a call for backup before heading into the warehouse after Daphne by herself, alone against all of those armed, masked men, without even the gun from Daphne's cereal box.

But her phone was dead, and that meant her plans were DOA as well.

Nora was on her own, and even if the thought of going in there after Daphne by herself was terrifying, almost crippling, really, she had no other choice. A hesitation in action now failed to fix the problem and put her client's life in danger.

She searched the station wagon for anything she might use as a weapon. The front and back of the cabin were both empty, but Nora found an actual disco stick in the trunk: a baton with a mini disco ball affixed on top. A garishly lame weapon, more suited to Daphne than her, but still many times better than nothing.

She held the disco stick with a fierce grip while slowly approaching the looming structure, bordered by a forbidding chain-link fence.

Nora followed the perimeter until she arrived at a bent segment with a hole just wide enough for a person around her shape and size to fit through.

The gnarled metal claws of the fence seemed to come alive as she crawled through it, scratching and biting at Nora as she moved. She ignored a sharp sting on her forearm, then an even sharper sting on her thigh.

But instead of slowing, she crawled faster, finally pulling herself free from the fence and its malicious grasp, then inspecting all of the fresh lacerations on her skin and figuring she would need to get an updated tetanus shot for sure.

She shook off the pain and took a moment to ground herself before tiptoeing toward the warehouse entrance.

To her surprise, she could hear the kidnappers chattering when she got within earshot, talking about Daphne like she wasn't even there, which made Nora wonder if she was maybe somewhere else, and none of their conversation was centered around what happened last night.

"Man, I loved her best in *Moonlit Serenade*. The chemistry between her and Amos Sans is fire."

"Fuck you," replied one of the men with a laugh. "*Desert Shadows* is her best work. The chase scene on the dunes? Fucking gold."

"I'm more into her earlier films," said the third voice, confirming that this really was some sort of weird and impromptu film club discussion about Daphne's classics that the kidnappers were apparently engaging in. "Summer's *Echo* is an underrated gem. That shit in the cafe made my wife cry."

"Indie films?" scoffed the first guy. "Fuck indie films."

"Why fuck indie films?" asked guy number three.

"The soundtrack to *Summer's Echo* was lit," opined guy number two.

"That's my favorite soundtrack from any of my movies!" Daphne yodeled with pure delight.

So this really was stranger than fiction, and Daphne was part of the conversation. She'd probably stoked the fires of the impromptu fan club herself.

Nora cautiously slipped past the Escalade and ducked into the dark warehouse, instantly dwarfed by the space, every inch filled with hulking storage crates. Monolithic metal structures of some kind reached for the rafters in high stacks to create a maze where long shadows danced on the walls and floor to give Nora a veil of concealment until she reached the door where the movie club conversation had inexplicably turned to which season of *Friends* was the best.

"Third season, hands down!" Daphne declared. "WE WERE ON A BREAK!"

Surely Daphne was still in danger and just acting brave, Nora thought as adrenaline flooded her system. She tightened her grip on the disco stick, peeking into the room and seeing a far cry from what she had expected.

Though, given Daphne, Nora should not have been surprised.

She expected to see the actress tied to a chair, maybe in front of some implements of torture on a table with a scary man who lived to inflict pain standing in front of it. Nora did see that table and the chair, but Daphne was unbound, and while the man wearing an apron in front of all the tools looked like he might have been scary as shit under different circumstances, he was presently seated in front of the actress and appeared to be engaged in his part of an amiable conversation. His torturous instruments were neatly arranged on the table, seemingly untouched.

"Nora! Finally!" Daphne shouted while motioning for her to lower the disco stick. "Meet Santiago."

The man in an apron raised a hand in acknowledgment.

"This isn't what it looks like," Daphne hurried to explain. "Santiago is with the Amigos Latinos. There's been a ... misunderstanding."

"Misunderstanding?" Nora echoed, looking from Daphne to Santiago, then to the other three men in the room — no one was wearing a mask anymore — before turning back to Daphne.

But Santiago answered, "We thought you two were with Chiflado's Latino Voices Alliance. It's been ... complicated lately."

Daphne leaned in to speak in a low and conspiratorial whisper that sounded almost gleeful as she caught Nora up. "There was an altercation last night. Things got heated between the gangs. They thought we were part of it."

"You can't be serious," Nora said, staring dumbfounded at Santiago as she assembled the events into a mosaic of understanding. "So you're telling me that this whole mix-up is because we somehow got caught in the crossfire of an escalating drug war?"

"Your friend Caroline had come to buy some fish scale." Santiago leaned back, sturdy hands resting on his knees. "Chiflado's LVA crew has been trying to establish dominance in this district for months. But they weren't expecting the Amigos Latinos to be present or for you two and Caroline to be there when the deal went down."

Daphne sounded almost professorial. "They thought Caroline was making the purchase on behalf of Chiflado's crew. Do you remember picking up Julio now? We dropped him off on Sunset Boulevard, all safe and sound?"

Nora didn't remember that at all, but judging by Daphne's tone and expression, she was obviously supposed to nod along. So she did.

Then Daphne changed the subject.

"Can you tell her what that one does again?" Daphne's finger landed on a sinister-looking contraption: a slender rod about two feet in length, with a series of sharp, angular hooks jutting out at intervals like the spine of some demonic creature.

Santiago grinned. "That's the Espina de Dolor or

Spine of Pain. An old tool used primarily to extract information. The hooks are designed to puncture skin without causing immediate deadly harm. By twisting the rod once it's inserted, one can inflict excruciating pain without causing a quick death. It's very effective."

"Isn't that gross?" Daphne's expression was somewhere between shaken and mesmerized.

Nora glanced at the time and said, "I hate to cut this lesson on medieval torture short, but we really have to go. My apologies for the intrusion, but we have an appointment that we can't afford to miss."

"Movie star stuff?" Santiago said.

"Movie star stuff," Nora agreed with a nod.

"I'm signing my next contract today," Daphne explained. "It's for a movie called *Sister Justice*. I play a nun with a heart of gold."

"I'll see it on opening day."

"It might go straight to a streamer." Daphne looked for disappointment for him.

But Santiago just shrugged. "I bootleg anyway."

"Oh, that's great then!" Daphne shocked Nora by giving her would-be torturer a warm hug goodbye. "Thanks for everything, Santiago! You're the best at knowing stuff about torture. If I ever need any tips, I know who to call!"

He scribbled his number on a piece of paper and handed it to her. "In case you need more ... insights."

Nora grabbed Daphne and dragged her toward the entrance, eager to put as much distance as possible between them and that dark room with its darker torture devices.

The bright Los Angeles sun slapped them hard as they stepped outside.

"I just want to get you to that contract meeting and try

to salvage whatever's left of this goddamned day," Nora muttered.

Daphne's phone rang.

"Uh-oh." She made a face when she looked at the screen. "It's Valentina and Vale."

Meaning, the jewelry store that loaned Daphne the brooch.

"This is Daphne!" She answered in a voice suggesting that she had not, in fact, lost their very expensive brooch. "Yes … that's right … oh my … yes, of course, that's my bad." She laughed. "I totally forgot that you guys were scheduled to pick it up from the safe today. I have it with me right now … right, because there was a photo shoot scheduled for today, and if I don't look good, you don't look good, or however that saying goes … of course! Absolutely … yes … yes … yes, by the end of the day. You've got it, Harmony — stay beautiful!"

Daphne hung up the phone and turned to Nora. "Shit balls. We're in trouble."

"I heard—"

Before Nora could say anything else, the warehouse door swung open behind them and Santiago emerged with his men.

"There was a news report about a bullet-riddled Rolls Royce found abandoned downtown," Santiago said. "It had blood smears on the trunk and a vanity license plate. You two wouldn't happen to know anything about that, would you?"

The women braced to run, but Santiago already had the gun in his hand, and whatever rapport he'd had with Daphne was gone along with his mirth.

"You two are going to tell me the truth about Julio's whereabouts and what really happened last night. Or I'm going to empty half of this gun into each of you."

Nora swallowed and started in on her bullshit story, hoping she could talk their way out of being murdered here in this warehouse.

But three words in, she heard the sound of yelling and gunfire coming their way.

Chapter Twenty-One

THE PUNGENT ODOR of gunpowder assaulted Nora as the air thickened with battle cries, gunfire illuminating the grim scene in a series of strobes casting shadows across the floor as Chiflado's LVA crew stormed the warehouse with their weapons blazing.

"Stay with me," Nora commanded, dragging Daphne behind a crate as the warring factions traded gunfire.

Bullets zipped through the air, embedding themselves into the crates with sickening thuds and sending splinters flying through the air.

The metallic clang of empty shells raining onto the concrete was a chaotic backbeat behind Daphne's choking breaths.

"It'll be okay," Nora promised.

"How do you know that? It definitely seems like we could die here!"

"Don't say that! You're supposed to be the optimistic one!"

"You're right!" Daphne seemed to gather herself

behind the crate, remembering who she was as she said, "I would rather die of embarrassment than let these bullets kill me!"

"I'm not sure those two things are related, but I do like that positive outlook."

Nora peered around the crate to catch a glimpse of Chiflado commanding his crew as they moved with synchronized precision. Ricocheting bullets and charging shadows ... it was a war zone, and if Nora didn't get her and Daphne out of it right now, they would be two more bodies buried among the rubble.

"We need to move!" Nora pointed toward the doorway.

"How are we supposed to do that without getting shot?" Daphne looked around at the fracas. "Shouldn't we just wait until all of this gunfire stops?"

"If we don't get out of here now, we'll be even more trapped in the middle of this chaos than we already are. We're dead unless—"

"Fine!" Daphne shouted over the gunfire. "What do we do?"

"Follow me." Nora swallowed and went for it, keeping low to avoid the hail of gunfire.

A bullet screamed past, grazing the space just above her head, forcing Nora to instinctively hunker down even lower.

Through the smoky haze, her eyes locked onto the exit door. She clutched Daphne's hand, and they pressed their bodies to the gritty floor, slithering like serpents through a tempest of bullets.

"Are you ready to run?" Nora asked.

"NO!" Daphne shouted. "But I'll follow you anyway!"

Nora made a mad dash for the exit with Daphne just

behind her as bullets hissed by them. Daphne belted out with a sharp cry, her momentum broken as she collapsed onto the concrete like a marionette with its strings cut.

Nora's heart constricted at the sight: Daphne had been shot.

She scrambled back to her friend's crumpled form.

With trembling hands, she rolled Daphne over to see the crimson stain seeping into her sleeve. A vicious gash from a bullet's unforgiving kiss on her arm.

"Thank God." Nora exhaled.

"What do you mean, 'Thank God'? I've been shot!"

"It could have been worse, Daphne."

Nora grabbed her by the good arm, but instead of heading toward the exit again, which was now under heavy fire, she yanked Daphne in the other direction, heading back behind the crates to where Nora had seen a first aid kit hanging on the wall.

"Why are you taking us back into the danger zone?" Daphne asked.

"This entire warehouse is a danger zone. But I think we're safer back over here for now, and I would like to take care of your wound."

"I would like that too." Daphne nodded. "Right now, this feels like I tried waxing my arm with sandpaper." She made a face. "Or like that time I tried a DIY chemical peel. Not a good idea."

"I wouldn't think so." Nora grabbed the first aid kit and opened it up to get what she needed to dress Daphne's wound.

It was an angry slash across her arm, the edges raw and inflamed, fresh blood oozing from the torn flesh. Nora gingerly dabbed at the wound with an antiseptic wipe, her hands shaky from the adrenaline rush.

But her patient kept wincing, gritting her teeth, and

doing an almost comical job of trying not to make any noise while the gunfire kept erupting all around them.

Nora placed a gauze pad over the gash, pressing down to stem the bleeding, before wrapping a bandage tightly around Daphne's arm.

Nora felt a surge of relief as she examined her handiwork. The bandage was still mostly white, with only a slight spotting of red. "You're going to be alright, Daphne."

"Well, it feels like my arm just got a bad perm. How about getting me some painkillers?"

Nora dug through the first aid kit and came up with a packet of ibuprofen.

"I said 'painkillers.' Because I'm in pain."

"Even if I had something stronger, I wouldn't give it to you. I need you to stay sharp until after you've signed that contract. Then, you can OD if you want to."

"You don't mean that."

"Of course, I don't mean that." Nora nodded at the exit, now that Daphne's wound had been dressed and their escape route appeared temporarily clear. "Are you ready?"

"Of course, I'm not ready!"

"Let's go." Nora started toward the open door, supporting most of Daphne's weight as she dragged her through the battling men.

A stray bullet ricocheted nearby and showered them with splinters. A distant shout and the sporadic drumming of boots on concrete as she and Daphne ran toward the exit, finally reaching the light and—

Nora expected to scream *Hallelujah!* when they finally made it outside, but instead, the bright Los Angeles sun smacked them in the face again, turning everything into a blur.

But even after blinking several times, their newest

reality still had not changed for the better: their garish disco wagon was gone.

"GODDAMMIT!" Nora bellowed.

"What?" Daphne looked around, then obviously noticed the car missing. "Oh."

"I guess we'll need to—"

"WHERE DO YOU THINK YOU'RE GOING?" roared an infuriated voice behind them.

Nora knew it was Santiago without turning around. His eyes were blazing with enough intensity to make the bloodstains all over his shirt look like finger paint by comparison.

She grabbed Daphne's arm again and breathlessly pulled her toward the street in search of cover — anything would do.

Santiago was closing the distance behind them fast.

Nora spotted a city bus ahead, pulling up to the curb. If they could reach it in time, that might be their only escape from the murderous thug in pursuit.

At least they were outside. Santiago was a lot less likely to shoot them in broad daylight.

"YOU THINK I WON'T SHOOT YOU?" he bellowed behind them.

Nora braced for the bullet and wondered if her brain would register the sound before it never registered anything else again.

Daphne whined right next to her as they double-timed it to the bus up ahead. "We're going to die—"

But that was all she got before the ominous black sedan that had been tailing them all day came screeching up in front of the bus, only a few feet away from them.

The passenger door flew open.

Nora didn't know what the fuck to do.

A thunderous shot sounded behind her, but it hit the sedan instead of her brain.

The metal screamed in protest as the driver's side door opened, and the driver returned Santiago's shot.

Daphne ran over and scrambled into the vehicle.

Nora followed, opening the back door and climbing onto the seat as the driver slammed his door and squealed into traffic.

"Who the hell are you supposed to be?" Daphne exclaimed.

"I'm Randolph."

"Randolph, who?" Daphne turned to Nora with a smile that should not have been possible, considering her fixer was still choking on their narrow escape. "It's like a knock-knock joke."

"Randolph, the guy from the private security company Valentina and Vale hired to monitor their precious brooch."

"You're a babysitter?" Daphne was appalled. "I take offense to that!"

"You take offense to the party who loaned you a two-million-dollar piece of jewelry wanting to track the location of their property?" Randolph asked.

"To be fair, Daphne, you haven't really been known for your reliability lately," Nora said. "So you've been following us all morning because of the brooch? Maybe it would have been nice if you had identified yourself."

"I was tracking the two of you to ensure the brooch's safe return. This was supposed to be simple. But my job just got a lot more hazardous, thanks to this one breathing trouble like oxygen."

He jabbed a thumb at Daphne before returning both hands to the wheel. "Right now, I'm the closest thing you ladies have to a guardian angel in this mess that you made for yourselves."

"What does gender have to do with it?" Daphne asked, even though that wasn't her usual fight.

Nora decided to intervene before Daphne said something that got them in even more trouble.

"We really appreciate the intervention, Randolph. I'm sorry that our mess has made your job more difficult. What can we do to help you?"

"You can answer some questions."

"I'll answer whatever you ask me." Nora gave him a nod he could see in his mirror. "But not right now. I need your full attention on the road. We're headed to Wilshire. You have my word that I will explain everything in detail. But right now the clock is ticking, with only fifteen minutes left until a critical appointment that I barely managed to reschedule. If we don't make this, Daphne loses out on her next role and maybe all the roles after that."

"Heard." Randolph returned her nod and floored the accelerator.

"I thought the meeting was later?" Daphne looked confused.

"I changed it," Nora replied because she was buying time.

If they made it to the contract signing before the incriminating footage was leaked to Sheryl, that would be one problem solved. After that, returning the brooch and dumping the body would be priorities one and two, though Nora wasn't sure in which order she would actually be able to handle them.

"Do you mind if we listen to some music?" Nora asked Randolph, wanting something to help obscure the call she was about to make.

"What do you want to hear?"

"Just pick something." Nora pulled up the number, ready to report the disco wagon stolen, covering their tracks. As Britney's "Toxic" filled the car, she breathed in deeply and hoped beyond hope that the nightmare was almost over and they could still salvage this day.

Chapter Twenty-Two

Randolph pulled up in front of the office building on Wilshire at exactly 12:16 p.m.

"You are a prince among men, Randolph. I definitely won't forget this." Nora slapped the security guard on his shoulder and opened her car door.

"I know you won't, and I'll be waiting right here for you when Daphne is done getting that contract signed so I can return your loaned brooch to its rightful owners."

"Jeez." Daphne rolled her eyes. "Like we need the reminders."

"Why are you looking at me like that?" Randolph asked Nora.

"I just need one more thing."

"Saving your life and getting you here on time wasn't enough?" He narrowed his eyes at Nora, still holding her stare in his rearview mirror.

"Shouldn't we hurry?" Daphne said.

Nora pointed to Randolph's jacket. "Can I borrow that?"

"What do you want my jacket for?"

"It would be nice if Sheryl didn't see that Daphne had been shot," Nora explained. "It would be a shame for you to have raced all the way here to our appointment only to see us getting turned away at the door."

"You make it sound like this Sheryl lady is some bouncer at a club."

"Well, she is the person who gets to decide whether this movie star sitting next to me gets to step back onto the Hollywood stage."

Randolph handed Daphne the jacket. "Well then, you better hustle up."

She shrugged into it like the jacket was just another costume change, and then the blood from her grazed arm and the red-spotted bandage were both buried.

"We only have like two minutes, and I'm already *so* tired of running!" Daphne whined as Nora led her through the sleek lobby with one hand while gripping her disco stick with the other. She was weirdly reluctant to throw the makeshift weapon away.

Floor-to-ceiling windows bathed the lobby in buckets of natural light, highlighting bold geometry on the black marble flooring as they raced across it, running too fast to appreciate any of the multiple pieces of minimalist art.

They dashed into the elevator just as it was closing.

A short woman with novelty-sized glasses looked over at them. Her hair was neatly pulled back into a tight bun, revealing a pinched face and high cheekbones.

"Have you two ladies been having a good day so far?" She had the tone of someone who wasn't expecting an answer so much as feeling the need to be polite in the twenty seconds they had together.

"I got shot this morning," Daphne told her. "So the day has been a *lot* so far."

"I know what you mean!" The woman surprised

Daphne with her exclamation before leaning forward and whispering, "*Me too.*"

She pointed to the pinpricks on her face where the Botox had gone in. "I've been doing it for ten years now, and I'm still not used to all the needles."

"I'm sure the bullet I took had a bit more kick, but at least we both look fabulous!" Daphne clapped. "Your forehead looks smoother than a baby's butthole."

"I think it's just a regular bottom," Nora corrected her.

The elevator doors dinged open, and she yanked Daphne away from the conversation.

"I was talking!" Daphne complained.

"You were just complaining that we only had two minutes and that you were tired of running."

"Exactly. We weren't running when I was talking to that nice woman. Did you see her forehead?"

"Yes. It looked like a butthole. Now move faster, or we're going to be late."

Nora didn't need an answer so much as for Daphne to move faster as they navigated the lush hallway from the elevator to Sheryl's office, arriving exactly on time as Nora opened the door and took in the view of bustling Los Angeles streets. Movie posters hung on every wall — Sheryl's productions, of course — while Jocelyn sat behind a sleek receptionist's desk in front of Sheryl's closed office door.

"She's expecting you," Jocelyn chirped as Nora pulled Daphne inside.

"Thanks!" Nora said as she opened Sheryl's door.

She and Daphne entered the office in unison, but Nora noted that the wall clock read 12:21 a beat before Sheryl griped, "You're late."

"I'm so sorry. It's been a week and a half already this morning," Nora said.

"You're both looking more than a little haggard."

"We had to run," Nora offered Sheryl a weak smile. "We didn't want to be any later than we already were."

"Would you like a bottle of water?"

"That would be great." Nora gave her a more genuine smile, although she had to ignore the chills rolling through her body as she heard Sheryl's offer.

She popped the cap and downed her entire bottle in a series of gulps. Daphne managed to sip hers.

"I guess you were dehydrated?" Sheryl narrowed her eyes at Nora as if trying to decipher an enigma. "Do I get to hear the story behind that little prop?" She nodded at the disco stick still firmly in Nora's grip.

"It was from a photo shoot earlier this morning. Daphne fell in love with it and asked the photographer if she could keep it. He told her to go nuts."

"Ah." Sheryl nodded. "Part of that week and a half this morning, I presume."

"Exactly." Nora nodded again as she and Daphne sat on the other side of Sheryl's desk.

Sheryl set the contract in between them. "I'm glad you could make it—" A buzzing phone cut her off. "I'm so sorry. I just need a second. I'm expecting an important text."

Nora didn't dare to utter a word about *this* also being an important meeting that deserved her full attention, because at least she was sitting in the chair right now and no longer sweating whether or not they would make it. Sheryl could take all the time that she needed.

But then Sheryl's face changed as she looked down at her phone screen.

And Nora felt a sickening clench in her stomach as she glanced down at the contract, just as Sheryl yanked it away and turned the phone screen to face them.

"Care to explain this?"

"Of course, I can explain that," Nora said.

"You mean spin it," Sheryl scoffed. "Fine. Go ahead. Give it to me."

"Daphne's drink got spiked last night. She wasn't in control of her faculties. So despite the usual drama that we all know is a part of Daphne's past, she was a victim of circumstance last night."

"Damn right I was," Daphne agreed with a vigorous nod.

"It doesn't matter." Sheryl shook her head. "The deal is off."

"Why is the deal off?" Daphne asked.

"The deal is off because we can't have our nun being naked all over town," Sheryl explained.

"I wasn't naked all over town — I was topless on top of Burt's tiki bar. I was also violated by someone taking that video without my permission, and then violated again when someone sent you that."

Sheryl nodded at her phone. "You don't look very violated."

"Daphne was violated when her drink was drugged!" Nora said. "This wasn't her fault."

"It doesn't matter," Sheryl said again. "This isn't the kind of publicity we want anywhere near *Sister Justice*. It isn't right for the project's image, and I'm sure that this will only come back to bite us if we're not careful."

"The project's image?" Nora repeated. "Are you kidding me? *Sister Justice* picks up an AK-47 and starts shooting people in church at the climax. That's not very nun-like behavior, either. Are you really saying that—"

"I'm sorry, but this is out of my hands."

"This is ridiculous!" Nora yelled. "What is wrong with

this country that we don't care about our body counts, but nipples are enough to inspire a riot?"

"I don't remember reading 'Thou shalt not bare thine beautiful bosom' anywhere in the Bible," Daphne interjected.

Like Daphne Belle had ever read the Bible.

"There must be something we can do to make this right, Sheryl," Nora tried.

"I'm sorry, but there isn't."

"You know what I'm capable of," Nora argued. "Please give me a chance to make this right."

"There aren't any more chances to be had here." Judging by Sheryl's expression, there was nothing left for either Nora or Daphne to do beyond getting up from their chairs and leaving the office.

"You look even more upset than I am," Daphne said once they were back in the elevator. "I'm the one who lost the role."

Nora didn't answer her. "I just want to get my phone charged. So I can give whoever texted me that video a piece of my goddamn mind."

"Ooh, I can't wait to hear that!"

They were halfway to the exit when they saw Scarlett entering the lobby with Melissa. Daphne didn't hesitate, taking one look at her rival and marching over with an accusation flying out of her mouth.

"You fucking bitch! You *drugged* us last night."

"No, she didn't." Melissa shook her head, looking stoically calm while walking over to Nora and showed her phone screen. "We got a message from an anonymous number asking us to stop by Sheryl's office."

Nora took out her phone and compared the numbers. "It's the same one that sent the photo."

"We need to go," Melissa said.

She and Scarlett started walking away.

"Convenient that you're here just in time to take my part!" Daphne yelled as Nora tugged her toward the exit.

She saw a small crowd huddled around Randolph's car as they stepped outside.

"What do you think is happening?" Daphne asked.

"I'm not sure. But I don't feel good about it."

"Maybe they're giving out free samples or something? I could definitely snack."

Sometimes, Nora couldn't even tell when Daphne was kidding.

She inched closer, dreading what she might see through the windshield.

As they approached the car, the murmuring of the crowd became a low hum of shared horror. Police lights seemed imminent, soon to bathe the scene in a wash of blue and red while blocking onlookers from what was still on display right now.

Randolph's head lolled to the side, and his white button-up had turned a shocking shade of crimson from the vicious gash like a horrifying smile across his throat.

Chapter Twenty-Three

Nora and Daphne traded a look.

"What the fuck is going on?" Daphne asked, sounding more sober than Nora had heard her in recent memory, which was saying a lot considering all that they had been through in the last couple of hours.

Nora dragged Daphne away from the car, hauling her toward the end of the block.

"Where are you taking me?" Daphne demanded.

"Away from the scene of that crime."

"But we didn't have anything to do with it!"

"Do you think that matters? Do you really want to answer questions from the cops right now? Do you want even *one* of those people over there to take a picture of you and see another embarrassing picture of Daphne Belle on some stupid BuzzFeed article?"

"No." Daphne pouted. "Of course not. So what are we supposed to do now?"

Nora shook her head. "I have no idea."

"You must have some idea. That is what you're paid to do, right?"

"Yes, Daphne, that is what you pay me to do. I appreciate you reminding me of my role yet again. But I'm not a fucking PEZ dispenser. So give me a second to think, and I will come up with a plan. Okay?"

"Great." Daphne smiled. "I'm glad we're communicating."

"I need to recharge my phone," Nora said.

"I remember. Because you can't wait to give the anonymous guy who's been one step ahead of us the entire time a piece of your mind when you call the number, he texted you from but almost for sure won't answer."

"Do you think they already cleared your stuff out of the suite by now?"

"Why would they do that?" Daphne asked.

"It might be past checkout time."

"I still have the room. I paid for an extra day."

"You are very quickly going broke and constantly complaining about how fast the money is running out, and yet you paid for an entire extra day on an overpriced suite at the Sunset Sovereign?"

"It's not that overpriced. Some of the hotels in that area are a lot more, you know."

"That so isn't the point."

"It's not like I wanted to pay for an extra day, but they said no when I asked for a late checkout, and I think we both know exactly how much I would have needed my beauty sleep this morning if things had gone according to plan," Daphne scoffed. "Whoever would have imagined that I'd wake up in my own goddamn house?"

"It doesn't seem like that far-fetched a place to wake up."

"Yeah, but with glitter all over my tits?"

"Let's go back to the hotel," Nora said, too exhausted to say anything else.

"Do you know where it is from here?" Daphne asked.

"It's not far."

"How far is not far? Because I think you and me might have different definitions of not far. I'm thinking if it's more than a short strut away, we should probably call a cab."

"We can get there faster than calling a cab."

"How far is it?" Daphne tried again.

"Maybe a strut and a half."

"What does that mean? How far away are we in actual miles?"

"One, maybe two. I'm better with directions than distances."

"I'm not so good with either. One time, I asked Siri to map me out to drinks with Jennifer Aniston, and I ended up on a three-day cruise."

"Was Jennifer Aniston with you?"

"Why would she be with me?" Daphne looked perplexed.

Nora didn't answer.

After another 20 minutes of walking, the Sunset Sovereign appeared in the distance, the hotel's art deco facade and gold accents shimmering on the palm-lined boulevard.

Nora was just about to remark that the hotel was obviously closer than she thought when Daphne declared, "More like 10 miles!"

"Where are you going?" she called out after Nora entered the lobby a full beat before her, heading toward the front desk instead of the elevator.

"Would you happen to have an iPhone charger I could borrow?" Nora asked when she got to the counter.

"Yes, of course," the clerk replied.

She turned around and dug through a drawer behind

her, then turned back around and handed a charger to Nora. The words *Sunset Sovereign Hotel* were written in large block letters on the side.

"Thank you. I'll return this soon," Nora said, then followed an impatiently waiting Daphne to the elevator.

The doors dinged open just as that same mother and daughter duo from last night joined them inside. Daphne didn't have a stunning piece of jewelry for the little girl to compliment this time, but the wee lass still had something to say.

She tugged on the hem of Daphne's shirt. "I hope your friend feels better today."

"Which friend?" Daphne clearly had no idea what the little girl was talking about.

Her mother said, "Striking woman. Expressive eyes. A regal presence?" And when that wasn't enough. "She starred opposite a young Bryon Roberson in *Seven Ate Nine*."

"That's my friend Caroline!" Daphne explained.

"I'm sorry," Nora interjected. "Are you saying that we were back here at the Sunset Sovereign last night?"

"Yes," answered the mom.

"What time was that?" Nora asked.

"We were coming back from a wedding late, around one in the morning or so."

"After midnight!" the little girl yelled.

"Yes, after midnight," continued Mom. "And all of us met up in the elevator."

"I guess we do that a lot," Daphne said.

The little girl giggled.

"Can you tell us anything else?" Nora asked.

"It was a short ride, but your friend was obviously very sick. You know, the kind of illness that goes away after a little prayer to the porcelain god."

The doors dinged open.

"What does that mean, Mommy?" Nora heard the girl ask her mother as they closed again. "Who is the porcelain god?"

"I kinda wanna hear her answer," Daphne said on their way to the room.

It was still a disaster inside, exactly like the last time Nora had seen it, with Daphne's clothes scattered in piles atop the bed. Daphne tossed her purse on the top of the pile. It shifted, sending a small avalanche of scarves and blouses to the floor and revealing a new layer of colors: cobalt blue, soft pinks and yellows, scarlet, and even a glimmer of gold.

They went into the living area, and Nora plugged in her phone. She patiently waited for a long minute until the Apple logo reappeared. Then she booted the thing up to see that she had several voice messages. Two seemed immediately important.

The first one was from Eric. "Hey there, Nora. I'm just calling to check and see if you're okay."

There was a long pause before he cleared his throat and finished the thought. "I saw that video of you and ... just know that I'm here if you need to talk or if you want me to tell stupid jokes while you just listen and try not to think about what a dork I am."

He gave her an awkward laugh before signing off.

The next message was from someone named Maria at Three Mile PR. Nora knew that much by the auto transcription accompanying her voicemail, and also knew that the call was not a good sign. Nora had never heard of Maria, and thus felt certain that her reaching out could only mean bad news.

"Hi there. I'm calling for Nora Bauer. This is Maria Sandoval from Three Mile PR. You were scheduled to come in for a job interview tomorrow at 3 p.m., but I'm calling to let you know that the firm has decided to go in a different direction. I really hope—"

Nora ended the message because she didn't need to hear anything else that Maria had to say.

"What's wrong?" Daphne asked.

Nora shook her head. "I don't want to talk about it."

"Do you really not want to talk about it, or do you not want to talk about it in the sense that you want me to ask three or four questions before we get into what made your butt hurt?"

"My butt doesn't hurt. And I really don't want to talk about it."

"Okay, but if you change your mind, I'm all ears. Well, mostly hair and heels and boobs, but you get the point."

Nora's phone buzzed with a new text.

"Aren't you glad you can get those now that your phone has juice?" Daphne asked. "I feel like actually dying when my phone is dead ... Uh-oh, what is it now?"

Nora turned the phone screen around to show Daphne another video, this one of her and Daphne dragging a body out of the trunk of her Infiniti.

Her phone buzzed again, this time with a message. *Double the money by 8 p.m., or this video goes to the press.*

"You fucking piece of shit," Nora managed to say before her phone buzzed again.

I hope you don't mind that I decided to send that first video to Sheryl. I just thought it was important that you understand I mean business.

Nora sagged to the floor and cradled her head, somehow managing not to sob.

This entire mess could have been avoided if only she had done the right thing and called Eric this morning after finding the body.

Instead, Nora listened to Daphne, and now they were being blackmailed because of it. Nora was A+ at working out various scenarios in her head or on paper, but there were few ways she could see of escaping this situation that didn't end up with her going to prison forever.

"...and that's when I realized leopard print isn't considered camouflage. HEY. YOU. NORA!"

"What?" Nora snapped at her.

"It doesn't seem like you're listening to a word I say."

"That's because I'm not listening to you. I'm trying to *think* so that I can come up with a plan like you pay me to do. Now, can you please just shut the hell up for once?"

That did the trick. Daphne didn't just close her mouth, she seemed to collapse into herself like a dying star. Nora suddenly felt terrible.

She knew exactly how Daphne was feeling right now because Nora had been down this spiral before. It was one she felt used to.

The same thing used to happen to her as a kid all the time — when she would get overwhelmed trying to take care of her mother, and nothing she did was ever good enough, and she would still go to bed hungry — and why the fuck did she ever think she could do this job in the first place?

Chapter Twenty-Four

DAPHNE WASN'T one to totally freak out in even the most totally freakoutable situations, but she had been watching Nora for a few minutes now and felt even worse about her supposed fixer's ability to snap out of it without some serious help than she had when the poor woman started muttering to herself while rocking back and forth on the floor.

Nora's brokenness was turning each minute into a quarter-hour of anxiety.

How was Daphne ever supposed to get out of this disaster with her life and sanity intact while also worrying about the person who cleaned up her messes in the cases where she failed to help her avoid them entirely?

"Nora." Daphne poked her again. "Hey, Nora! Say something annoying. Please? I just need to see that the bossy pants know-it-all who's always telling me what to do is still in there somewhere."

But Nora still didn't answer, so Daphne got out her phone and gave Burt a call.

"Daphne," he said after the first ring, "I do like this

little frenaissance we're having lately. Are you calling because you want to come over and take turns shooting my rocket launcher?"

"I think I broke Nora."

"What do you mean? Is she okay?" Burt whispered into the phone. "*Nora isn't dead, is she?* Wait. Don't answer that."

"Nora is very much alive, but I need you here at the Sunset Sovereign."

"Don't tell me — I'll find out when I get there."

"You're a good man, Burt, and not just because you play one in every goddamn movie you're in."

"See you soon," said Burt in his hero's voice before ending the call.

Daphne paced the room while waiting for Burt. She briefly considered cleaning up a bit, except that was what they paid the cleaning staff for, and it wasn't like she had the energy required to pack all of those piles of clothes back into her bag.

Really, the only thing Daphne had a mind to do right now was to collapse on the floor and worry about Nora — the bed would have been more comfortable, but only after the discomfort of having to move all of those clothes — and what her incapacitation might mean when it came to Daphne's decaying career.

Twenty minutes after hanging up with Burt, there came a strong knock on her hotel room door. She scurried over to answer it, slightly surprised to see that Nora was still fully catatonic but also kind of glad because a part of Daphne had pictured Burt coming into the room only to find Nora already back to being her bossy pants self, and that would make Daphne look dumber than she wanted to in front of him.

Daphne opened the door to see Burt in his silk

bathrobe, standing in the hallway with his hair perfectly tousled and a smile that radiated charisma.

"Come in." Daphne took Burt by his wrist and pulled him into the suite, all the way over to the plush sofa in their living area, where Daphne sat next to him and spilled the beans about everything.

She told him about the car and about the drug dealing.

She confessed that Caroline had gone missing and that she and Nora had gone to The Disco Stick after leaving his party, where Nora had apparently gone full Coyote Ugly-Showgirls.

It all came out of Daphne in manic bursts of fragmented and grossly out-of-order language.

"I think I've got that," Burt said when she finished.

"I'm sorry." Daphne sagged down into the cushions. "I just really can't remember what happened last night."

Burt went over and tried talking to Nora, but she didn't respond. He poked her, and Daphne said, "I already tried that, and a lot harder than you're trying right now."

"I'll be back." He stood, then disappeared into the kitchenette area, returning two minutes later and dumping an entire coffee pot full of cold water on top of Nora's head.

She lurched to her feet, instantly furious.

"What the hell was that for?" Nora screamed.

"You were catatonic, dear," Burt explained.

"I was thinking. That's what happens when I go deep in thought, which is where I need to be if Daphne expects me to fix the mess that none of us would be in right now if she had just let me call Eric earlier this morning like I wanted to — *and suggested at the time.*"

Daphne shrugged. "Maybe you should have insisted."

"Excuse me?"

"If you had insisted, then I would have listened. That's kinda sorta our deal, right?"

"Sure you would have." Nora rolled her eyes. She was about to start in on Daphne, but Burt redirected her.

"Who is Eric?"

Nora grabbed her phone and went into another part of the suite without answering.

Daphne brought her a towel to dry off. "Tell me what's wrong, honey."

Nora tried to ignore her.

But Daphne wasn't having it, looking down at Nora with obvious concern as she pulled her into a hug. Once in the embrace, Nora stiffened, then went limp.

"What is it, honey?" Daphne nudged Nora nearer to a confession while petting her.

"I lost my job at Three Mile PR. Some bitch named Maria called to let me know that the firm was going in a different direction."

"Sounds more like some cunt," Daphne said.

Nora laughed and wiped the snot bubble away from her nose.

"You'll find another job, honey. I promise not to hold you back."

"But that's the job I've been wanting forever. I only worked with Vivian as long as I did so I could get good enough to eventually become one of the best. That's what Three Mile looks for more than any other virtue."

"What?"

"The potential to be great."

"Well, fuck them! You're a lot more than 'potential,' darling. You're *already* great."

"Thanks, Daphne, but that doesn't change my actual situation. No one is going to hire me after they see that video of me."

"I know what you need." Daphne let go of Nora and walked to the nearest phone.

"Who are you calling?"

"You need to eat," Daphne exclaimed.

"I'm not hungry," Nora told her.

"Sure you are," Daphne argued. "We're always hungry. It's called evolution, baby."

"I'm seriously not hungry, Daphne."

"Well then, good news. Hunger's got nothing to do with it."

"Hi there, darling," said Daphne into the phone, "you might want to grab a pen because this will be hard to remember, not that I'm calling you dim or anything, I'm just saying that I don't even know what I'm going to order until it's out of my mouth so I'm sure that will make it harder to get it all. I talk fast, so just let me know if you have any questions after I'm done, because ready or not, here I go, starting with a charcuterie board and extra blue cheese — smells like feet but tastes like heaven — plus a few sliders if you have 'em, and if not, just three of your best sandwiches will work. Do you have truffle fries? Extra crispy if so, and if not, then I guess you can give me two orders of regular fries and an order of onion rings. There's no ignoring my sweet tooth once it starts aching these days, so throw in a chocolate lava cake, extra molten if that's a thing, and maybe a lobster bisque or something creamy now that I'm thinking about it."

"You're going to go broke soon," Nora said after Daphne hung up the phone. "You can't keep ordering like that. The prices in this place are ridiculous, and you just bought enough food for a football team."

"Honey, you have obviously never been around an actual football team. And I'm never going broke because you're going to get me that role in *Sister Justice*. After that, the industry will be tripping over itself to throw parts at me again in no time."

"I'm glad you have faith in me."

"You know it, sister!" Daphne exclaimed with a laugh before adding, "*Justice!*"

Burt knocked on the door and then entered the room with a question. "Might I ask again, who is Eric?"

"Her boyfriend," Daphne answered.

"Eric is not my boyfriend," Nora clarified with a shake of her head. "He is a detective for the LAPD and a friend of mine who happens to be male."

"I've had a few 'friends' like that, too, but none of them had a badge. Just the occasional cowboy hat. And handcuffs, of course." Daphne laughed.

"I think that Nora might have a point here," said Burt. "If all of that has been happening to you since this morning, it might be time to alert the authorities."

But Nora said nothing. For the first time since Daphne had met her, she didn't seem to know what to say. But Burt read her mind like they were two actors sharing a stage.

"Would you like me to call this Eric for you, dear?"

"Yes, please."

He dialed the number and wasn't even finished identifying himself before Eric announced his intentions on speakerphone. "I'm off work right now. I'll be at the Sovereign in twenty."

Daphne hovered over her, handing out an occasional pat on the shoulder until they finally heard a knock at the door, and everyone jumped.

But it was just room service, storming into the suite with a pharaoh's banquet.

Daphne stared down at the spread. "Honey, you better help me out, or my next role will be as the leading lady in *Attack of the Muffin Top*."

Nora picked at her truffle fries.

"I think we need a distraction," Burt said as he went over to turn on the TV.

Of course, it was a news program covering Randolph's murder. The ticker at the bottom of the screen referred to the killing as a *drug deal gone wrong*.

"See?" Daphne crowed. "Nothing to do with us."

But then the footage flipped over to the bloody Rolls Royce that had been found in downtown Los Angeles, and the ticker on that story informed them that police were still searching for any information.

Daphne turned to see Burt's mouth open, his jaw hanging low.

"Is that my car?" he asked.

Chapter Twenty-Five

NORA HAD SPENT a total of ten minutes catching Eric up on all that had happened, both before and after he came to pick her up at the museum, but the five minutes required to process that information felt like five times as long, if not longer.

"You can stop staring at me if you want to," Nora said.

"I'm sorry. It's just…" Eric stopped talking again.

And now it was her turn to poke him. "Eric. Please, talk to me."

He stood from the sofa and started pacing the room while Burt, Daphne, and Nora all watched him.

"I can't believe you moved a dead body." He shook his head in admonishment. "Do you have any idea what you could get charged with?"

"You sound like Nora," Daphne snorted.

"You're not helping." Nora swallowed and turned back to Eric, looking into his eyes without flinching, needing him to understand that she wasn't trying to play him. "I'm sorry. I completely see how terrible this looks. How terrible this *is.*" She shook her head. "I never should have listened to Daphne, and honestly, I have no idea why I did."

"I can be very persuasive," Daphne crowed.

"That's nothing to be proud of." Eric was still fuming.

"Well, sure it is," Daphne had the terrible sense to argue with him. "It just depends on who you're talking to. One time, I convinced a spa to give me an all-day massage for the price of a half-hour session. And another time, I persuaded this bakery in Anaheim to name a pastry after me."

"Daphne," Nora interjected. "Please stop talking."

Burt leaned back in the armchair, enjoying the show.

"I ought to arrest you both," Eric said.

"Oh, honey, you don't have to do that!" Daphne waved her hand in the air as if she was slapping his suggestion aside.

"I'm going to Daphne's house to take a look at the body." Eric turned to go.

"We'll come," Nora said.

Burt was already standing.

"No." Eric shook his head. "I want all three of you to stay here."

"Including me?" Burt asked.

"That math does check out." Eric offered the actor a thin smile.

"Why me?"

"Because this situation is already out of hand, and I would like to keep it contained as much as possible until I know more."

Burt nodded. "Fair."

"Stay here, I'll be back fast," Eric told everyone before turning to Nora. "A word?"

"Of course." Nora nodded and followed him into the bathroom.

He closed the door behind them.

And Nora started blathering. "I'm so, *so* sorry, Eric. And I really mean that this isn't me just spinning you, I swear. I wouldn't *ever* spin you, and I hope you know that. I should have called you, of course I should have called you, but it's not every day that you find a dead body — even this business doesn't prepare you for that! Anyway, I just couldn't remember any of the shit that happened last night and—"

Eric stopped her with a kiss.

Nora fell silent, her world narrowing down to just the two of them with both urgency and comfort, giving her a momentary yet deeply needed reprieve.

Eric pulled away, but she wanted him back. Kissing him was the sole bright spot in what had been a brutally tumultuous day.

And besides, this might be her final kiss before a lifetime behind bars.

Their breath synchronized as the kiss deepened, then they reluctantly parted ways.

"I should have known that something was off this morning," Eric said. "Dammit. I *did* know that something was off this morning. And you knew that I knew and promised to tell me later. You were evasive with me, Nora. You should have told me that you had been drugged."

"I know. I'm sorry."

"I could have done a drug test."

"You're right."

"We could know what you had been given already, and that would at least be a lead," he continued. "I'm just trying to understand *why* you would keep that from me?"

"Because when I first called you this morning, I thought that Daphne had drugged me. She's always been a lot to handle, and I figured this was more of the same. A little whipped cream on her usual dessert. Once she signed the *Sister Justice* contract, I would be able to add some less demanding clients to my roster and ... I'm sorry."

Eric kissed her again gently on her forehead. "I'll be back within the hour."

"Thank you for helping me." Nora nodded while holding his eyes. "I don't expect you to break the law just because I did. I'm ready for my consequences, whatever they might be."

He kissed her on the forehead again, then they left the bathroom together.

But neither Burt nor Daphne appeared to be in the suite at a glance.

And those suspicions were confirmed after a swift investigation.

"Motherfucker!" Nora exclaimed.

"I could not agree more. Where do you think they're going?"

"I'm guessing they're on their way to Daphne's house."

"Think we can beat them?"

"You're the one with a siren on his car, so I'm going to say yes."

"It's actually called a beacon," Eric said. "Or a magnetic mount siren."

"Thank you for the seminar."

They ran down the hallway and into the elevator.

They dashed through the lobby and burst through the hotel doors.

They cast rapid glances up and down the street, searching for any sign of Daphne or Burt. Even if Eric might have seen the Jeep at the next interaction first, only Nora knew what it meant.

"Over there." She pointed at the military vehicle. "I saw that same Jeep at Burt's place earlier this morning."

Eric was already jogging toward his car.

Nora followed, ducking into the passenger seat thanks to an open door when she got there. The engine roared to life as he put the car in gear, and she buckled up.

Eric scanned the lanes and locked onto the Jeep as his car screamed into traffic, sailing through the yellow in a blink before it turned red.

Good thing because the Jeep was barely still in sight as it turned the corner.

Eric followed him. Two blocks later, the Jeep had to stop at a red.

He threw the car into park, unbuckled his safety belt, and lunged out of his car, striding with purpose toward the Jeep.

"What are you doing?" Nora called out.

The light turned green before Eric could get there.

Its engine revved, and the Jeep screeched forward, tires clawing asphalt as it left Eric in its wake. He raced back to his car, muttering curses, inaudible to Nora, though she could easily imagine the swears.

The Jeep turned a corner up ahead.

And apparently, another one after that because by the time Eric was turning, the Jeep was no longer in sight.

"It's okay," Nora assured him. "We have the address."

Even so, Eric stewed about the loss all the way to Daphne's, where they arrived to find both her and Burt standing by the Jeep, laughing as the detective marched over to them.

"I told you to stay at the hotel!"

"This is my house!" Daphne exclaimed.

"That doesn't mean—" Eric stopped short when he spied the front door. More than ajar, it looked busted wide open. "Have you gone inside the house?"

"We just got here," Burt said.

"We were waiting for you guys. Nora gets her butt hurt when I do stuff without her."

"That's not true," Nora said.

But Eric didn't care. He pulled his gun and started toward the front door.

"Wait here." He was halfway to the porch when he noted that all three of them were following him. "I'm going in alone."

"I can be backup," Burt offered.

"Thank you, but no." Eric turned his back to the actor, clearly unimpressed with his performances in *Moonlight Killer*, *Silver Foxes*, or any of the *Avenge Her* movies.

Eric entered the house, and time seemed to stop entirely.

"It feels like he's been there for hours," Nora said after a half hour at most.

"It's been six minutes," Daphne reported.

"That can't be possible." Nora shook her head, not really disbelieving so much as needing to express her incredulity out loud.

Daphne showed her the still-running stopwatch she had set on her phone, now at six minutes and seventeen seconds.

Nora paced in front of the shrubs until Eric finally emerged.

She held out her hands, wrists exposed to facilitate her arrest.

"You all need to come inside," Eric said, turning around and reentering the house.

"I'm not sure that's such a good idea," Daphne protested. "We don't want to contaminate the crime scene."

Eric turned back around. "Inside. *Now.*"

Moments later, they were all in the living room looking down at the couch, but there wasn't a body anywhere in sight.

Chapter Twenty-Six

Nora stared down at the couch in disbelief, willing to consider that she was going out of her goddamned mind, except that Daphne had been here with her earlier this morning, and she had seen the same bloody man on the same bloody sofa as Nora.

And yet, right now, there wasn't so much as a speck of red on the fabric.

Nora could barely find the words to voice her disbelief.

Eric finally broke the silence. "Was the guy actually dead?"

"Of course, he was dead," Nora said.

"Well, yeah." Daphne sounded anything but convincing.

She and Nora traded a glance.

"Please tell me that you checked to make sure he was dead," Nora said.

"Why would I check? You're the fixer! I thought you checked."

"I assumed that you did before you told me he was dead." Nora shook her head. "Jesus Christ."

"Looks like you made an ass out of both of us again, Nora!" Daphne yelled at her.

"So he could have just been passed out then?" Eric asked. "I need you both to think about this."

"He was completely covered in blood," Nora said.

Daphne nodded. "It really looked like the guy had been shot."

Eric pinched the bridge of his nose.

"So does this mean we're not going to be arrested?" Nora asked.

Eric turned to her. "Arrested for what?"

Nora raised her eyebrows. "Did you want a list?"

"I'm surprised that you think there's anything. Your job is to put the best spin on something, not the worst one. Tell me, fixer, where is the crime?"

"What about Burt's car?"

"Totaling Burt's car isn't a crime."

"Totaling a Rolls is *absolutely* a crime," Burt chimed in.

Eric shook his head. "Unless you're planning to press theft charges, which you're not because the car wasn't stolen."

"Burt would never press charges against us," Daphne said.

Nora thought Burt was a little slow to nod at that.

"What about the drug deal?" Nora pressed.

"Do you *want* me to arrest you?"

"Maybe she just wants you to use the cuffs on her." Daphne laughed. "You don't have to spend your life behind bars just to—"

"I just want to make sure I understand all of this," Nora cut her off. "Because there *was* a drug deal."

"Did you buy any drugs?" Eric asked.

Nora shook her head. "Not that I can remember."

He shrugged. "Well, there you have it."

"YAY!" Daphne clapped. "Now we need to celebrate, and since we're already at my place, I get to pick the champagne. I still have a bottle or two of the good stuff, and if it's still too early for anyone, I can add orange juice. Burt, would you be a dear?"

Burt started toward the kitchen but then stopped when Nora spoke.

"We're not celebrating," Nora told her. "Because this isn't over yet."

"The large lady is singing, since we're not supposed to say 'fat' unless it's with a P-H. We should pop some bubbly."

"Who killed Randolph?" Nora asked. "That feels like a pretty big fucking mystery to walk away from considering—"

"Who is Randolph?" Eric wondered aloud.

"A security guard. Specifically, a security guard paid to watch the spider."

"The spider?" Eric repeated. "Is this a movie thing?"

"A spider brooch. Daphne lost it—"

"I didn't lose it!"

"—and Randolph was hired to make sure she didn't lose the jewelry. We—"

"I didn't lose the jewelry."

"—told him that it was at Daphne's house. And then someone killed him."

"Another body?" Eric was aghast.

"The one with its throat cut on Wilshire." Daphne almost sounded proud. "That was us."

"It wasn't *us*."

"Jesus, Nora," Eric said.

"*And* Daphne," Daphne reminded him.

"What else aren't you telling me?"

"That's it," Nora assured him. "Now you know everything."

"I'm heading back to work. I'd like to see what else I can find out about this Randolph fellow."

"Maybe it was just a random mugging," Daphne tried. "It was in a bad part of town, you know."

"Why would you say that?" Nora asked her. "It was right outside of Sheryl's office." Then back to Eric. "Do you think we should put out a missing person's report for Caroline?"

"I'll take a look. You said her assistant's name was Sophia?"

Nora nodded. "I'll get you the number.

"The brooch was worth two million smackers." When no one responded, Daphne added, "I just thought that might be relevant to the case."

Burt put a hand on her arm. "It's okay, dear."

Nora gave Eric Sophia's contact information and said, "Should I walk you out?"

"That would be great." He nodded. "Thanks."

Their exchange felt weirdly formal. But the energy was even more awkward outside. They hesitated in unison, holding a mutual gaze as an unspoken question hung in the air between them.

Nora considered leaning in, but then Daphne's silhouette in the doorway caught her eye and she backed away, leaving Eric with an almost chaste kiss on his cheek before making an about face to go back inside.

"Promise to call me if anything else comes up, okay?" Eric called out behind her. "Anything at all. Nothing is too small — you never know how the elements come together in the end."

"I promise to call if anything comes up," Nora replied without turning back around. She didn't want to hurt him or feel like she had hurt him. Not with her breaking the law earlier or with whatever this was in between them.

Not that there was anything.

"Looks like it's been a great day for your love life," Daphne said once Nora was back inside.

"What's that supposed to mean?"

"Besides exactly what it sounds like? It means that maybe all of this was worth the hassle, assuming you get some private dick."

"Please stop saying that," Nora begged.

"What were you doing at Sheryl's?" asked Burt.

"We were supposed to sign Daphne's contract for *Sister Justice*, but that didn't happen."

"Why not?"

"Someone sent Sheryl an episode of Daphne's Sexiest Home Videos," Daphne explained.

Nora flushed, wishing she could disappear into the floor so she wouldn't have to hear them talk about it.

"Another video?" said Burt.

"There's another one of Nora." Daphne had the sound of ratting her out. "But I was talking about the one with me going all glitter tits on your tiki bar."

"What about a video with Nora?"

"Apparently, I was dancing at The Disco Stick."

"No apparently about it, Sister Fister!" Daphne laughed. "We both know you were there."

"Please don't call me that."

"She never likes my nicknames," Daphne complained to Burt. "Do you want to see the video again?"

"Of Nora dancing at the Disco Stick?"

"No, silly!" She waved a hand at Burt. "I mean the one of me."

"Well, of course." Burt acted like he had a choice, but Daphne was already shoving her phone in his face.

"My tits still look like a million bucks."

"They are magnificent," Burt agreed. "And I'm sure they only cost a fraction."

"Practically a rounding error." Daphne laughed again. "But worth it, right, Nora?" When she didn't answer, Daphne turned back to Burt. "She only listens to me half the time. Do you think I should only pay half of her bill?"

"I'm thinking," Nora said.

"She's always thinking." Daphne made it sound like an insult.

"What are you thinking about?" Burt asked.

"If Vivian hadn't retired after her big payday, I would say that her fingers were all over this mess."

"I don't think Vivian has quit the business," Burt said.

"What do you know?" Nora asked.

"Not much of anything." He shrugged. "Only that I heard she was taking a sabbatical."

Nora felt confused, unsure of what to believe. "I heard that Melissa was taking all of her clients."

"And I heard that she's looking after the business for Vivian but that the queen bee definitely plans on coming back to her hive."

"Well, fuck." Nora was back to thinking. "This changes everything."

"What does it change?" Daphne sounded clueless.

"It's possible that Vivian is behind this," Nora began to theorize. "Melissa was at the party. She could have spiked our water because—"

"Vivian wanted the role for Scarlett," Daphne finished.

Chapter Twenty-Seven

"Has anybody ever told you that you make a big deal about everything?" Daphne didn't let Nora answer before finishing her thought. "If life were a potluck, you would be boring everyone with your drama casserole."

"I'm just not sure why you didn't think that this nugget of information wasn't important enough to share with me."

"I don't know how you want me to say it differently, Nora. I already told you. I didn't think about it until just now."

"So just to clarify," Nora continued like the wrong kind of bitch, "you're sitting in Vivian's office with Melissa, and she offers you a bottle of water, and it's the same cheap-ass brand that we were given last night that knocked us both on our roofied asses—"

"I'm not sure it actually knocked either one of us down. With me tits out atop the tiki bar and you waving what the Good Lord gave you down at The Disco Stick."

"My question remains."

"And what question is that? I'm not sure I've actually heard you ask one yet. Just a lot of letting me know all about the things I should have told you sooner."

Nora sighed. "Jesus."

"You say that a lot."

"I guess you make me feel religious."

"Hallelujah."

"When you saw that bottle of Oasis water in Melissa's office, did you think about the bottles that we were handed last night?"

"I don't know." Daphne shrugged. "Probably?" She shrugged again, giving Nora a look that plainly was asking what the hell she expected from her right now. "I told you the literal second that I remembered Melissa having that brand of water in Vivian's office because you just identified her as a suspect. How about, 'Great job, Daphne!' Or something like that. You can surprise me."

"Great job, Daphne."

"It makes me so mad!" Daphne clenched her fists. "What can we do to expose Vivian and her meddling ways?"

"Are you auditioning for Scooby Doo?"

"What are we going to do, Nora?"

"Nothing yet. We don't have any evidence."

"We could entrap her," Daphne suggested.

"I'm not sure Eric would like that suggestion."

"I bet he doesn't like that you haven't blown him yet either, but I don't see you moving to fix that problem."

"That's not a problem. Maybe I should call Vivian?"

"On the phone?" Daphne asked.

"No. I figured I would go out to the street and scream."

"If you scream 'casting couch favors,' I bet Scarlett will come running right over."

Nora took out her phone, swiped for Vivian's contact info, and then made the call.

Her attempt didn't go straight to voicemail, but it did ring four times before clicking over to Vivian's outgoing message.

"Hey there, Vivian, it's Nora, I was hoping we could talk. I just need a few minutes, and you know how it is: *you can call me back at any time.* I hope you're well."

"That was a very cordial call for someone who's trying to destroy your only client," Daphne said after Nora ended the call.

"We don't know that as a fact. And besides, you know what they say about catching more flies with honey."

"The only time I'm willing to deal with flies is if they come with cabana boys."

"I'm going to try Melissa." Nora dialed, but it rang until she got voicemail from Melissa too. She tried to leave a message, but Daphne talked over her.

"That was rude," Nora said.

"Fuck her! It's rude for Melissa to ignore your phone call."

"It's after hours," Nora defended her.

"So what? She's a fixer. You guys aren't supposed to have hours."

"That's not actually how it works. You just have no sense of space or personal boundaries."

"What if you were her client right now and you were having an emergency?" Daphne asked.

"Well, in that case, I am sure that I would have been given a special number that Melissa answers 24 hours a day. But since I am not her client and she doesn't have *my* personal number, I don't blame her at all."

"You mean I can get a hold of you when other people can't?"

Nora nodded. "Exactly."

Daphne smiled, seeming almost delirious with silent appreciation.

"I bet Melissa is still at the office and just ignoring calls," Nora said. "I want to go down there right now before it gets too late. Maybe I can talk to her."

"I'll drive," Burt offered, appearing in the doorway as if awaiting his cue.

They all piled into the Jeep, which Nora found horrifically uncomfortable. Every bump and jolt on the road echoed through her spine with unforgiving clarity.

"Where did you get this thing?" Nora asked after a mile or so.

He glanced in the rearview mirror and smiled. "Would you believe it if I told you that I picked this baby up at a salvage sale?"

Nora would have zero difficulty believing that, but Burt apparently thought he needed to convince her by telling the story anyway.

"Buddy of mine gave me a heads up about an old military storage being cleared out. I thought, why not take a look?" He shrugged, then drummed the steering wheel. "I spotted this baby, and then I practically stole her. A little restoration and she was good as new."

What had it been restored from? And why was good as new when it came to the Jeep so much worse than most other old vehicles that were total pieces of shit?

Burt approached the spot where Randolph had parked on Wilshire earlier, and Daphne pointed out the obvious. "His car is gone."

"It went from being a car to a coffin," Nora said. "Did you expect the police to keep a murder scene parked on the street?"

Daphne pouted. "Well, I don't know, but you don't

have to ask me like I'm stupid. There's not even crime tape or anything."

"I think you're confusing real life with an eighties cop show," Nora told her.

"Ladies." Burt gestured at the building. "Shall we get going?"

The trio found the lobby unlocked, but after a short ride in the elevator followed by an even shorter walk down the hallway, they ended up in front of Vivian's office door, feeling a lot less lucky. The place was locked up, and it was too dark inside for them to see anything past the frosted glass.

"It looks like they're gone for the day," Daphne said.

"Obviously," Nora agreed.

"So now what?"

"Could anyone else go for a milkshake?" asked Burt.

"Please don't tell me that you can actually drink milkshakes." Daphne seemed genuinely offended. "I might have to strangle you dead with my own two hands."

"How else would you strangle me?"

Daphne rattled a few ideas off the top of her head. "With a scarf or an evening glove, maybe a belt. I have this beaded flapper headband, or—"

"Have you actually been giving this some thought?" Burt gave Daphne a smile, but Nora thought he seemed slightly unsettled.

"We should go back home," Nora suggested. "There's nothing more we can do."

"Bullshit!" Daphne snapped. "There's always something more we can do. Why not talk to Vivian? We haven't done that yet."

"Vivian didn't answer when I called her."

"So. Fuck her for ignoring your calls. You know where she lives, don't you?"

Nora made a face. "That's a bad idea, Daphne."

"This whole entire day has been about bad ideas, Nora. Why not keep that streak going? Burt can drive us, and you can fix it."

"I can drive you guys." Burt somehow managed to make his offer sound like a brand-new idea instead of him simply repeating what Daphne had said. Then he added, "I haven't had this much fun in ages!"

A few minutes later, Nora was back to clenching her stomach in the backseat of the Jeep on their way to Vivian's house. The vehicle's suspension seemed nonexistent, each pothole and rough patch of road jolting her like another crack to the skull.

"This is fun!" Daphne shouted.

Then after several minutes of only the rumbling Jeep, Daphne turned back to Nora and said, "I'm really sorry for the mess that I got you in."

"That's nice of you to say, but it's not your fault, Daphne. This mess is just as much mine as it is yours. I knew better, but I panicked."

"Well, I'm sorry anyway. And I guess I also want to say thank you for taking such good care of me over the last two years."

Nora gave her a smile, talking loudly enough to be heard over the rumbling. "It goes both ways. You taught me a lot about the business, and I've not always been as patient with you as I should be, considering you're my only client."

"That's not exactly a news flash."

"I could learn to be a little more flexible when it comes to my rules," Nora said.

Daphne nodded. "Yes, you could."

Nora's stomach felt better as they rode in silence until

Burt was finally swinging the Jeep onto Vivian's street. The hairs on Nora's neck stirred in the breeze.

Vivian's small estate was full of sleek lines and wooden panels. By no means massive, but stately enough, especially for a lone occupant. The windows were dark, and the place felt as dead as it appeared.

"It doesn't look like anyone is home." Daphne looked from the house back to Nora. "What do you think we should do?"

"I'm thinking."

Daphne was already grinning as she opened her door, with a plan clearly already in mind. "As long as we're here…"

Nora jumped out of the vehicle to stop her. "We can't break in, Daphne."

"We're not 'breaking in.' We're just stopping by to visit an old friend."

"Why would we be visiting an old friend when that old friend is clearly not home?"

"Emergency PR," she answered.

"We can't do this, Daphne."

"We *have* to do this, Nora. What were you just saying on the drive over here about being more flexible with your own rules?"

"There's a difference between being flexible and breaking the law. We're already out on a limb as it is."

But Daphne was already walking away from Nora, marching toward the front door.

It must have been locked, because she turned around and picked up the nearest large stone statue without hesitation.

Nora came running over, yelling, "You can't just smash your way in, Daphne!"

"I'm not." Daphne laughed while pulling a key out of

the cherub's fiberglass bottom. "I bought this thing for Vivian."

Nora exhaled.

Burt laughed.

Daphne unlocked the door and waved them all inside.

Chapter Twenty-Eight

Vivian's home was eerily quiet as the trio entered and gingerly closed the door behind them. A slow chill slithered down Nora's spine as she curled her fingers into a fist and released it. Again.

"I'll find the lights," Daphne declared, then stumbled into the darkness and immediately stubbed her toe or something. "Sweet cherry cheesecake, why do tables always jump out at my toes?"

Nora wasn't sure that she wanted the lights to go on before she figured out why this heavy sense of unease was settling all throughout her body. But before she could articulate that thought, Daphne found the lights, and the living room went bright.

Nora absorbed it all in a blink:

The expansive living room was bathed in a sophisticated palette of neutrals, with deep charcoal accents and a plush cream-colored sectional lined with a curated selection of velvet and silk throws atop a soft geometric-patterned rug.

Windows framed one side of the room, floor to ceiling,

with an unobstructed view of a presumably manicured but entirely dark backyard. An abstract painting added a splash of color on the opposite wall.

Minimalistic glass shelves showcased a range of art pieces and sleek vases, with a glass coffee table harboring three matching stacks of glossy art books (that Nora was sure Vivian had never opened) and a massive square pot stuffed overflowing with moth orchids, bright white with blush-colored throats.

"Turn the lights off!" Nora shouted after taking it all in.

Daphne responded like a reflex, and the room was doused in darkness again.

"Is everything okay?" Daphne almost sounded scared.

"Everything is just perfect, dear," Burt assured her.

Nora felt a breeze tickle her neck, then a certainty she felt compelled to voice. "Someone's broken in."

"How do you know that?" Nora didn't answer because she was already on her way to the kitchen. Daphne turned to Burt. "How does she know that?"

"It's her job, dear," Nora heard him say.

She circled around to the back of the house, through to the kitchen, and saw that someone had indeed broken in. The floor was littered with glass, shards glinting ominously in the faint moonlight that filtered in through the broken window. Crushed flowers from an upended vase lay among the glittering fragments. A jagged edge of windowpane dangled in the frame.

Nora returned to the living room, ready to tell Daphne and Burt that they all needed to get the hell out of there, but they were already gone.

She returned to the kitchen and collected two sets of rubber gloves, pulling one on as Burt appeared in the doorway.

"Where did you run off to?" Nora asked.

"Just a little bit of exploring," he didn't explain. "Daphne went upstairs."

"*Goddamn it.*" Nora leaped to her feet and bolted after her, finding Daphne in a second-floor office with a light on, of course, going through the paperwork.

"Daphne!" Nora shouted. Daphne looked up from the desk. "We need to get out of here right now!"

"Why?" Daphne looked perplexed. "We just got here."

"Somebody else just got here before us."

"What do you mean?"

"The same thing I meant downstairs before I confirmed it in the kitchen: *somebody has already broken into Vivian's house.*"

"What do you think they were looking for?"

"I would love to know the answer to that, but I don't. I just know that we need to get the hell out of here."

"I'm not going anywhere until we find evidence that Vivian did this."

Daphne was just like Nora's mother. She had to have her way, even when that put other people in danger. But Nora knew she wasn't going to talk Daphne out of it, and if she wasted time trying, they were even more likely to get caught.

So she chucked the other pair of gloves onto the desk. "Then put those on."

Daphne donned the gloves and began to rifle through the drawers.

"I found something!" she exclaimed a few moments later.

Nora looked over at the bottle of pills in Daphne's hand as she shook them.

But then Daphne looked down at the label, and her

face fell. "Never mind. They're just for migraines. And that actually makes me feel sorry for the bitch."

"What about—"

"OH!" Daphne exclaimed, cutting Nora off as she abruptly stood from the desk and marched over to a gaudy portrait of Vivian. "She keeps her important documents and stuff in the safe."

Daphne pulled the portrait away from the wall.

"Don't do that," Nora warned her. "You're going to get us caught. You don't even know the code to that thing."

"The code," she snorted. "I'm sure it's something idiotic like her birthday."

The words weren't even out of Daphne's mouth before Nora heard the agreeable beeps declaring that Vivian's cryptic code had been cracked.

She swung the safe open with a giggle.

Nora rushed over, peering into the safe and seeing stacks of crisp one-hundred-dollar bills sitting neatly arranged on one side, pristine like a movie prop. Beside the money lay an assortment of jewelry: sparkling diamond necklaces, emerald earrings, and a few intricately designed gold bracelets. On the other side of the safe lay a pile of official-looking documents sealed in clear plastic envelopes.

"This is Vivian's All the Things I Never Told the IRS About Collection." Daphne ignored the cash and jewels but gathered the plastic envelopes into her arms and brought the stack over to the desk.

She started going through them as Nora got comfortable on the opposite side of the desk and started going through a second pile.

They each found their own haunting evidence in unison, looking up from their individual documents in tandem and saying the same exact words.

"This is in Russian."

"That is strange, right?" Daphne said. "Documents aren't normally in Russian, are they?"

"Not without reason. But without knowing Russian, I couldn't tell you if what we have is evidentiary."

"You don't need to speak Russian to know that Vivian has something illegal going on with that stash in her safe."

"Sure. But we need to focus on what's in front of us."

Daphne gestured at the desk full of documents. "This all seems pretty goddamned evidentiary to me!" She started gathering the envelopes that were obviously in Russian and stuffing them down her shirt. "If these documents have value to Vivian, then we can trade them for her admitting that she drugged us."

"So now we're becoming blackmailers?"

"No! Of course not." Daphne shook her head as if offended by the accusation. "We're just trading information."

"That's exactly what blackmail is. And now Vivian will know that we broke in."

"No, she won't. We'll just say that we received them in the mail. There isn't anything linking us to this. Remember?" Daphne raised her rubber-gloved hands. "You're the one who's always prepared. I'm surprised this is taking you so long to get."

"Where is Burt?" Nora asked, thanks to a sudden yet insistent instinct that also had her turning to look out the window just in time to see Burt burning rubber in the Jeep.

Daphne's phone pinged with a text: *GET OUT NOW! SECURITY IS COMING!*

"We need to get out of here!" Daphne exclaimed, like it was her own big, brilliant idea and not something that Nora had been begging her to do.

They ran toward the stairs, but tromping boots sounded like sudden thunder in the house.

"HANDS WHERE WE CAN SEE THEM!" bellowed a terrifying voice.

"WE ARE ARMED AND NOT AFRAID TO SHOOT!" added the man's even scarier-sounding partner.

Nora turned around and shoved Daphne back into Vivian's office.

"*Stop it!*" Daphne whispered and shouted at Nora. "We're better off facing these guys. We're on the second floor. We can still talk our way out of this. There's no escaping if we—"

"You can't talk your way out of everything," Nora argued as she dragged Daphne into the office and quietly closed the door behind them.

"Oh yeah, that'll keep them away. We're safe now, for sure!"

"We're going out onto the balcony."

"And what are we supposed to do out there? Wait for them to shoot us in the breeze?"

"No." Nora pointed to the tree as she stepped out onto the balcony. "We're climbing down to the ground and getting the fuck out of here."

Chapter Twenty-Nine

THE BARK WAS rough and unforgiving under Nora's palms, making her wince with every grip. Daphne, ungracefully sliding down just behind her, let out a muted yelp every time a branch tickled her skin in the wrong way.

"Why do trees have to be so handsy?" Daphne grumbled, trying to keep her balance as she made her descent.

A particularly stubborn twig snagged in Nora's hair, yanking her head back as she tried to lower herself. An involuntary yelp escaped her.

"I thought we weren't supposed to be making any noise!" Daphne yelled down at her much too loudly. "What's taking you so long?"

Nora was going as fast as she could. She had also started her descent first at Daphne's insistence, but the tree's uneven surface and erratic branches made each step test her agility.

Daphne froze above her. Nora looked up to see her eyes widen as she said, "Oh, that is *not* a pleasant place for a branch!"

By the time Nora dropped the final few feet onto the ground, she was a mess of disheveled hair, scratches, and leaves in places where foliage should never be. Daphne looked even worse, with twigs in her hair and torn clothing, but still, she wore an expression of victory.

A dog began to furiously bark, the canine tattling on their escape.

"Do you think they know we're down here yet?" Daphne asked Nora in a whisper.

"They will any second. We need to keep moving."

They ran around to the back of the house, pushing through the shrubs and into the neighbor's backyard. Compared to Vivian's shadowed enclave, the soft glow of twinkling fairy lights washing over a trim lawn looked like day instead of night.

"Daphne! Wait!" Nora called out.

But, of course, it was too late. Daphne triggered the motion sensors, and the entire property was suddenly bathed in bright white light.

"Over there!" shouted the first security guy again.

"This is your last chance!" warned the second.

Nora had warring instincts, half of her wanting to find the deepest recesses of shadows and hide in the darkness until danger had finally passed them by. But her smarter part knew that was only cowardice, and that shivering amid false security was a shortcut to ending up dead.

What they needed to do, despite it screaming loudly against the logic her body wanted to believe, would be running two homes over to where a lively party was in full swing.

"Goodie!" Daphne exclaimed as she chased Nora to the party. "I was hoping this is where we would be going."

Guests sipped champagne and mingled around an

infinity pool amid a canopy of lights, the water shimmering with reflections of the night sky and Los Angeles lights. Sporadic laughter punctuated a soft hum of conversation as servers in crisp uniforms floated among the clustered attendees, offering hors d'oeuvres from silver trays.

Nora scanned the crowd, spotting several familiar faces: Greg Anderson, a prominent movie producer; Helena Martinez, a talent agent with WingMan, wrapped in conversation with a trio of up-and-coming actors; Martin Rhodes, a critic she had sparred with on a few unfortunate occasions, was sipping a drink by the bar; and Clarice Li, debuting an even more audacious hairstyle than Nora remembered ever seeing on the director, a vibrant cascade of neon streaks full of shocking pinks and electric blues.

Nora gently steered Daphne toward the bar.

"Finally!" Daphne clapped.

"We're not getting drinks. We're disappearing behind the crowd. And just in time."

Nora nodded at the two towering figures now pushing their way into the party's perimeter. One was a broad-shouldered man with a sharp buzz cut and a tattoo peeking out from under his shirt collar. His companion was even taller, with a hawkish gaze and a neatly trimmed beard. Both of them were bulging out of their suits.

"Have you seen two women who don't belong here?" asked the taller guard, who had no idea that Nora had ducked behind an elderly couple just a few feet away.

Nora couldn't see who the guard was talking to, but she could hear the rolling eyes apparent in her voice. "Sorry, no. Good luck ruining the party, though."

She and Daphne managed to get inside without being spotted by either of the security guards or anyone from the party who appeared remotely capable of giving a shit.

They went into the bathroom upstairs and cleaned themselves up. Daphne went first, reentering as Nora was finding fresh clothes for them from the closet.

"Whoever lives in this place," Daphne declared on her way back out of the bathroom, "the bitch has great taste."

Nora and Daphne descended the staircase down into the foyer like they owned the place, arriving just in time to see an amorous-looking couple about to leave the party.

Daphne gave them a wave as she walked over to them. "Hey there."

"You're Daphne Belle," said the woman.

"That's me!" Daphne giggled on cue.

"I love you so much!"

"I'm really glad to hear that." Daphne laughed again. "Because I'm about to ask you for a favor."

"We were just on our way out," said the guy.

"Of course you were! And I don't want to intrude, but my friend and I here really need a ride, and while I'm sure you two are super eager to get your fuck on, and I really want that for both of you, I can't exactly call an Uber right now since my bestie Nora here is dealing with the kind of mess we really shouldn't be talking about and she really wants to—" Daphne lowered her voice "—*stay off the grid*. I wish it was for some exciting CIA-type stuff instead of stupid, boring, stalker boyfriend nonsense, but we can only choose our own adventures if we read that series. Am I right?"

"There's plenty of space in our limo," the woman offered.

The man looked like she had kicked his puppy.

"That would be wonderful!" Daphne exclaimed.

Nora had to hand it to her: the bitch knew how to get what she wanted.

"I'm Angelica, and this is Christopher," the woman introduced them.

"Daphne, of course." She touched her chest and gestured to Nora. "And that's Nora. Don't let our age difference fool you. She keeps me young, and I give her wisdom."

Daphne laughed again as Christopher impatiently opened the door and waited for them all to exit before scurrying to the front of the line and leading them all to the limo.

"Would you like some champagne?" Angelica offered them once they were on the road. This was clearly not how Christopher had expected this ride in the limo to go.

"Yes, please," Daphne replied.

Nora shook her head. "No, thank you. For both of us."

Angelica turned toward Daphne, seeking confirmation.

"I usually just let Nora steer the ship," Daphne explained. "I'm the fun-loving pirate, but she's the grouchy captain who gets us all the treasure."

"Where are we taking you?" Christopher asked.

Daphne turned to Nora. "Where are we going?"

"To any place where we can make copies."

"The nearest Kinko's or FedEx or whatever," Christopher said to the driver, then added in a whisper that was still loud enough for her to hear, "*the faster, the better.*"

Nora didn't bother to point out that Kinko's no longer existed.

Fast meant just under eight minutes, then Nora and Daphne bid their farewells to the couple that was probably already getting it on before the next red light. Daphne waved at the retreating limo while Nora entered the fluorescent-soaked copy shop.

Hardly a FedEx, the Copy Club seemed out of time,

with off-white linoleum floors scuffed from decades of customers and walls crammed with rows of humming and beeping machines. Old wooden countertops were overstocked with papers, print samples, and a smattering of markers and pens. A bulletin board boasted flyers, business cards, and community announcements, a few colorful and many surprisingly ancient.

"I feel like we're in a spy movie," Daphne said when she came over to where Nora was photocopying the documents.

"A spy movie would have much better lighting than this dungeon."

"If this is a dungeon, then the lighting is actually great. Or I guess not, because a dungeon is supposed to be dark. So I guess it's actually terrible lighting for a dungeon."

"Do you ever think anything that you don't say out loud?" Nora asked.

"Thinking without speaking is like cake without frosting."

Daphne kept saying all kinds of things that didn't need to be voiced out loud, and Nora did her best to ignore most of them until she finally finished photocopying all of the documents. She was still talking while following Nora to the front counter, where she paid for a manila envelope along with some stamps.

"This is so exciting!" Daphne clutched the copies as Nora stuffed the original Russian documents into the envelope.

"How about you wait outside?" Nora suggested, because holy shit did she need a reprieve from Daphne's incessant chatter.

She was about to address the package to herself when Nora suddenly changed her mind and addressed it to Eric

Guerrero, care of the LAPD. She scribbled a note and tucked it inside: *In case anything goes sideways, this might be something you need to see.*

Then she sealed the envelope and dropped it into the mail slot.

She went outside to where Daphne was waiting with the photocopies.

"Burt is coming to pick us up. Twenty minutes or less."

"Great." Nora nodded at the coffee shop next door. "That's just enough time for me to get some coffee and pie if they have it."

"They have pie!" Daphne reported with glee. "I already looked in the window to peruse their menu. They have all kinds. And you know what, Nora? You're a lot more fun today than I thought you would be."

The cozy aroma of freshly brewed coffee and baked goods enveloped them as they entered Café Dulcet. Vintage wooden tables and mismatched chairs gave the space a quaint charm and old-fashioned pendant lights bathed the room in a buttery glow.

The glass display case contained exactly what Nora had been hoping for, showcasing an array of delectable pies: apple cinnamon with a lattice top; rich, dark chocolate pecan; tangy key lime crowned with a soft meringue; creamy banana cream with delicate wafer crumbles; and a classic blueberry bursting with ripe, juicy berries and a dusting of powdered sugar. That was just the first row.

"You look like you really love pie," Daphne said.

"This place reminds me of a little shithole where my mom used to take me. A place called Mugs and Crumbles. After a long day on set, we would stop by on our way home. It would be way past my bedtime, but stuff like bedtimes rarely ever mattered to my mom. Probably not the best parenting decision, bringing a kid out for midnight pie, but those moments ... those were some of the only few genuine times we ever shared."

Daphne touched her hand. "She loved you, in her own complicated way."

Nora blinked back the sting of tears. "Not enough to stay sober."

Chapter Thirty

Nora was taking the final bite of her chocolate silk pie as she answered Daphne, the third slice she'd tried in the 20 minutes they had spent waiting for Burt.

"No." Nora vehemently shook her head. "Absolutely not. I can pay for our coffee and pie, especially after that obnoxious monument to gluttony earlier at the hotel."

"That was fun," Daphne said, audibly patting herself on the back.

Burt came barreling into the parking lot, waving at them through the window as he pulled into the nearest space.

Nora paid the check with a generous tip, then she and Daphne both stood from the table and walked out to greet him.

"I'm so sorry for leaving you ladies in the lurch back at Vivian's, but I trusted Daphne's extraordinary ability to wiggle out of trouble and Nora's professional hand. But if they'd caught me, we would *all* go down."

"It's okay." Nora patted him on the shoulder. "We all understand your cowardice."

"That's not fair," Daphne defended him. "Burt is conditioned for retakes, not real takes."

"So what did you find?" Burt asked as he drove.

"Russian documents!" Daphne announced, making it sound like the word 'treasure' when used by the Goonies. "We're going to trade them for Vivian's confession."

"What kind of documents?" Burt asked.

"We don't know," Nora admitted, "because they are all in Russian."

"Russian?" Burt was already pulling over. "Can I see them?"

Daphne handed him the documents.

"Can you speak Russian?" Nora asked.

"No." Burt shook his head.

"I can," Daphne declared.

Nora turned to her in abject surprise. "Seriously?"

"Of course!" Daphne exclaimed, shifting into an accent that sounded more like a Bond villain than actual Russian, every single word of her terribly offensive monologue in English. "In Mother Russia, we do not read documents. We feel them deep in our cold, vodka-loving hearts!"

Daphne dramatically placed her hand over her chest and continued. "Why, I remember, as a little babushka-wearing girl, dancing with bears and playing balalaika under the glow of the Kremlin's golden domes." Her voice took on a deep, gruff tone, now sounding more like Boris Badenov. "Da, and in the winter, we would wrestle Siberian tigers and take shots of vodka to keep warm, da?"

Nora was not amused.

"These are all copies," Burt said, looking up from his pile of documents.

"We put the originals in the mail," Daphne told him.

Nora said, "My landlady speaks Russian. Maybe we can ask her what the documents say."

Burt shook his head. "We should use my masseuse. Irina is Russian, and she works all hours. She also owes me favors from here to Temecula."

"What does that mean?" Nora asked.

"It means that she would be happy to help us out."

"Why Temecula?"

"It's a long story involving a winery, a hot air balloon, and some very confused geese," Burt said.

"I remember that!" Daphne declared.

"You weren't there, dear."

She pouted. "Oh."

"What kind of masseuse?" Nora asked Burt.

Burt looked at her in confusion. "How many kinds are there?"

"She's asking if your massages have a plot twist." Then, in case he didn't get it, Daphne clarified. "Does she get a bigger tip after licking yours? Is she the kind of masseuse that is willing to touch you anywhere?"

"Are there other kinds?" Burt shrugged. "Anyway, if you want to ask Irina what these documents say, then she can almost for sure translate tonight without us having to wait long. Would you like for me to text her or not?"

"Yes, please," Daphne said.

"Yes, please," Nora echoed begrudgingly.

Burt texted and got a response immediately.

"Great, we're on." Though that didn't explain the look on his face.

"She just sent you a picture, didn't she?" Nora asked.

"Yes," Burt admitted with a grin. "Irina is very proud of her body, as she should be. Her tits are like coconuts."

"Coconuts are hard. And hairy," Nora argued.

"I was thinking about the fun I have cracking them open."

Nora shook her head. "You're a pig."

"You can drink my piña colada anytime, sailor!" Daphne offered.

"Oink-oink." Burt grinned, turning back around and pulling back into the street, driving as Nora stared out at a dark city that seemed both empty and alive at the same time. Shimmering streetlights cast a light glow on the road as they headed into South Central.

Burt pulled up in front of a small broken-down rancher lit up from inside. He practically hopped out of the Jeep and trotted toward the door.

Daphne and Nora disembarked, then followed him to the porch.

The door swung open, and Irina appeared in the doorway.

She was tiny, barely more than five feet, with a slender build and wavy brown hair that cascaded past her shoulders. She looked over at Nora from Burt's embrace with expressive eyes that were a startling shade of blue.

Burt pulled her into an even tighter bear hug, lifting Irina right off of her feet before setting the tiny woman back down on the ground with a giggle.

"Lucky," Daphne said, sounding greener than a kale and cucumber smoothie.

Irina stepped away from Burt and opened the door to her home all the way, calling out to Nora and Daphne in a thick Russian accent. "Come in. Everyone now, you are all welcome. My home is your home, as they say."

But as the door closed behind them, Nora didn't think that there was anything homey about the place. Rows upon rows of shelves dominated the space, each one packed with handbags of every conceivable design, shape, and hue.

Imitation leather gleamed beneath the harsh lighting to reveal subtle yet obvious imperfections in the product. And the room reeked of synthetics and glue.

"Deep discount," Irina explained with a sweeping gesture across all of her many stacks. "Gucci, Prada, Louis Vuitton, Chanel, Fendi, YSL, Hermès." She rattled the brands off with evident pride in each familiar yet mispronounced name.

"Do you have any buy one, get one free deals or anything like that?" Daphne moved toward the nearest mountain of merchandise, clearly interested in whatever Irina had to offer her.

"Daphne!" Nora snapped. "You need to stay focused right now."

"You're doing great, dear."

"Thank you, Burt!"

Irina shrugged. "Just let me know. I have everything if you change your mind." Then, she led them through to the kitchen and made them another offer. "How about some vodka? Straight or with juice? What is better?"

Daphne glanced over at Nora, but of course, Nora shook her head.

"No thanks," Daphne said.

Irina shrugged. "I need a drink for me before I can think in both languages. Yes?"

Nora wasn't sure if that was rhetorical, but she nodded just in case. "Yes."

Fifteen minutes later, Irina looked up from her second empty glass of vodka. "Bad news, this woman, Vivian, she is laundering money for our mafia."

"Our mafia?" Nora repeated.

"Russian mafia," Irina clarified. "My people."

"Aren't you mafia?" Daphne glanced at all the handbags.

"Fashion-forward does not mean criminally inclined."

"How sure are you?" Nora asked.

"There is no mistaking." Irina shook her head. "This is a shadow you cannot outrun, even in the brightest of suns."

"What does that mean?" Daphne asked.

"That we need to return these documents right now," Nora answered. "This entire situation just exploded into something that's ten levels above our pay grade."

"I'm not getting paid anything," Daphne said. "Besides, if you're scared about having these documents right now, then I bet Vivian is even more scared. That means she'll be willing to negotiate."

"I think she's right." Burt turned to Irina. "Thanks for your help. Still on for Tuesday?"

"Of course. But feathers cost extra."

"Have I ever complained?"

"Not without paying me after," Irina said.

"Please don't tell me what that was all about," Nora told him on the way to the car, certain that Burt was about to explain what she didn't need or want to know.

"It's not butt stuff if that's what you're thinking," he felt compelled to tell her. "Not that there's anything wrong with butt stuff."

"Definitely not," Daphne agreed. "So, what are we doing next?"

"I need to think," Nora said.

"Great." Daphne nodded. "You can do that at my house."

Chapter Thirty-One

They had been at Daphne's for an hour already but were still on the same path to nowhere fast. Nora paced the living room while Burt and Daphne traded ideas. Some were decent, most were laughably bad, and a few were clearly the two of them working out elevator pitches for stories that could star their character types while also involving the Russian mob.

Once they got going, their work on the case turned into them trading loglines.

"So what about a quirky hairdresser from some small town in Ohio discovers she's the sole heir to a Russian mob fortune. Good so far, right?" Daphne clapped. "She has to navigate her lavish new life in Moscow, but then she quickly learns that controlling an empire requires more than just good hair and a sassy attitude."

"A suave, retired intelligence officer is pulled back into the world of espionage—"

"You didn't let me finish!"

"Sorry, dear."

"It's okay, love." Daphne smiled and continued with

the pitch. "But with her eccentric charm, she might just win over the mob and bring a touch of Midwest warmth to the icy Russian underworld."

"That's very good."

"Now you go," Daphne encouraged him.

Nora wished she could get her ears to stop working.

"A suave, retired intelligence officer is pulled back into the world of espionage he left behind when he's tasked to intercept a dangerous deal between rival factions of the Russian mob. Getting lost in the shadows of Moscow, the handsome rogue finds himself in a cat-and-mouse game of seduction and betrayal."

"That's great, honey, but let's give it some sparkle."

"Glitter me."

"Amid the opulence and danger, this dashing hero will need every ounce of his charm and wit to outsmart his adversaries and prevent an international crisis," Daphne finished his pitch.

"This is why I love you. Your turn."

Nora's phone rang and saved her from hearing Daphne's next logline. She looked at the screen and answered, "Hey, Melissa."

"Hey, Nora. I'm just returning your call. What's up?"

"I'm trying to get a hold of Vivian. I was hoping you could help me."

"You know as much about how to get a hold of Vivian as I do, Nora."

"I'm not sure that's true."

"What do you mean by that?" Melissa asked.

"I heard that Vivian hasn't actually left the business."

"That's bullshit. Vivian has definitely fucked the hell off. I've actually been looking for her myself. But I've not had any luck. She isn't answering any of her phones."

"Why are you looking for her?"

"For a few reasons," Melissa replied.

"When was the last time that you and Vivian spoke?"

"I don't know. It's been a while," Melissa replied, sounding evasive.

"You know how we are in this business. We love specifics. So *specifically*, can you tell me when was the last time you and Vivian had a conversation?"

"I don't know. Like a month ago? Are we done now? Can I get on with my night?"

Melissa was clearly lying right now. The question for Nora was *why*?

"I'm not sure I believe you," Nora said.

"When you think of a reason why I should care, call me back."

Melissa hung up the phone, and Nora instantly redialed, ready and prepared to shove up to a hundred reasons down her throat.

"You tell that bitch!" Daphne jabbed a finger at the sky as if reading her mind.

But Nora never got the chance because her call went straight to voicemail. She hung up without leaving a message.

"Do you have a Sharpie anywhere around here?" Nora asked Daphne.

"Give me one sec." She left with a nod, then returned a moment later and handed Nora a Sharpie with glee.

"How about a large piece of white paper?"

"No, sorry." Daphne shook her head. "I don't think so. I have lots of smaller pieces of paper from the printer, or you could just write on that wall over there."

Daphne pointed to a white wall with nothing hanging on it.

"I'm not going to write on your wall," Nora protested.

"Why would I care?" Daphne shrugged. "We can just

paint it over again later. Right now, we have some fixing to do, right?"

"Ruining walls can be fun," agreed Burt.

Nora found herself smiling on her way over to the white wall, which she immediately began to mar with her Sharpie while plotting out the points of their prior evening, retracing steps while trying to determine if any of the Russian stuff could have anything whatsoever to do with them.

"Let's make a list of everything that's still missing," Nora said.

"Caroline is still missing."

"I know. I asked Eric to look into that. But we know that the last place Caroline was seen was at the hotel, and so…"

"What?" Daphne asked when Nora didn't finish her sentence. "What is it? Why is your face doing that?"

"The security footage," Nora said. "The hotel would have some, wouldn't they? Why didn't I think of that sooner?"

"You probably needed to ruin a wall first," Burt told her.

Five minutes later they were all piled into his Jeep again, barreling down the nighttime road on their way to the Sunset Sovereign Hotel.

They approached the front desk manager, moving through the lobby like a single unit, but Nora felt discouraged before they arrived at the front desk, both because it was a different clerk than the one she had been dealing with over the last two days and because the pinched look on the man's face implied that he brooked no nonsense and considered them the kind of guests who were likely to shove it down his throat.

Edgar was his name.

"Probably not," Edgar said when Nora asked if they could possibly see the security footage. He answered through the tightest expression before she had even finished her question.

Daphne took over. "Is the answer still no, even if I buy a bunch of bathrobes from the hotel for all of my family and friends, but I let you keep the bathrobes and also all of the money I spent on them?" Daphne was anything but subtle.

Edgar's expression tightened even further. "I am quite sure that it would not."

"Come on, Gaston," Daphne continued. "Let us be your guest."

"I am sorry, but this hotel is simply not that type of place."

"Are you kidding me? All hotels are that kind of place." Daphne sighed and crossed her arms. "I really hoped that it wouldn't come to this, but you're leaving me no choice."

"Whatever are you talking about?" Edgar sounded exhausted.

"I had a spider brooch in my hair yesterday. I wore it to the gala. And guess what, Gaston: that brooch cost two million smackers. We need to see the footage because we're trying to find that brooch. My friend Nora is a little too nice for her own good, and she was *trying* not to make a big deal about this. She asked me to please not make a big deal about this so as not to embarrass her, but we think the brooch was stolen from here, buddy, yeah, that's right, stolen right out from under me at the Sunset Sovereign Hotel. If you don't let us see the security footage, we'll have to turn Nora's assumption into a fact when we announce this awful loss to the press, and I do think that would tarnish the reputation of this fine establishment, and turning this hotel into 'that kind of place' anyway."

Edgar stared back at Daphne, obviously on the fence as to whether he should go ahead and let the entitled actress have her way or stand his ground and preserve the integrity of both himself and the culture of refinement he was representing.

Nora and Burt stood on either side of Daphne as she poured it on thick, drawing in a melodramatic breath, eyes glistening as if on the verge of tears as she started.

"The Sunset Sovereign used to be my sanctuary. A place I felt where I could feel safe in this big, bustling city. But that stolen brooch wasn't just diamonds and gold — it was *trust*."

Daphne held a hand over her heart as her voice began to tremble. "To think that something so precious was taken from right here? It's not just the brooch that was lost, I'm telling you, but my faith in this place!"

A hand to her forehead. "How can I ever see the Sunset Sovereign as my safe haven again? It is truly a tragedy for both my heart and this once-grand establishment to—"

"Fine." Edgar sighed heavily, running a hand through his meticulously styled hair.

He grabbed a placard from behind the counter with *Be Right Back* in ornate lettering and slapped it down with an air of resigned exasperation, then motioned for them to follow him.

Edgar led them down a dimly lit corridor to a door labeled *Security*.

He swung the door open without so much as a knock and barked at the lone guard sitting in his chair, maybe thirty years old, but already flabby and balding.

"Please show our guests whatever they need to see before they leave the hotel."

Edgar left and they found the footage in question fast.

Soon Nora, Daphne, and Burt were watching Nora, Daphne, and Caroline onscreen, standing in the elevator with the couple that had just returned from the wedding.

All three of the women were laughing and could barely stand straight.

Caroline, with a mischievous glint in her eyes, pulled Daphne close, their lips meeting in a playful, drunken kiss as the elevator continued its descent.

Nora looked over at her, but Daphne just shrugged.

The elevator doors opened, and the trio stepped out of the elevator.

Nora pointed to another screen showing a separate elevator. "Can we look at that one?"

The security officer pulled up the second feed, and a moment after that, they were all watching Tim Bowen stepping onto the elevator, followed a beat later by Scarlett.

The doors closed, and the elevator went into motion.

So did Tim and Scarlett, with the reporter reaching over to stop the elevator so that he and the actress could start going at it. One of his hands flew up her shirt while the other one yanked her panties down.

"That's enough," Nora said. "Let's go back to the other elevator again."

They watched that first scene on repeat, seeing Nora and Daphne leaving sans Caroline.

"So that means we left her at the hotel?" Daphne sounded like the question was as much for herself as for Nora.

"It looks that way. But where we went from there, no one knows."

Nora and Daphne traipsed like drunk leprechauns through the lobby onscreen, then onto another camera outside, where they both climbed into a waiting taxi.

"I'll call the cab company and find out where we went," Daphne offered.

The call connected. She asked her questions and was put on hold.

Then, a minute later, Nora saw a look on Daphne's face.

And for some reason, the expression scared her.

"Do you have an address?" Nora asked.

Daphne nodded.

"Then what's wrong?"

Daphne shook her head. "I don't want to tell you."

Chapter Thirty-Two

It was silent inside the Jeep as Burt drove headed toward an address that Nora didn't even want to think about, let alone visit. But they had no other choice. The only way to reach the other side of this fiasco was for them to go all the way through it.

And right now, considering where they were going, *them* meant Nora.

Daphne turned back to look at her, crouched down low, and curled into a comma on the bench seat. She reached out and took Nora's hand and gave it a long and meaningful squeeze. She expected Daphne would try to comfort her with words because language was like air for the actress, but instead, she gave Nora what she deeply needed: silence serving as proof that Daphne really did understand her when it mattered most.

"We're almost there." Burt made the unnecessary announcement as if needing to break the too-quiet tension.

A few minutes later, the Jeep was pulling up in front of the Hollywood Forever Cemetery. Though deadly silent under the veil of night, the graveyard held a stately air of grandeur as moonlight glinted off ornate gravestones and mausoleums.

The wrought-iron gates were wide open, but the cemetery was obviously closed.

And Nora felt herself curling into an even tighter ball.

"We don't have to do this," Daphne assured her. "I'm sure Burt would be happy to flip a bitch and take us back home."

"Burt would just love to know what we're doing here at the Nightmare Before Christmas," said Burt.

"There's nothing spooky about a graveyard," Daphne said. "It's a place where all the drama ends so the peace can finally begin. Especially *this* graveyard, where the stars in the ground meet the stars in the sky."

"Is that their tagline?" Burt asked.

"It should be." Daphne turned back to Nora. "Do you want to go home, honey?"

"No." Nora sat up straight. "I need to do this. What if there's some key to what happened last night here and it answers all our other questions? We wouldn't have come to this place without a reason. At least I sure as hell wouldn't have."

"Do I get to know what's going on now?" Burt tried again.

Daphne shook her head. "Definitely not, honey."

"What can I do to help?"

"You can wait right here with your big manly Jeep."

"I don't like the thought of abandoning the two of you," he protested.

"You're not abandoning us. I—"

"You're definitely not abandoning us," Nora agreed.

"—promise we'll be fine."

"Going into a graveyard at night."

"I told you, graveyards are nothing to be scared

of!" Daphne laughed as she climbed out of the Jeep. "I'm more scared of my phone battery hitting red."

Nora got out after her.

"Are you ready, dear?" Daphne held out her hand.

Nora took it. "Absolutely not. But I don't know that I could ever be readier."

As they ventured into the cemetery, the world seemed to whisper around them. Nora heard the distant rustling of leaves as soft moonlight bathed their walk in a silvery hue, elongating shadows on the tombstones and statues.

She could smell more than see the flowers.

"You know, we don't have to walk in the dark," Daphne said. "It's not disrespectful to the dead if you want to turn on your flashlight app."

"Are you asking me to do it because that uses a lot of battery, and you don't want to dip any closer to ten percent?"

"You know me so well."

Nora got out her phone and turned on the flashlight app.

"Stop walking," Daphne said when the illumination washed over a headstone just in front of them. "We're here."

"Well, that's weird."

"The universe is weird, honey. You just have to listen to what she's saying. You'll find that most of the time when you really surrender, you'll end up near wherever you were supposed to go."

Nora shone the light on her mother's headstone:

KATHERINE BAUER

HER STAR BURNED EVER BRIGHTER

Something red flashed in the light.

Nora reached out to snatch it, but Daphne got there first.

"Holy crap! It's my spider brooch!"

"Your borrowed spider brooch," Nora reminded her.

"Who cares? It's two million dollars just sitting right there for any bum to grab off the grave."

"I don't think bums are hanging out in the cemetery. I also don't think we're supposed to call them bums." Nora paused. "It must have come unpinned while we were here."

"Or I left it here as a tribute."

"Why would you do that? She wasn't your mother."

"She was my friend," Daphne replied. "I was quite fond of her."

Nora dropped to the ground, glumly sitting cross-legged. "You probably spent more time with her than I did. When she wasn't on set, she was out at a fancy party. Sometimes, I don't think she even remembered that I existed."

Daphne sat down beside Nora. "You okay, kiddo?"

"Of course, I'm okay."

"But you really want to sit here in the creepy graveyard and cry?"

"I'm not crying. And you said that graveyards aren't creepy."

"I said they aren't scary. They're plenty creepy." Daphne put a hand on her knee. "Your mom really did love you. I promise that from the bottom of my heart."

"I always figured that Katherine didn't love me because she was always working. Or partying."

"That's not true at all. It was hard in the early days. She was always working *because* she loved you. Your mother wanted to keep a roof over your heads, and when success comes and goes at the speed of Hollywood, well, honey, you've been around this business enough to know it."

"My entire goddamned fucking life."

"You know how fleeting fame can be. You can't blame your mom for wanting to strike while the iron was hot and have something more to give you."

"I just wanted more of her time."

Daphne pulled her into a hug. "I know, honey."

"Do you think she would be proud of me?" It was a hard question to ask, and it choked Nora twice before making it all the way out.

"Of course, she would be proud of you! She always used to tell me how well you took care of her. That was one of the reasons I knew you would be able to take great care of me when I needed someone to do that. And you have, Nora. You've always done a great job despite how hard I've made it on you."

"Maybe I'm tired of taking care of everyone."

"Maybe that's because you never take care of yourself," Daphne said. "You should consider putting everyone else in your life last for once. Not permanently or anything, because that would definitely suck for me. But maybe for a week or even a weekend. One long day—"

"Got it. Give myself a hug and then get right back to you." Nora laughed when she said it, and then Daphne joined her.

"Let me finish hugging you first."

They steeped in the cemetery silence for a while longer, neither of them in any seeming hurry to leave, despite the creepiness, and Burt waiting in his Jeep on the other side of the gates. Just as Nora was starting to wonder how much longer Daphne could go without starting to worry about her friend, she said, "We should probably find Burt."

"That sounds about right," Nora agreed.

"He's probably worried sick about us."

"Or at least you."

"If you're important to me, then you're important to him. That's how Burt is."

"Why didn't you ever get married? It definitely seems like you two have a thing."

"Oh, we have a thing alright." Daphne laughed. "But that doesn't mean that I'm not also too old for him."

Daphne stood and extended a hand to Nora. She took it, and then together, they started back toward the cemetery entrance.

"I just need to make a call real quick," Nora said.

"Are you calling anyone we both know?" Daphne didn't wait for an answer. "If so, tell them I said hi!"

Nora dialed Lavigne.

"Nora. To what do I owe the pleasure?"

"I'm calling about that favor you owe me."

"Of course. Why would I ever think you were calling just to chat?"

"Never going to happen." Nora lowered her voice and stepped away from Daphne to finish the call, only fueling the fire of her curiosity.

"I thought we weren't supposed to talk to Lavigne," Daphne said when Nora returned. "He was specifically on the no list, and you totally gave me shit about him."

"Well then, I guess it's time that I broke some damn rules. Especially mine."

"Atta-girl!" Daphne held out her hand for a high-five and waited for Nora to comply before she continued. "But don't sell yourself short; you've been breaking rules all day."

Nora gave her a smile. "Yeah, I suppose I have."

They passed through the gates to see Burt leaning against the Jeep while talking on the phone, ending his call when he saw them.

"The cops finally figured out that I'm the owner of that Rolls they found. It was registered under my LLC, so I just confirmed it was stolen. Where to next?"

"How about you go home and leave the rest of this to us? You've already gone well above and beyond the call of duty."

"No way am I leaving the two of you to deal with Vivian alone." Burt shook his head. "Especially not if the Russian mob is involved."

Chapter Thirty-Three

THEY WERE all about to pile into Burt's Jeep when Nora's phone rang.

She was surprised to see that it was Vivian calling. "Hey there, Vivian."

"I heard you've been looking for me. What do you want?"

"You don't sound very happy to hear my voice."

"Am I supposed to?" Vivian asked.

Daphne mouthed, *Put her on speakerphone!*

Nora did. "It's been a while since we talked."

"You're sniffing around, Nora. And doing it poorly. I taught you better than this. Tell me what you want, and be fast about it."

"I want to know why you drugged me and Daphne. Or what made you think that you could get away with it?"

"I have no idea what you are talking about." Vivian's voice was void of emotion, and without her present, Nora didn't have the clues she needed to read this situation.

"I have the documents."

"Congratulations." But a note of concern crept into her voice. "What documents?"

"The Russian documents. And unless you start talking, you won't be getting them back."

Vivian replied with an agony of silence. It seemed like Daphne was about to say something, but Nora stayed with her by raising a hand, shaking her head, and mouthing, *Make her wait.*

Another twenty or so painfully long seconds passed, and Nora could practically feel her former mentor calculating through scenarios until she finally broke the silence.

"How did you get the documents?"

"Hey there, Vivian!" Daphne shouted to answer her question.

"You broke into my fucking house?" Vivian screamed at Daphne.

"It's not breaking in if you use a key, bitch! And I would break into your house nine times on a Sunday after the bullshit you pulled on me and Nora!"

"I didn't pull any bullshit!" Vivian protested.

"Bullshit!" Daphne yelled, and then a second later, she added, "Bullshit squared!"

"I can see you've lost none of your elegant levels of articulation."

"I will articulate the fuck out of your face, you stupid cunt!"

"That's exactly what I'm—"

"You have the morals of a pirate! I'm surprised you didn't have children just so you could sell them to the highest bidder!"

"Fuck you, Daphne! Everyone on this call knows that you're a professional goddamned disaster."

"Does Russian dick taste like borscht or Communism, you—"

"Okay, ladies," Nora cut her off before it got even worse.

Burt looked disappointed.

But Daphne didn't push it as Nora continued. "We have way more important things to discuss, like the Russian documents and what we're going to do with them if you don't start talking."

"You were always great at circling back," Vivian said to Nora. "How about we start with your ridiculous drugging accusation? I have never, and would never, drug anyone. If somebody drugged you, and you're sure that it was connected to me, then I'm guessing this has something to do with Melissa."

Nora opened her mouth to protest, but Vivian was already talking louder and faster. "Second thing: *I want my documents back*. You two have no idea what you got yourselves involved in, but I can tell you from personal experience that you won't like the results of continuing to do whatever it is you're doing."

"That's a lot of words to say nothing, Missy!" Daphne yelled at the phone.

"If you know what's good for you, you'll return the documents," Vivian pressed. "And I mean that."

"I'm glad you've finally learned to say what you actually mean," Nora said. "We should meet."

"Somewhere public," Vivian agreed.

"The Grove in twenty minutes." Nora hung up the phone.

"Irina just texted," said Burt to Daphne. "She wants to know if you want any handbags. She said buy two, get one free sounds great to her and suggests you make a list."

"Not now!" Nora snapped.

"It's not like I can afford the real ones," Daphne argued.

"Irina will give her a really good deal—"

"NOT RIGHT NOW!" Nora should not have had to yell.

"I'll tell her 'maybe later'," said Burt.

A quarter hour after that, they pulled up to the Grove and they all clambered out of the Jeep. The place was deserted, with its usually bustling pathways eerily silent, and only the soft glow from ornamental streetlamps to illuminate the empty cobblestone walk.

"Why are you taking that?" Nora asked as Daphne grabbed the disco stick and gripped it like a bat. "You should leave it here."

"No way." Daphne shook her head as she started walking toward the shopping center. "We might need to beat a confession out of Vivian."

Nora shrugged and started following her.

"It's kind of creepy at this time of night, don't you think?" Daphne said.

"Not as creepy as a graveyard," Nora replied.

"Where do you think she is?" Burt asked.

"Right over there." Nora nodded to a vague shape in the distance — surely Vivian.

Nora walked toward her. Halfway there, a pair of Russians emerged from the shadows, one not too far and another uncomfortably close, both converging on Nora and Vivian as she quickly closed the distance between them.

Nora recognized them both as the "guards" who'd shown up at Vivian's house.

The first halted abruptly, looming over them with an air of calculated menace as the second attacker closed in with a predatory gallop.

"Run!" Nora told Daphne and Burt.

Buzz Cut grabbed Vivian.

Nora picked up the nearest potted plant and hefted it overhead before smashing it down on his skull.

"Asshole," she said as he released his grip on Vivian and fell to the ground.

They raced to the parking lot.

"I can't believe you betrayed me!" Vivian shouted.

"I had nothing to do with any of this!" Nora's voice pierced through the hail of bullets streaking past them.

Most of the shots seemed to tear through the air overhead, a few rounds zipping dangerously close before thunking into the wall ahead of them.

"*Fuck*," Vivian grumbled to herself as she pulled out a gun, then turned around and fired three times at their two pursuers.

"Holy shit! Where did that come from?"

Vivian finished hauling Nora over to her car, and Nora felt some amount of empathy for Daphne, who she had been dragging around like that since early that morning.

Vivian turned around and fired at their attackers again, then popped the trunk of her car and waved her gun at the opening. "Get in."

Nora shook her head. "Not a chance."

"You're dead if you don't. Even if I don't pull the trigger, you have ten seconds before they get here."

"Fuck you, Vivian," Nora said as she climbed into the open space.

As Nora settled uneasily into the cramped trunk, Vivian slammed it shut and plunged her into darkness perforated only by a dim glow seeping in from the taillights.

Vivian's car roared to life, tires squealing against the asphalt as she executed a reckless U-turn.

Nora's body was thrown from one side of the trunk to the other as Vivian swerved and accelerated. The muffled yet unmistakable retorts of gunfire echoed outside.

She heard the guttural revving of engines behind them.

The chorus of bullets and engines was a symphony of danger and pursuit, with every bumping jolt of the road sending another shiver down Nora's spine.

"LET ME OUT!"

She never should have agreed to get in the trunk. Vivian had only been bluffing. She never would have pulled the trigger and left Nora for dead in a place where a camera or ten had surely captured her presence in the area.

Though the Russians would have shot her for sure.

She shrank down, making herself as small in the confined space as she possibly could, then felt around for any possible weapon.

Her fingers found the edge of a jack, and she pulled it toward her.

The car swerved with purpose, and soon the relentless drone of pursuing engines grew fainter and fainter, until they were finally drowned out by the rapid thumping of her own heart.

The car came to a sudden halt.

Moments later, the trunk lid creaked open and flooded Nora's cramped space with the relief of fresh air and light.

Vivian looked down and noted the jack in her hand. "You won't be needing that."

Nora got out of the car but for damn sure wasn't leaving the jack behind. If Vivian suggested it again, she would have to wallop her former mentor over the head.

"We're at your office," Nora observed.

"You never miss a thing. And even so, you still don't have a fucking clue about what's going on here."

Vivian started toward her office.

"Why are we here?" Nora asked.

"Because you never know when—"

Vivian's head exploded into a burst piñata of gore as a thunderous gunshot rang in Nora's ears.

Chapter Thirty-Four

Nora was paralyzed.

It was the kind of cliché she would never believe if she were seeing or reading it. Nora had hated every book or TV show where the heroine just stood there frozen in one place while danger screamed all around her. She always called bullshit when fright kicked in over flight, picturing herself fleeing the scene post-haste if a nightmare were to happen right in front of her.

But it didn't get much more nightmarish than having her former mentor's head explode like a smashed watermelon right in front of her, even though Nora was right now realizing that she was painted in blood and covered in brain with little bits of bone, and that someone must be shooting at her because Vivian was very much lying dead on the ground with her brain looking like a dropped bowl of oatmeal covered in cherry syrup.

"Get a hold of yourself, Nora," she said out loud.

And that was all she needed to get herself bolting toward the door, expecting another shot to ring out before she arrived. But none came, and the lobby was still unlocked, with the door swinging open to her relief.

But every single office door she attempted to open after getting inside was locked. Nora was downright frantic by the time she was racing across the lobby to the elevator, desperate to make it before her attacker (or attackers) got inside.

She screamed when Buzz Cut burst through the lobby doors, carrying an even larger-looking gun than the one she had seen him with at the Grove.

Nora ran to the rear of the building, blindly turning corridors fast to escape her pursuer. Instinct led her to a fire exit, and she tried to shove the door open, but it appeared to be stuck. Until she slammed her entire body hard against it and managed to force the door open after triggering a screaming alarm that echoed through the corridor.

Nora was outside but disoriented, the panic clearly getting to her.

She fumbled for her phone and realized it was gone — surely lost somewhere in Vivian's trunk.

Nora tried not to think about the nightmare of Vivian's head or grieve her dwindling odds of survival as she bolted down the nearest alleyway, still terrified that Buzz Cut would catch up and turn her head into pasta.

Her heart pounded like a hammer on an anvil as she veered sharply into a narrow alley, her shoes skidding on the grimy pavement.

Nora thought she had gained some distance, but it wasn't enough.

She saw the glint of headlights illuminating the alley entrance ahead as a black sedan moved toward her with predatory intent.

She veered right into another dark alley, her breath ragged but determined.

But another car was already screeching to a halt at the other end, its headlights flaring up like the eyes of a demon.

Car doors popped open and slammed shut, ominous silhouettes emerging — guns gleaming dully in the scarce light.

"Nora!" they shouted, their voices echoing down the narrow corridor of brick and shadow, making her name sound like a death knell.

She pivoted on her heels and sprinted back the way she came, running and running and running and running until she found herself flying right by a bodega.

She stopped short, took a breath, glanced around, and then ran back to the store and darted inside.

She looked down at her clothing once under the wash of fluorescent lights and noted yet again that she was painted in blood.

The old man standing behind the counter had graying hair peeking out from under a worn baseball cap and wire-framed glasses, eyes widening in unmistakable worry as he took in her bloody appearance.

His eyes lingered on Nora for a blink before he sprang into action, moving from behind the counter and locking the bodega door, turning the sign from *OPEN* to *CLOSED*, then hurrying back to his post behind the counter to dial 911.

"Yes, hello! I would like to report a disturbance at…"

The old man's voice was drowned out by the Russians screeching to a stop outside.

Moments later, they burst into the bodega with a shower of bent metal and broken glass. The man raised his fist at them. "You have no right to be here!"

His head didn't explode like Vivian's, but a neat hole there turned black for a blink before blood spilled from the wound, pooling on the ground after his body hit the linoleum floor.

Nora ran out the back door, bursting through the bodega's exit doors and falling hard onto the alley ground, scrambling back up and ignoring the agony of gravel biting into each of her kneecaps as she ran.

Tires squealed behind her, and she knew this was it, finally, her time to die. There would be no outrunning the bullets this time.

But as Nora reached the end of the alley and pivoted to her left, she stole a glance to see it was Burt behind the wheel of his Jeep.

He yelled out to her from the middle of the alley, pulling up alongside her as he opened the passenger door.

She clambered in and slammed it shut.

Burt tore down the street.

Nora turned around and looked into the back seat, but she didn't see Daphne.

"Don't worry about her, Daphne's safe," Burt said, as if reading Nora's mind.

Nora exhaled with relief, but she was also confused about how Burt had found her and a bit unsettled by the sudden sense that maybe the back seat hadn't been as empty as she thought at a glance.

Instinct turned her head back around, and she noted that someone was indeed hiding in the back seat, but an arm was already around Nora's neck, a sticky sweet substance on a cloth covering her mouth.

"Help!" she screamed to Burt while trying to fight off her attacker. "You have to help me — someone is in your back seat!"

But Burt kept driving, ignoring Nora as if he couldn't hear a word she yelled.

A police car pulled up behind them.

Burt flipped on his blinker and made a right turn.

The police car did not follow.

What the hell is going on here? was the last thing Nora thought before passing out.

Chapter Thirty-Five

NORA WOKE UP, surprised to find herself restrained on a wooden chair, which was sitting atop a large piece of plastic sheeting in the middle of what was clearly a soundstage.

Her head was still foggy, and her memories were muddled, like so much of last night had been, ever since she'd opened her eyes next to that homeless man, Frank. But the little she could remember just before losing consciousness wasn't adding up, and the situation she was in right now felt perfectly deadly.

But that was a problem for Future Nora to solve. Present Day Nora had to do everything possible to get loose and escape this situation.

Not that there was much she *could* do, and even after several minutes of trying, Nora only felt worse about her predicament.

Her hands were zip-tied, and so were her feet, both ankles bound to the chair.

She clenched her jaw and drew a deep breath, steeling

herself before thrusting her full weight forward in an attempt to scoot the chair inch by inch to the door.

The wooden legs squealed against the plastic sheeting, snagging and refusing to glide. With a frustrated growl, Nora tried using her heels for leverage, pushing against the ground as if she could row her way to freedom.

But her ankles were bound too tightly to the chair, rendering her lower body almost useless when it came to maneuvering.

The chair finally spilled over, and Nora landed hard on her face.

"Help!" Then, after wondering what the hell she was doing by not belting it at the top of her lungs, she let the empty room have it. "HELP!"

Nora stopped screaming when she finally heard footsteps, but even after the door opened, she couldn't tell who was in the room with her because it was still too dark, and she was lying on her side.

Then bright lights suddenly illuminated everything for a second of excruciating brightness. Nora blinked and realized that she was looking at Burt, then a beat later, she also realized how terrified she was of him.

And how justified those emotions were, considering he had been behind the wheel when someone had attacked her from the back seat before driving her here to where she woke up tied to a chair.

"I apologize that you ever had to find this out, Nora." Burt shook his head in a performance of true regret while proving that he was indeed the bad guy. "But when you wouldn't let go of those documents, you left me no other choice. I do hope you can understand that."

"I have no fucking idea what you're talking about. If you're working with Vivian, then why did you just kill her?"

"For a fixer, you're awfully stupid. I'm working with … Well, I should just let you see for yourself." He stopped talking as the sound of heels clacked across the concrete.

Nora could only see the woman's feet when she stopped in front of her, but she recognized the voice.

"Get her up!" Sheryl snapped.

Burt reached down and turned Nora's chair upright until she was staring at Sheryl.

"So, you're the one laundering Russian money," she said.

Sheryl laughed. "Burt's right, you're too stupid to be a fixer. I'm not laundering money at all."

Nora finally got it. "You're laundering weapons."

"That's right." Sheryl nodded. "Talk about easy. I take the fake ones overseas for a shoot in Europe and bring back the real ones. Easy peasy. I'm the Spielberg of smuggling, and no one on either continent has ever been the wiser."

"Until recently, you mean."

"Yes, until recently." Sheryl gave Nora a thin-lipped smile. "Until Vivian caught wind of what I was doing and stole some documents. She held them over my head, daring to blackmail me like a fucking bitch who was begging to die."

"And how did Burt play into it?"

"This one?" She jerked her thumb at the actor. "Burt knows a good investment when he sees it. Besides, where do you think he got the tank, the military weapons, and that rocket launcher from?"

"Burt has plenty of money, and I've heard of scenarios where people with money can buy literally anything. Even seen a few." It churned her stomach to say it out loud.

"How do you think Burt knows Russians? Did you really think that woman was his masseuse?"

That is not the way Nora would use that word, but yes, she definitely thought that Irina was Burt's masseuse, and she still did. But everything else was also making sense to Nora, now in 8K clarity compared to that black-and-white bullshit she had believed just a short while ago.

"So Burt told the Russians we were meeting Vivian?"

"Yep," Sheryl nodded.

"I promise not to say anything if you let me go," Nora reasoned. "Why create another problem, with another body to dispose of? Let's be practical here, Sheryl. You know that discretion is my business. I don't see any reason why this needs to leave this room."

"It's too late for you, and I'm not about to give you false hope that you'll be leaving here alive without surrendering the documents."

"You have the documents."

"Burt gave me photocopies. I want the originals."

"I already mailed them."

"Well then, I'm sorry, Nora Bauer. It's time to take your final breaths." Sheryl put the gun to her temple.

"WAIT!"

Sheryl lowered her gun.

"I can get the documents back!"

"Say more things like that," Sheryl commanded her.

"I just need to leave and come back here."

Sheryl laughed while raising the gun again. "Yeah, right."

"You or Burt can come with me. I just need to—"

Sheryl cut her off. "Not gonna happen."

"Daphne can get the documents for you!"

That one did the trick.

Sheryl took out her phone. "No funny business."

"I promise. I want this to go well for all of us," Nora said. "Of course, I'll be good."

Sheryl dialed Daphne and then put the call on speaker.

"Does she know about you?" Nora asked Burt as it rang.

"Of course not. Daphne Belle is one of the dimmest bulbs in Hollywood. It's one of the things I love most about her."

Chapter Thirty-Six

Daphne's pulse beat along with the low hum of an unseen generator as she crouched behind a grime-smeared dumpster, the air soaked with decaying refuse.

She tilted her head, peeking beneath the garbage bin's rusting underbelly.

Her eyes, adjusted to the shadows, scanned the narrow alley for signs of movement but caught only the distant flicker of a dying neon sign.

She gripped the cold metallic hilt of her disco stick and crawled out from her makeshift hideout, knees grazing the concrete and sending prickles up her skin.

A dead Russian was sprawled on the sidewalk, his eyes emptier than a Hollywood promise. Panic churned in her gut as she swiveled her head around, desperate to locate Burt and Nora.

"*Burt!*" she rasped into the void. "*Nora!*"

A cacophony of sirens ruptured the silence and started getting loud fast.

Daphne's adrenal glands went into overdrive as she sprinted onto the road.

She fumbled for her phone, pulling it out of her pocket with a pounding heart.

Nora — no answer.

Burt — no answer.

Vivian — still no answer.

Each unanswered call tightened the knot in her chest until most of the air had been squeezed from her lungs.

But she refused to let paralysis grip her.

What would Nora do?

The thought was a bright red lipstick amid a dull sea of nudes.

Because Daphne knew without a doubt that Nora would call Eric.

Grim determination settled in as Daphne strode away from The Grove, leaving the palm trees and cobblestone streets behind her as blaring sirens tore through the air.

Any second now, a fleet of police cars would come screaming past her, red and blue strobing like lights at a rave. She needed to get the hell out of here. There was no way she could call Eric right now with all the background noise, anyway.

Daphne surveyed the streetscape until her gaze locked onto a glowing red sign.

CHEE'S: FULL STEAM AHEAD 24 HOURS A DAY.

Despite boasting round-the-clock hours, the restaurant looked like a film set after wrap. *Perfect.*

She crossed the street and pushed through the glass door, its bell tinkling an out-of-tune welcome as she entered the sanctuary of empty booths and dim sum carts.

Daphne sat at a corner table, glancing down at the white porcelain cups as a middle-aged woman approached her. She had a weathered face and a few strands of silver hair escaping from an otherwise tidy bun.

"Do you have a pen and paper?" Daphne asked before the woman could greet her.

She stared back at Daphne as if seeming to assess her before finally leaving with a tight nod, walking behind the counter, then returning with a pen, a piece of paper, and a fresh pot of steaming oolong tea.

"Would you mind sitting down with me?" Daphne gestured to the empty seat across from her. "I need to go over something with you."

"Would you like to see a menu?"

"No, thank you."

"Did you want to order some food?"

"I always want to order some food, dear." Daphne laughed. "But right now, I'm more interested in getting a little work done. Are you the owner of this place?"

The woman narrowed her eyes as if trying to figure out why her customer might want to ask such a question.

"I'm not trying to rob you." Daphne laughed again. "Are you Chee or not?"

The woman nodded. "I am Ling."

"Nice to meet you, Ling." Daphne smiled at her, using her first name just like Nora would. "I was hoping you could help me with something."

"What do you need help with?"

"I want to lay out all the facts as I know them and have you help me to sort through everything. You seem like a woman who knows her way around a puzzle. Am I right about that, Ling?"

Nora would use her name again while giving the woman a compliment, so that's what Daphne did. And Ling honestly seemed like the kind of lady who could help her put these pieces together after she said them out loud.

Ling gave Daphne a nod, so she got right into it.

"I'm in a bit of a kerfuffle because my friend Nora and

I were at this fancy rager last night, and someone slipped something in our drinks, and then each of us woke up to our own nightmare. Ever since, we've been on this wild goose chase, trying to figure out what happened last night and who drugged us, but these scary mafiosos started chasing us, and now I need a place to sit and get my thoughts together so I can figure out what to do next and hopefully find Nora before something awful happens!"

Ling nodded again, clearly unsure of what Daphne wanted her to say.

"We're looking to answer two questions here, Ling. First, where did the Russians come from? And second, if Vivian is working with the Ruskies, then why where they shooting at her? Do you got that, Ling?"

Daphne was trying to sound like Nora but realized the tone of that last Ling might have sounded a little insulting.

Ling simply nodded and gestured for Daphne to continue.

"We were trying to get some dirt on Vivian because we thought she was the one who drugged our drinks before we went to Burt's party last night. But then we broke into her place and found a bunch of these papers written in Russian in her safe. We had no idea what they said because the only Russian I know is Arnie Schwarzenegger, but Nora decided to mail the docs to the cops, just in case. Burt knows a Russian who gives him lingam massages and has some really great handbags designed to sell fast — not that I got to buy one even after Irina offered me a BOGO because these scary Russians with guns started chasing us all over town! Are you following me, Ling?"

Daphne couldn't tell if she sounded nice that time or not.

Ling nodded, so she continued.

"Nora wanted to meet up with Vivian at the Grove and

maybe get some answers, but more of those Russian thugs popped up out of nowhere and started going bang-bang at us, but with real bullets. I just don't know how to make that sound. Me and Nora got away, but we couldn't find Burt."

Ling leaned forward as Daphne drew another breath.

"This Burt, he was with you and Nora earlier in the evening?"

"Burt's been helping us out the whole time. That man is a prince!"

"Are you sure about that?"

"What are you trying to say, Ling?" Daphne wanted to hear her out — she was asking for her help after all — but Daphne didn't like where this conversation appeared to be headed.

"It sounds to me like this Burt might be your bad guy."

"Why would you think that?" Daphne whispered, even though they were the only two people in the restaurant. "This is *Burt*. As in Burt Randolph from *Vanishing Act*."

"He was okay in that." Ling shrugged. "But he still sounds like the bad guy."

"Why?"

"Did you or your friend Nora call the Russians?"

"No." Daphne shook her head. "Of course not."

"Well, neither did Vivian if they were shooting at her. And the only other person who knew where you two were was Burt, and he was also the one with a Russian friend."

"*Masseuse*," Daphne corrected her while shaking her head for an entirely different reason. "I just can't see old Burtie-Boo doing that."

"He did it in *Confidence Manor*," Ling reminded her.

"Only in the show," Daphne corrected her as if Ling didn't understand how the whole acting thing worked. "Burt isn't actually a bad guy."

"Okay." Ling shrugged. "Are you hungry now?"

Daphne's phone rang.

She grabbed it and looked down to see *Sunset Studios* on the caller ID.

"Hey there!" Daphne answered like she was about to get offered a role. "This is—"

"Daphne. It's Nora."

"Why do you sound so weird?"

"I need you to listen—"

"Where are you?" Daphne tried a different question.

"I need you to pick up the documents I left at the Copy Club and bring them to me at the Sunset Studio soundstage. Can you do that for me?"

"I *can*." Daphne looked across the table at Ling to share her WTF expression with someone. "But aren't we supposed to be protecting the documents? Didn't you say—"

"I need you to do this for me, Daphne. Can you help me or not? The Sunset Studio soundstage, as soon as you can get here."

There was something in Nora's voice that Daphne could no longer ignore. She didn't understand the details of whatever was happening here, nor did she need to. The reality of this situation was clear enough: a good friend was in danger, and she needed Daphne to help her.

"I'll get there as soon as I can." Daphne swallowed a lump after making the promise. "You take care of yourself."

"Daphne!" Nora called out before she could hang up.

"What is it?"

"Can you pick me up a box of Honey Nut Cheerios for breakfast tomorrow?"

"I guess?" An odd request to make at a time like this.

"See you soon—"

The call went dead, and Daphne looked across the table at Ling.

"It's probably a trap," said Ling with a knowing nod.

"Yeah." Daphne sighed. "Fucking Burt."

"Do you want some food before you go?"

"No thanks, Ling. But I do want you to have this." Daphne emptied her purse, handing over every shred of lettuce inside it. "I would give you more if I could."

Ling looked down at just under $300 as Daphne stood from the table to go.

But she couldn't help herself, turning back to Ling before leaving. "I'm just curious … do you know who I am?"

Ling smiled. "A fancy rager, drugged drinks, and Russians? Sounds like a Daphne Belle movie that I would never change the channel on."

Daphne wished she had more money for another tip.

Chapter Thirty-Seven

SHERYL YANKED the phone out of Nora's hand and disconnected the call. "What was that bit about the cereal?"

"I was trying to keep things light. I didn't know what to say."

"You yelled her name before asking the question," Sheryl argued. "It sounded more like you knew exactly what to say."

"Daphne was about to have a meltdown. You know how she can be. She was rattling off too many questions, so I cut her off. Redirecting Daphne is like getting a dog to chase a ball. I just need to know the best place for me to throw—"

"Honey Nut Cheerios?" Sheryl narrowed her eyes at Nora, then turned to Burt. "Does that mean anything to you?"

"Nope." Burt shook his head. "But Daphne *really* likes her breakfast cereal. She's actually taken boxes home from my pantry before."

"I needed to keep her from panicking in order to get

your documents so I don't end up dead. Satisfied? Or would you like to grill me some more about the secret Honey Nut Cheerios code word that me and Daphne worked out this morning just in case one of us got kidnapped by Sheryl?"

Sheryl and Burt traded annoyed looks.

"How about we talk about whatever has to happen next?" Nora tried.

"I'm assuming you mean after Daphne delivers the documents to me?"

Nora gave her a nod.

"Vivian's murder will be attributed to you." Sheryl nodded at Burt.

He grabbed Nora's wrist and squeezed it hard until her hand flinched open, and he pressed the murder weapon into it.

"Why would I ever want to kill Vivian?" Nora asked.

"Revenge for leaking that video of you to the press," said Sheryl. "Of course."

"No one will believe that."

Sheryl laughed. "Only the nut jobs will doubt it."

The door opened, and one of the Russians — one Nora hadn't seen before — entered the scene.

Burt dropped the gun into a plastic bag and handed it over to him. "You know where to take this."

The Russian nodded and left Nora alone with Burt and Sheryl again.

The room reeked of her inevitable death.

"Now all we have to do is wait for Daphne to arrive," said Burt.

"Then the two of you will be stuffed into a shipping container and sent to Siberia. There will be nothing left but bone dust by the time you arrive," added Sheryl.

Burt shook his head in disgust. "I'm not sure that's necessary."

But Nora would never make it to the shipping container — at least not alive, given the plastic sheeting on the floor. She needed to figure a way out of this mess, and right now, that meant keeping both of these sociopaths here in the room with her.

"Why did you kill Randolph?" Nora asked.

"Who is that? Never mind, you're dead." Sheryl turned to Burt. "Who is Randolph?"

"The man outside your office."

"Ah." She nodded and turned back to Nora. "I thought he worked for Vivian. *My blackmailer.* The man was following everyone all around town. It was a natural assumption."

"So you just killed him without checking to make sure."

"You don't succeed in this business by leaving loose ends untied."

"He didn't know anything! He just wanted Daphne to return the brooch she'd borrowed."

"That is what he insisted," Sheryl replied with a nod. "But let's be real with one another, Nora: once he was involved with your little investigation, my men still would have cleaned up the mess. There was no way to be sure you hadn't told him something that could lead back to us later."

"You're a sociopath."

Sheryl rolled her eyes. "That's a bit dramatic. I have people to tidy up after me so that I can live a free life and spend the mountains of money I'm making. Your Randolph was a risk to me."

"He's not 'my Randolph.' Stop saying that! And how about the shopkeeper running his little bodega? Was that tidying up after you, too?"

Burt looked over at Sheryl, perhaps curious to see how his boss might answer.

"Of course it was." Sheryl shrugged. "And sure, that old man was a little more unfortunate than the others, but you still know the score, Nora. Some people live on the backs of others. Do I look like the heel or the spine to you?"

When Nora didn't answer, Sheryl commanded Burt to put the gun against her head.

"Heel or spine? Which one do I look like to you?" Sheryl asked her again.

"Heel." Nora swallowed, half-expecting that to be the last thing she ever said.

Sheryl nodded and gestured for Burt to lower the gun.

"Randolph and bodega grandpa are both on you. If you had stayed out of this in the first place, those men would still be alive. I'm not responsible for the Russians going off leash. *That's what Russians do*. Come on, Burt."

Then they walked out together, their footsteps echoing down the hallway in a receding tide of menace.

With the room now a mausoleum-in-waiting, Nora was back to nursing what would almost certainly be her final thoughts if she failed to figure out a way out of this mess.

Summoning reserves from her waning strength, Nora's muscles tensed as she yanked her arms upward until the zip-ties bit into her wrists like a tightening python.

The chair creaked ominously, but this time it did not fall.

She took a breath before trying again, but the door swung open, and another towering Russian entered the room.

He said nothing, standing with his arms crossed while keeping a lingering eye on Nora. She tried one more sneaky pull on her restraints, hoping for fractional progress, but the man was on her immediately.

"Stop now, or you make worse for yourself." His flat tone was clearly a promise.

After five or so minutes (it could have been ten or twenty, time crawled at a painful pace when zip-tied to a chair with a Russian watching her), she broke the silence, this time while trying for friendly conversation.

"Have you ever been interested in a Hollywood career?"

The Russian ignored her.

"You have the bone structure. I don't mean like in leading man roles or anything. Doing exactly what you're doing now. I bet you could make more as an extra than you're making here as a killer."

The Russian was still ignoring her and acting like Daphne wasn't helping.

"I have to pee."

"Piss yourself," the Russian finally responded.

Nora lapsed into a heavy silence as the slurry of fear, regret, and mounting despair swirled through her mind.

What if Daphne had missed her message about the Honey Nut Cheerios?

Or what if she had understood? Would Daphne call the cops or show up here at Sunset Studios to play the role of hero herself?

If she showed up to save Nora, locked and loaded or not, there was a better than decent chance that they would both end up dead.

Nora had not only failed to fix this situation, she had put her only client in mortal danger. She felt lonelier than she ever had before, though that was probably a normal emotion to experience shortly before leaving this life forever.

Eric would never even know what happened to her. And that made her the saddest of all.

Chapter Thirty-Eight

DAPHNE WATCHED the taillights of her Uber dissolve into the night.

A chill wind cut through her as she turned around to look at the dimly lit lot, its daytime charm now swallowed by elongated shadows and unrecognizable corners of darkness.

She clutched the box of Honey Nut Cheerios and started toward the entrance, barely making it ten feet before her ears caught the rhythmic patter of footsteps echoing faster than her own, coming from behind her and getting closer.

She saw a parked golf cart ahead and ducked behind the vehicle with a burst of adrenaline, crouching low to make herself small — the opposite of her usual moves.

She held her breath.

"Daphne!" Burt called out. "Where are you? I just saw you getting out of the car — where did you go?"

She swallowed and emerged from the shadows.

"Burt!" Daphne called out with glee.

But that was just her acting even better than usual,

making sure that all the doubt now roiling inside her didn't show up on her face.

Of course, Burt was the bad guy, here to make Daphne feel safe before she and Nora both ended up dead.

He parted his arms to give her a hug, and Daphne fell into them on cue.

"I'm so glad to see you," he said.

"I'm glad to see you too," she lied.

He pulled away from their embrace. "What took you so long?"

She shrugged. "I thought I was fast."

"You said you would get here as soon as possible, but it's been over an hour."

She held out the box of cereal. "The first Ralphs didn't have it and neither did the second one, so maybe they're at war with General Mills or something, because I finally found it at Vons, and they had plenty." She shrugged again. "It's not my fault that Nora got the munchies. What are you doing here?"

"I followed the Russians. I know where they're holding Nora for Vivian." Burt seemed to remember a particular box he might have left open and added, "I was eavesdropping on Nora's call and have been waiting for you to get here ever since."

Burt sucked at this.

"Good thing I'm here now," Daphne said.

He held out his hand. "I'll take the documents."

"That's okay." She shook her head. "I should hold onto them. That's what Nora would want."

"She is a stickler." Burt was only pretending to agree with her.

Daphne nodded vaguely at the soundstage. "Lead the way."

Burt escorted her to a door, then stopped dramatically

in front of it, pressing his ear against the wood and waiting several long seconds before quietly opening the door and gesturing for Daphne to enter.

"I'll watch your back," whispered Burt.

Only so you know where to stab it, thought Daphne.

It was dark and shadowy inside the room. She could barely make out the blurry figure sitting in the middle of the room next to a second empty chair.

"Nora?" Daphne called out.

The lights flicked on and told her what she already knew despite the momentary blinding. That was Nora in the chair, for sure.

"RUN!" Nora bellowed.

Daphne turned around to do exactly that, but Burt was holding a gun on her.

"What are you doing?" Daphne asked, acting as baffled by his audacity as she was clueless to his intent. "Why are you waving that at me?"

Burt wasn't really waving it, but Daphne liked the line a lot better that way.

Sheryl entered the picture.

"What the fuck is going on?" Daphne shouted. "Where the hell is Vivian?"

Burt waved his weapon at the empty chair next to Nora, and yes, this time, he really did make the gesture. "Take a seat, Daphne."

She pretended to be shocked. "Are you a bad guy, Burt?"

He waved his gun at the empty chair again instead of answering her.

Daphne sat, still clutching the box of Honey Nut Cheerios to her chest, as Nora turned around and ripped into her.

"Are you seriously so incredibly stupid that you couldn't

figure out that I was asking for help?" Nora turned to Sheryl. "Do you see what I have to put up with all the time?"

"You should shut up right now," Sheryl said.

But Nora kept going. "You can use me. And you're smart enough to know it."

"I said shut up!" Sheryl walked over and grabbed the gun from Burt, then turned it on Nora. "I'm serious."

"I would already be dead if you weren't at least a little bit curious about what I have to say," Nora kept pressing.

Daphne couldn't believe the balls on her. Go, Nora!

Sheryl didn't respond or stop Nora when she kept talking.

"Daphne is as useless as we all think she is. I would rather work for someone who is competent and clearly going places. Someone who knows her mind instead of an idiot who can't ever read between the lines, or figure *anything* out for herself."

Daphne figured that was her cue to jump in and start improvising.

"That's not nice, Nora! I'm the only reason you haven't been eating Top Ramen for the last two—"

"I wouldn't have had any problem finding other work if I wasn't spending sixty hours a week cleaning up your bullshit!"

"—two years, and I really don't appreciate your comments! After all, I did come here to try and save you. Or did you forget that I'm the one you called when—"

"I called you because you had the documents, Daphne! Even if I needed to be saved, I sure as shit wouldn't expect help from *you*, of all people! And in case you're having trouble following the timeline: *I didn't need any saving until this morning when you started fucking up my life even more than normal!*"

"—your panties were all full of poopy because you had

been kidnapped and were apparently fine with *me* getting kidnapped too!"

"ENOUGH!" Sheryl shouted. "Both of you."

She walked over and snatched the documents from Daphne's hand, leaving her with the cereal.

"Deal with them," she said to Burt before leaving the soundstage.

"This won't give me any pleasure." He shook his head, looking apologetically at Daphne.

"I don't need the performance, Burt," Daphne said in the midst of a little performance of her own.

"Daphne—"

But his eyes were already widening as she reached into her box of Honey Nut Cheerios — which now that he looked at it clearly, he probably realized it could not have come fresh from the store — and pulled out a pistol.

Daphne had the weapon aimed at him before Burt could even raise his arm halfway.

"You don't want to—"

"Wrong, asshole! I *do* want to!" She pulled the trigger.

He jerked and tried to shoot back, but Daphne yanked the gun from his hand as his fingers involuntarily flexed open. He lurched forward, clutching his bloodstained chest.

She pointed both weapons at Benedict Arnold and barked, "Untie her!"

"I can't untie her!" Burt wailed, but this time, it was definitely not a performance, though it was dramatic. "I'm bleeding out!"

"You should have thought about that before turning into a pile of shit," Daphne said as she turned to Nora. "Are you okay, honey?"

Nora nodded at Burt as blood gushed between his fingers. "Check him for a knife."

He tried to grab Daphne when she searched him, so she stepped on his wound and plugged her ears after he started screaming, his lungs raw. When the scream turned to pained gasps, she resumed her search.

"I found one!" Daphne declared.

She went over to Nora and cut her free with the knife.

"That is what you meant by bringing the Honey Nut Cheerios, right?" Daphne just wanted to make sure.

"You did perfect," Nora told her.

Chapter Thirty-Nine

"I KNEW YOU WOULD GET IT!" Nora ran over and threw herself at Daphne, hugging the woman harder than she ever had before. Not that they had ever really hugged it out before. "You saved me and I love you, and I would still love you even if you didn't just save me!"

Nora hugged her harder while Burt writhed on the ground like a gutted fish, his face contorted in agony, wheezing in a ghastly fusion of whimpers and growls as if his soul was being grated.

Daphne pulled out of her embrace. "Where does it hurt, honey?"

He groaned even harder and pointed to a blood-drenched spot on his chest.

Daphne made a sympathetic face, but then it turned into something grotesque as she pulled her foot back and launched it right into the bullseye he had just given her.

"That's for hurting Nora, you big-headed piece of shit!" She kicked him again. "I hope you choke on that big fat tongue of yours!"

"What the fuck is this?" Sheryl asked as she entered the

room, waving the paperwork that Daphne had brought with her. "It's all blank!"

Sheryl saw that Burt had been overpowered just as Nora grabbed his gun from the floor and raised it to aim at her.

Sheryl turned around and started to run.

Daphne fired first, but their adversary was already out the door.

"YOU BETTER RUN — YOU EXPIRED CAN OF HAIRSPRAY!" Daphne yelled after her.

She turned back to Nora. "Did you really mean all of that stuff?"

"EEEAAARGHUUUNNNGGG," Burt groaned on the floor.

Nora looked down at Burt, his guttural anguish like a discordant cello. Then she returned her gaze to Daphne, her eyes softening. "You mean about loving you? Of course, I do."

"No." Daphne shook her head, looking upset but trying not to show it. "The mean stuff about me being useless."

"Of course not. I was just trying to buy us some time."

"That's what I thought ... but you said, 'Daphne is as useless as we all think she is.'"

"I'm sorry. I swear I don't think that."

"EEEAAARGHUUUNNNGGG," Burt said again.

"Should we leave him here?" Nora asked.

"Definitely." Daphne kicked him again and turned to Nora. "You should try it."

Nora did.

"AAAAAHHHH!" Burt bellowed as they ran outside.

"She has a fucking helicopter?" Daphne yelled as she pointed at Sheryl running toward a waiting chopper, sleek and black with its rotors already starting to spin as a cadre of stern-faced Russians boarded it.

"Sheryl has an army of Russians, and the *helicopter* surprises you?"

Nora and Daphne were sprinting hard toward the helicopter when Daphne abruptly veered off course.

"Daphne!" Nora shouted. "We have to stop her!"

Daphne skidded to a stop in front of a hedge, then dropped to her knees and started to frantically forage through the foliage.

"DAPHNE!"

"I got it!" Daphne emerged from the bush looking triumphant, waving the disco stick over her head like a prize before handing it over to Nora.

"I'd rather keep my gun — what else do you have back there?"

"This fucker." Daphne grinned as she fondled Burt's rocket launcher. "I didn't just stop at my house for the Cheerios. I went to Burt's place to get the good stuff."

"You're not actually planning on—"

"Of course I am, honey. You call action, and I dish out an encore they'll never forget!"

Daphne narrowed her eyes while hoisting the rocket launcher onto her shoulder and aiming it squarely at the chopper full of Russians buckling themselves in.

One of them looked over and realized what Daphne was holding. He bellowed. Guttural screams from his comrades followed as panic exploded in the cockpit.

The helicopter blades spun faster, lifting the machine skyward and leaving Sheryl sprinting even faster in a frantic attempt to board.

But before Daphne could pull the trigger, Burt appeared in the doorway behind them, his face a mask of twisted yet determined loathing.

Bloodied but unbowed, he raised a new gun procured from who knows where with an ugly gleam in his eye.

Time seemed to congeal, the air thickening as his finger settled onto the trigger, and a snarl curled onto his lips.

Nora's heart was a war drum in her chest.

Daphne finally pulled the trigger, with her eyes almost comically narrowed as she did so. But to Nora's surprise, Daphne had been holding the rocket launcher facing in the opposite direction.

The roar was explosive, shaking the marrow in Nora's bones as the rocket blasted backward — launching out of the rocket like a furious demon flying right at Burt.

His eyes widened with a millisecond of realization before he was consumed in a ball of flame and smoke, his newly acquired weapon dropping from his charred hands.

The rocket blast ruptured the soundstage in a spectacle of devastation, sending a maelstrom of wood, metal, and burning fabrics into the air with cyclonic fury.

A piece of framing from the stage spiraled upward, hurtling toward the helicopter still clawing its way into the sky as if choreographed by Michael Bay.

The chopper erupted into a hellish fireball, plummeting back down to earth in a dissonant symphony of flame and debris.

Sheryl's eyes widened for a blink of disbelief before a razor-sharp piece of shrapnel impaled her leg with a gruesome *thwack*.

Blood spattered like abstract art on the ground beneath her.

Sheryl started dragging her punctured body in obvious agony, leaving a smearing trail of liquid life behind her, clawing at the concrete as if trying to disappear into it, gasping for breath between gritted teeth as she tried to distance herself from the inferno of her shattered ambitions.

Lavigne appeared from the shadows with a smile, lowering the camera from his face as Nora called out to him.

"You got that?"

Lavigne gave her a nod. "Sure did."

"Including the footage of Sheryl shooting Vivian?" Nora asked.

"I would say that's the most viral part." Lavigne nodded at the inferno. "If not for that."

Nora had called in her favor to have Lavigne follow along after them, but considering what the reporter had captured on his camera, he might end up owing her.

Sheryl was still several feet away from Nora when she scrambled to her feet and lunged forward, barely making it two awkward steps before Nora clocked her hard on the skull with the disco stick as the LAPD came roaring onto the scene with brazen lights and blaring sirens.

"I thought it was a good time to call your private dick," Daphne explained.

Nora looked around at all the dead Russians, the still-burning wreckage from both the helicopter and the soundstage, and Sheryl lying injured on the ground.

"Lavigne has it all on tape," Nora said.

"What does that mean?" Daphne asked.

Nora exhaled. "That we can finally go the fuck home and start pretending that last night never happened."

Chapter Forty

UNLIKE THIS MORNING when Nora had been riding shotgun in Eric's sedan, she was now sitting on the rigid backseat next to Daphne so her friend didn't feel alone.

Eric started the car and drove in silence, making it past several lights and what was probably at least two miles before finally breaking the silence.

"Home?" Eric looked into the rearview mirror, and Nora could see all the questions he wasn't asking her. *Yet*.

"Can you take us to the Sunset Sovereign first, please?"

"Sure thing." He gave her a nod, and then they drove in silence.

Even Daphne had nothing to add.

Nora looked over at Daphne, who seemed even worse for wear than she did, having been nearest to the explosion. Her hair was frazzled, with a few strands singed to a crisp, sticking out at unruly angles as if electrified by their harrowing night. Nora had only glanced at her reflection a couple of times since the bloodbath, and not even once on purpose. Like Daphne, she had smudges of soot on her face like war paint, plus scorched hems and small holes in her clothing that looked like she had been attacked by a raging sewing machine.

Nora and Daphne strode through the lobby with Eric, all three of them staring ahead, avoiding all possible eye contact as they walked briskly toward the elevator.

"We're calling it 'crispy chic!'" Daphne shouted to a couple whose staring was just a little too obvious.

The elevator doors were opening as if expecting the trio.

Eric paused to let the ladies enter, then ducked in right behind them.

Nora felt a flush of relief as the doors began to close.

"WAIT!" The voice was young and familiar.

Eric put his hand out to stop the doors from closing, and the relief went away.

The doors parted back open to a familiar family, two of whose members Nora and Daphne had already met before. But this time the girl and her mother were there with Dad. His hair was a tousled blond mop, and he wore a slightly befuddled smile.

He seemed excited, though not especially surprised to see Daphne as the doors closed and his daughter turned to the movie star.

"I saw you dancing on the TV today," said the girl.

"Oh yeah?" Daphne was obviously delighted by this news. "Great boobs, right?" She held them up so the little girl could get a better look.

The little girl giggled. "You're funny!"

Mom and Dad obviously had no idea what to do with that.

The elevator doors dinged open.

"Stay in school!" Daphne told the girl, adding a series of PSAs while trailing Eric and Nora down the hall. "Don't listen to the haters — you do you! Life's a party, so don't forget to dance! Go break some hearts, but don't let yours get broken!"

The elevator doors had already closed again when she bellowed, "BE THE GIRL WHO WALKS IN A ROOM AND OWNS IT!"

They stopped in front of the suite door, but Daphne turned to Eric and Nora before opening it. "Do you think I changed her life?"

"Unfortunately," Nora said.

"Hey. I thought we were being nice to each other now."

"Your words can shape worlds when you're a star. It's unfortunate that few celebrities choose to be architects of anything meaningful. It's not personal."

Daphne pouted. "Sure sounds personal."

"Nora is just saying that influence is a double-edged sword. It's not a judgment on how you wield it, Daphne." Eric came to Nora's rescue, despite surely knowing that there was indeed at least *some* judgment around how she was wielding that sword, whether Nora wanted there to be or not. "You both have your stages and on those stages, each of you shines. That's what counts."

They entered the suite and went straight to Daphne's room.

"You've gotta be fucking kidding me!" Daphne exclaimed upon opening the door.

"What?" Nora looked around the room and then back at Eric to see if he knew what she was talking about.

"Right there!" Daphne jabbed a finger at the mountain of clothes, but Nora still had no idea what she was talking about.

"You mean your closet vomit on the bed?"

Eric snickered.

"It's Caroline!" Daphne pointed harder, then walked

over to the pile of clothing and swatted the first layer off until a small patch of Caroline's gold-sequined gown was visible. "We just didn't see her because I like to keep my clothes in an advanced state of organized chaos for maximum creative freedom."

"What the fuck is going on?" Caroline asked the room after sitting up and slowly blinking her eyes into awareness. "I feel like I've been drugged. Why…"

Caroline fell back onto the mattress and immediately started snoring again.

"We should let her sleep," Daphne said.

"Agreed." Eric nodded, looking with curiosity at Caroline and the half-closet's worth of clothes that garnished her body. "I'll drop Daphne off first."

Daphne laughed. "So you guys can do it afterward?"

Nora and Eric both ignored her, but Nora was pretty sure that she saw him grinning.

Daphne was surprisingly silent on the way to her house, though she was right back at it, and louder than ever when Eric pulled up to her place, and they saw an Escalade parked in the driveway. She belted out the obvious observation with Broadway-worthy projection as if the detective couldn't see the SUV for himself.

"THERE'S AN ESCALADE RIGHT THERE!"

And not just an Escalade, but several Latino men standing in front of Daphne's door, all five of them looking like the definition of serious.

Eric killed the engine and drew his gun while getting out of the car.

"My friends!" Santiago emerged from the shadows and came walking toward them. He nodded at the front door and explained. "We are fixing your door right now because we broke it earlier." He bowed his head. "We would also like to apologize for the misunderstanding."

Before either Nora or Daphne could respond — while Eric continued to study the situation — Julio came out of the darkness to join Santiago by his side.

He bowed his head to Daphne and Nora. "Thank you for saving my life the other night at Action Channel. I got myself shot, but you got me out of there."

Julio lifted his shirt and showed them his bandaged chest. "I'm going to live, thanks to you two crazy ladies. I won't ever forget that." He shook his head. "You ever need anything, anything at all—" He pounded his chest. "You just tell me what it is so I can make sure you get it. Whatever that means." A glance at Eric. "No offense."

No reply from the detective.

"I got a present for you." Julio grinned, pulling something out of his jacket and prompting Eric to raise his gun.

"*Relax!*" Santiago raised his hands at Eric and nodded at Julio to show that the man was unarmed, holding a small bundle of something wrapped with paper that read *Happy 40th birthday!*

"Sorry." Julio nodded at the paper. "My *tia* turned forty a few weeks ago, and that was all I had."

"I would love to be forty again!" Daphne exclaimed as she unwrapped her kilo of coke.

Eric plucked the package out of Daphne's hand. "I'll hang onto that for you."

"We were just finishing up. I am glad we got to see you before leaving." Santiago nodded to his men, and they moved toward the SUV in a herd. "Like Julio said, you need anything, just let me know."

"I'll be right back," Nora said to Eric as the Escalade shrank in the distance.

"Make him show you the key before you let him handcuff you to anything," Daphne advised after closing the front door behind them.

Nora pulled Daphne into a hug without dignifying her with a response. "Get a good night's sleep."

"I'm way too wired for sleep," Daphne replied as she pulled away. "I'll probably have to use my Hitachi."

"I'll see you on Monday." Nora ignored that one, too.

She took a step toward the door but then turned back to Daphne.

"What is it, honey?"

"I just remembered, we have to return the brooch," she said wearily.

"I dropped it when the Russians grabbed me at the cemetery."

"After all that?"

"What can I say? I'm not a tough fixer like you. I panicked."

But Daphne didn't seem at all worried about it.

"We should go back and look."

"This is exactly the kind of situation that insurance is for, honey. Don't you worry about it. I'm not."

"You pay me to worry for you and to tell you when—"

"Right now, I'm paying you to not worry about it, okay? Go let Eric inspect your gadget. There was a helicopter crash, honey, and the brooch is insured. No one will be talking about missing jewelry when there's so much juicer stuff to talk about. And if anything, poor old Randolph can take the fall since he's sleeping with the fishes and everything."

Randolph's death had nothing to do with the mafia and, therefore, nothing to do with that saying, but Daphne still sounded half-fixer herself. And she wasn't wrong. If everyone else considered the situation resolved, that meant that there wasn't anything left for Nora to fix.

Back in the car, Eric took Nora's hand. A simple yet profound gesture. In the aftermath of a day with Daphne, followed by the most explosive night of Nora's life, their shared silence throughout the drive was exquisite.

Eric pulled up to her apartment building. Nora eyed the Art Deco facade with intricate details that made her wonder about a Hollywood that no longer was.

"Do you want to come in?" she asked.

"I'm sure you're tired." His eyes were less gentlemanly than his voice.

Nora felt a magnetic fatigue fueled by adrenaline. "I'm still too wired for sleep. But I can think of a few ways to expend some of this pent-up energy."

Eric grinned and got out of the car.

Nora followed, gripping the disco stick.

Chapter Forty-One

Nora was sitting at PastaMio, waiting on the other two in her party of three at a table for four. She found herself enjoying the trendy, fast-casual Italian vibe that had mastered the art of blending efficiency with ambiance and the exposed brick walls dressed with pop-art canvases of Italian icons and playful neon signs full of declarative phrases like *Mangia Bene* and *Vivi Felice*. It all felt wonderfully … normal.

"Welcome to PastaMio, my name is Cecelia. Have you dined with us before?"

"I have not, Cecelia. But I have smelled this place many times while walking to my car. I finally had to try it."

"Would you like to wait for the rest of your party?"

"We can start with a bottle of water for the table. And an appetizer. Which one is your favorite?"

"Most popular, or my favorite?"

"Popular is what you tell people when you want to move the table and earn a good tip. I want to give you a great tip, Cecelia, but I would also like to have the best of whatever while I'm here. I want to know *your* favorite.

Imagine you're having a really shitty day, and you need something from the kitchen to cheer you up. The only requirement is that it has to be something for sharing, even if this isn't something on the regular menu. Or maybe, *especially* if it isn't on the menu. What's your favorite thing to order on a bad day, Cecelia, and why?"

Her eyes brightened, just as Nora had expected.

"On a bad day, I would go for our off-menu, family-style Pappardelle Al Ragu. Wide pasta ribbons tossed in a slow-cooked Bolognese with a sprinkle of Parmesan." She smiled. "It's a warm hug with just the right amount of sauce."

"I was thinking finger foods."

"Can it be a dessert?"

"Sure." Nora shrugged. "Why not?"

"Then, oh my God, the cannoli nachos."

"Say more."

"Cannoli shells drizzled with chocolate and served with a ricotta dip."

"Sold." Nora smiled. "I'll take an order of cannoli nachos and an order of that Pappardelle Al Ragu. But that's for you to take home after work, okay, Cecelia?"

"Why? I mean, thank you." She bowed her head. "And I do mean that. But why are you being so nice to me?"

"Because there might be a disturbance at this table later, and I just want you to know both before and after whatever happens that I appreciate you." Nora gave her a smile. "And the Ragu doesn't count as a tip."

Cecelia returned her smile and then practically skipped away from the table.

Nora's first guest came waltzing into PastaMio as if he had no idea that his life was about to change forever because this was the end of a story where the dickhead got what he deserved.

Tim took a seat across from Nora as Melissa entered the restaurant. She suveyed her options and decided on a seat beside Tim instead of sitting next to her frenemy.

"Do you have a scoop for me?" Tim asked, as if there was a chance in hell that that was happening.

"I know it was you," Nora said to him.

"Me what?" But Tim knew exactly what she was talking about, and Nora could tell by the look on his face.

"You're the one who released the footage of Daphne dancing to Sheryl." Nora narrowed her eyes. "You're the one who threatened her."

"You have no proof." His voice barely quivered, but if it was enough for Nora to hear it, then Melissa could hear it too, and she was surely shitting those Prada panties right now.

Nora got out her phone and dialed the number for whoever had tried to blackmail her. The phone in Tim's pocket started to ring.

"It was just a joke. A harmless prank. I never meant for it to be anything more than—"

"A lark? How is it harmless when you're blackmailing someone?"

"She has the money—"

"Hardly."

"—and I need it."

"Let me guess: it's expensive keeping Scarlett in furs and champagne?" Nora said.

Tim traded a knowing glance with Melissa, then turned back to answer her question. "More like it's expensive keeping up with her. She can buy her own damn furs and champagne, but I have to pay my way in the relationship, and it ain't cheap."

"But *blackmail*. That's your solution to bridging the income gap — committing a federal offense? And you …"

Nora shook her head as she turned to Melissa and stared at her with shaming eyes. "You might even be worse. Worse than Tim for sure, but maybe even worse than Vivian."

"And why is that?" But Melissa knew her role in this play just as much as Tim had known his.

"Because you drugged me and Daphne so that Scarlett could get the part."

"Drugging you makes me worse than defending pedophiles?" Melissa laughed like she wasn't a human monster.

"This early in your career?" Nora nodded. "It sure does. The devil took a while to take total hold of Vivian. You're already in bed with him."

"First of all, if that was my plan, then it obviously worked. And second, you can't prove shit, so fuck you six times, Nora."

"Six times." Nora nodded at Melissa. "I like that you're always specific. And just so we're clear, I don't want to prove it, and I don't need to prove it. Daphne dodged a bullet with *Sister Justice* and soon everyone in the world is going to know it. *No one in their right fucking mind* would want to be associated with that movie now."

The color was already draining from Melissa's face, and Nora had yet to close her argument. Tim was still sitting right next to her, apparently oblivious to the reality that his federal offense had its consequences coming, too.

"Scarlett's career is about to tank. And this won't be like Daphne mouthing off about Me Too. Scarlett will be done for because we both know that she barely had a career to begin with."

"What the hell are you talking about?" Melissa snapped.

Nora just smiled.

Melissa turned to Tim, but he didn't know.

Cecelia arrived at the table with a bottle of chilled water, an order of cannoli nachos, and three small plates.

"Thank you, Cecelia," Nora said as their server set everything down at the table.

"You got it." Cecelia nodded, then gracefully disappeared from the table, having been warned of the tension beforehand.

"You should really enjoy those cannoli nachos." Nora looked down at the dessert, then back up at the baffled faces in front of her. "Think of it as a last meal sort of thing."

"What is all of this, Nora?" Tim asked. "What are you actually getting at?"

"I'm getting at the fact that I had the biggest scoop of the century, but I gave it to someone who didn't try to blackmail me instead of you."

She nodded at the TV where Lavigne was onscreen, breaking the biggest story to ever rock Hollywood. The reporter looked better than Nora had ever seen him, rocking an impeccably tailored suit, and his smile had never looked warmer. The anchorwoman's poised elegance and attention were basking fully on him with a ticker beneath them that read, *Hollywood Rocked By Deadly Underground Russian Weapons Trafficking*.

"I would suggest that we watch the news together, but it looks like we have company." Nora glanced down at the dessert nachos again. "And you're running out of time to get your sugar rush on."

Nora nodded at Eric as he entered the restaurant and immediately walked over to their table.

"Hey there, Eric," Nora said when he arrived at the table. "This is Tim. He's the shithead I was telling you about." As if her performance hadn't made it perfectly clear already, she added, "The one who blackmailed Daphne."

"It's good to meet you, Tim!" Eric gave him a wave. "I'm here to arrest you for extortion."

"You can't prove anything," Tim tried.

"That wouldn't be true even if you were smart enough to not bring the incriminating phone to this restaurant."

Tim finally got it and sagged down low in defeat.

Melissa was still in shock, watching the TV with a gobsmacked expression as Eric turned to her and grinned.

"You must be Melissa." He gave her a friendly smile. "I'll be arresting you for assault."

"I'll leave you guys to it," Nora said. "Have fun with Eric. He's a good time. I bet you he'll even let you eat those cannoli nachos if you promise to share with him."

"You bet right!" Eric said.

Nora paid and left PastaMio with a smile, holding her head high as she stepped out onto the street with a ringing phone.

Three Mile PR.

"This is Nora," she answered.

"Hi there, Nora! This is Maria from Three Mile PR!"

"Hey there, Maria."

"I was just calling because we've been hearing about your work over the last few days, and it sounds like exactly the kind of exceptional service we offer our clients here at TMP. I was wondering if you would be open to an interview?"

"I really appreciate the kind words," Nora said. "But I'm going to pass."

"Are you sure?" Maria sounded surprised.

"I'm taking a sabbatical, so that means I'm sure for now."

Nora ended the call.

Then she took a moment to bask in the sunshine.

Chapter Forty-Two

Nora approached Daphne's set without having any idea what she might see.

That wasn't new because Daphne still lived her entire life as a surprise, but at least they weren't surprises for Nora to manage because she was no longer Daphne's fixer. She had plenty of other annoying clients to keep her busy, teaching her that Hollywood was full of nut jobs and that Daphne was never really all that bad compared to what she could have been dealing with.

And these days, if Daphne ever needed help with a little emergency PR, Nora would be happy to help her out as a friend. Daphne was still newsworthy, but the public cared less about directors than they did about actors and actresses, and Daphne had decided to move behind the camera for this next phase of her storied career.

She was still interested in acting, including being the star of her directorial debut, but Daphne saw her future in directing. And producing, since she had been the one to come up with all of the money for *Last Night Never Happened*. She was banking on the film to be a hit, with a big enough return on its two-million-dollar budget for Daphne to outlive her aggressive spending.

"Let's take a break!" Daphne shouted at everyone in earshot when she saw Nora approaching. "Ten minutes! Unless I'm not back, and then we'll start whenever!"

Nora laughed and gave her good friend a hug, heart-to-heart, like Daphne always insisted.

"It's great to see you!"

"It hasn't been that long," Nora said as they pulled back.

"It's been long enough. And I'm getting older, you know. You should visit me more."

"You sound like my grandma."

"That's what I was trying to sound like, Nora. I need to keep my acting sharp since I'll be using it less these days. How is work?"

"I love it. I have six clients, all annoying in their own way."

"And not a single one of them even close to inspiring the love you felt when working with the legendary Daphne Belle, am I right?"

"As rain," Nora agreed.

"Where did that saying come from, I wonder."

"It's British, I think. Because it rains there all the time."

"Speaking of golden showers, how are things with Eric?"

Nora ignored the first part. "Never better."

Daphne nodded. "Same for me and Caroline."

"Are you comparing the two relationships?"

She nodded again. "Sometimes."

Nora's phone buzzed with a text.

She sighed while looking down at the screen.

"Duty calls?" Daphne asked.

Nora sighed. "The universe clearly doesn't care about

my dinner plans. Harmon Dean just eloped. In Vegas. With his costar."

"Maria Inez?"

"The one and only."

"Looks like love is in the air and on its way to breaking the internet." Daphne laughed. "So I guess that means we really are back to it. I'm not sure if everyone will be happy about that or not."

Nora stood to kiss Daphne on the cheek. "Break a leg, sister."

"Lunch tomorrow? We can have it here. Craft services makes these sriracha-glazed cauliflower bites, and they taste like heaven decided to throw a rager and you're gonna be its guest of honor."

"Cauliflower? That doesn't sound like Daphne Belle."

"I'm new and improved, darling." Then, because she couldn't help it, "#DaphneDoesn'tAge. A star has to keep shining, you know."

"How did you get the funding for this film?"

Daphne grinned. "I already told you."

"You said it was an anonymous benefactor."

"Right." She nodded. "Exactly."

"Too bad that spider brooch never turned up," Nora said.

"Some lost things have a way of helping us find ourselves," Daphne replied, admitting nothing as she glanced at her set. "That brooch might be gone forever, but now I have *Last Night Never Happened*."

The End

About The Authors

Nolon King writes fast-paced psychological thrillers set in the glitzy world of entertainment's power players with a bold, insightful voice. He's not afraid to explore the darker side of human nature through stories featuring families torn apart by secrets and lies.

Nolon loves to write about big questions and moral quandaries. How far would you go to cover up an honest mistake? Would you destroy your career to protect your family? How much of your soul would you sell to get the life of your dreams? Would you cheat on your husband to keep your children safe? Would you give in to a stalker's demands to save your marriage?

Sean Platt has always been an entrepreneur, but knew he'd rather tell stories. When his wife bought him a laptop for his birthday in 2007 he dropped everything to start writing fiction.

Since making the leap, Sean has written hundreds of novels (including the international best-sellers Yesterday's Gone and Invasion), penned dozens of scripts, and founded the IP Incubator Sterling & Stone where more than thirty storytellers work together to create world changing IP. Sterling & Stone's stable of writers come to Sean for ideas, mentorship, and "better words."

Originally from Long Beach, California, Sean now lives in Austin, Texas with his wife and dog, Fisher.

Also By Nolon King

Replaced

Replaced

In Her Place

Irreplaceable

Cold Vengeance

Cold Vengeance

Cold Reckoning

Cold Retribution

Hidden Justice

Hidden Justice

Hidden Honor

Hidden Shame

Hidden Virtue

No Justice

No Justice

No Escape

No Hope

No Return

No Stopping

No Fear

Once Upon A Crime

Once Upon A Crime

Twice Upon A Lie

Three Times a Murder

Dead For Good

Dead For Good

Left For Dead

Dead Of Night

Wake The Dead

Dead For Life

Stand Alone Novels

Pretty Killer

12

Blown

Miserable Lies

The Target

Secrets We Keep

Close To Home

Heat To Obsession

A Simple Kill

Tell Me No Lies

Red Carpet Black

Fade To Black

Victim

Last Night Never Happened

Also By Sean Platt

The Dead World Series

Dead Zero

Dead City

Dead Nation

Dead Planet

Empty Nest

The Beam Series

The Beam Season One

The Beam Season Two

The Beam Season Three

The Beam Season Four

The Beam Season Five

Robot Proletariat Series

En3my

Robot Proletariat

The Infinite Loop

The Hard Reset

Cascade Failure

Reboot

The Tomorrow Gene Series

Null Identity

The Tomorrow Gene

The Tomorrow Clone

The Eden Experiment

Karma Police Series

Jumper

Karma Police

The Collectors

Deviant

The Fall

Homecoming

Yesterday's Gone

October's Gone

Yesterday's Gone Season One

Yesterday's Gone Season Two

Yesterday's Gone Season Three

Yesterday's Gone Season Four

Yesterday's Gone Season Five

Yesterday's Gone Season Six

Tomorrow's Gone

Tomorrow's Gone Season One

Tomorrow's Gone Season Two

Tomorrow's Gone Season Three

Available Darkness

Darkness Itself

Available Darkness Book One

Available Darkness Book Two

Available Darkness Book Three

WhiteSpace

WhiteSpace Season One

WhiteSpace Season Two

WhiteSpace Season Three

Z2134

Z2134

Z2135

Z2136

The Dream Engine Series

The Tinkerer's Mainspring

The Dream Engine

The Nightmare Factory

The Ruby Room

The Pandora Core

The Engine Convergence

Stand Alone Novels

Burnout

The Island

Crash

Emily's List

Pattern Black

Devil May Care

The Secret Within

The Sleeper

Last Night Never Happened

www.ingramcontent.com/pod-product-compliance
Lightning Source LLC
LaVergne TN
LVHW031537060526
838200LV00056B/4534